HELLBENDER

A Fangborn Novel

Also By Dana Cameron

Fangborn
Seven Kinds of Hell
Pack of Strays
"The Serpent's Tale" (short story)
"The Curious Case of Miss Amelia Vernet" (a short story)

Emma Fielding Mysteries
Site Unseen
Grave Consequences
Past Malice
A Fugitive Truth
More Bitter Than Death
Ashes and Bones

DANA CAMERON
HELLBENDER

A Fangborn Novel

47NORTH

Text copyright © 2015 Dana Cameron

Published by 47North, Seattle

www.apub.com

Amazon, the Amazon logo, and 47North are trademarks of Amazon.com Inc. or its affiliates.

ISBN-13: 9781477849385
ISBN-10: 1477849386

Cover design by Cyanotype Book Architects
Illustrated by Chris McGrath

Library of Congress Control Number: 2014951972

Printed in the United States of America

For Mr. G, who dares me.

Prologue

"Hi. I'm Zoe Miller and I'm a werewolf, one of the Fangborn. If you don't know about the Fangborn already, well . . ." I took a deep breath. "You're going to very soon. It's not like you see in the movies—we're the good guys, and have been fighting evil in secret for as long as . . . well, as long as there've been people to protect. Werewolves, like me, we can smell evil, track it down, and eradicate it. Vampires can, too, only they can also heal people and make them forget they ever saw us. And oracles—"

I paused, raising my hand against the bright lights, trying to get the guts to go on. "I'm sorry, talking about this, knowing I-Day is here . . . It goes against everything I've been taught. Everything's going to change. For everyone."

"Zoe, you know, you don't have to go over all this. The basics are in the report we present to the president."

"Yes, ma'am, I do, but I have it in my head a certain way, and if I don't follow that, I'll lose track of everything else." I turned back to the camera, trying to get my thoughts in order, trying to find my place. "Oh, okay, right. The rest of our Family are oracles. They're lucky, or some of them can tell the future, and some of them are very powerful indeed. We all work to fight pure evil, and we're never wrong. Like I said, we've been working on the side of good for as long as human history; you could say it's our basic nature. But now, we need some help. The Order of Nicomedia has been persecuting—no, that's too mild a word. Hunting us down, torturing us, killing us. And it's getting bad. But that's not the reason I'm here tonight. It's worse than that.

"I'd rather be doing archaeology—that's what I used to do, what I still dream of doing, but for the moment, I'm what stands between us and *them*. By us, I mean everyone, Normal and Fangborn. By them, I mean . . . I don't know what. I just call them the Makers because . . . they're whatever made me, whatever 'made' the Fangborn. I don't know for a fact that they're dangerous—well, they *are*, but I don't know that they mean us any harm, if you see what I mean. I figure, you can bend time and space, you've probably got *some* game, so I think we should be careful. Careful and polite, because I doubt we have the tech to shoot first and do anything but make them angry. We've had some trouble communicating, but we . . . I'm still trying to see if we can work out a real dialogue.

"I know, this is all a lot to take in. I mean, the Fangborn? We look pretty scary, we're strong, and we heal superfast—and that's good when fighting the bad guys. But we're on your side. Trust me, I grew up not knowing what I was and it was a big relief to find out I was still Zoe . . . plus. Plus some fangs, plus some fur, plus some claws. It took me a while to understand, but I'm getting there, and I hope you will, too.

"But you may have heard about these other guys, the Fellborn. They look like bad copies of us werewolves when we're in our bipedal form, and were created by the Order I mentioned, by chemicals and arcane methods on unwilling victims, to eradicate us. I can assure you, we're not the same. They seem to be built only to destroy, and we were born—not bitten, by the way, not cursed—and seem to exist only to protect. The Fellborn have killed my friends, they've wreaked havoc on my Family—"

My throat started to close up, but I took a sip of water and continued.

"We're working on containing the Fellborn, but for now, please understand, we are not the same thing.

"So what I'm going to ask you to do is three things. First: keep calm. We're all working on this situation. You'll know when we do, because that's one of the agreements I have with the folks I'm working with: transparency. From now on, no more secrets.

"Second: cooperate. We're all in this together. We don't know what's coming next with the Makers, but I'm convinced we need to stick together on this one. All of us, all across the world.

"The third idea, well, that's more my idea of something to do until we have a solid plan. Hug someone. We could all use a hug right now. I know I could. This kind of contact is unprecedented, and we should learn from our own colonial mistakes if at all possible. We want to make sure we can't be friends before we know we can't."

I took a deep breath and another sip of water. "So here's what's going to happen. I'm going to remain in contact with the Makers. And to answer a question I've heard an awful lot of lately, why am *I* talking to them and not someone else? I'm doing it because I'm the one who can. I'm representing all of us. I think this will be easier to get through the more cohesive we can be, so if you can find it in your hearts to try and set aside any animosity against your neighbor, the guy who doesn't look like you, the Fangborn, even the jerk who cuts you in line, that would be good. Thanks."

I was about to walk away but thought of something and stepped back onto my mark. I looked back into the camera, trying not to squint against the bright lights.

"One last thing: I'm doing the best I can."

Chapter One

"Quarrel?" I whispered frantically, trying to get my bearings. "You there, my friend? I really could use some help here."

I was rain-soaked to the bone, in a world of pain, and nowhere that I recognized, with my worst enemy, Jacob Buell, dazed and muttering quietly across the dark alley from me. It looked like Japan, and the train station across the street had a sign that said "Kanazawa." I should have been in Boston; an instant ago, I had been there with my friends and Family, fighting the Order of Nicomedia, who had apparently started an all-too-public campaign to wipe out us Fangborn once and for all.

I should have been in Boston. Somehow I wasn't.

There was nothing, just the pelting rain, the cool humidity, and the unfamiliar sounds of traffic in the street just beyond. Not a word from Quarrel. I'd never tried reaching out to him on my own before the first time I traveled to meet him; he'd always contacted me. Since the dragon's "voice" usually threatened to dissolve my insides with its volume, I didn't know whether he couldn't hear me, didn't want to answer, or couldn't respond.

None of these were reassuring. I needed a friend. I needed to know where I was. And I needed to know what had happened to my powers—which had become pretty impressive, when I knew what I was doing. The flat stones of the bracelet mystically embedded in my right wrist looked dull and dead, and last I'd checked, the other elements, which had been gradually covering my body like jeweled armor, had vanished entirely.

I'd apparently done something so awful, my powers had been taken away. So terrible, a dragon had gotten frightened and fled from me.

The only thing I could think of was that the unseen Makers, who had been "inspecting" me just before I arrived here—had taken offense when I'd told them to fuck off with the riddles and tell me what they wanted, plain and simple.

Maybe dropping the F-bomb was going too far, but I'd had a pretty grueling day. I at least hoped it was still the same day, and that somehow, I'd find myself back in Boston before too long, fighting the Order and their revolting creations. I might be a were-wolf, but my Fangborn Family—including vampires and oracles—were the good guys.

Actually, it had been a tough week, what with the jet-setting, the search for Fangborn artifacts, and their "integration" with me as they took over the surface of my body and enhanced and added to my werewolf powers. The discovery that my dead friend Sean really *was* dead, and that those artifacts were using my memories of him to communicate with me. The torture at the hands of Jacob Buell, who had accompanied me here, clinging to my leg and the knife that he'd stabbed me with. I didn't think my transporting him, however accidentally, was going to improve our relationship. Basically since the self-described werewolf hunter was dedicated to eradicating my kind and using them for experiments.

Actually, looking back at it, the last couple of months had sucked pretty bad.

"Quarrel?" I tried again, still keeping my eyes and ears open for Buell. "It's me, Zoe. Uh, the Hellbender, like you said?"

Still nothing. Calling the dragon with a name or title I didn't know the meaning of made me feel like a dope. Werewolves can't move through time and space, I'd thought. Not without a plane.

The stab wound in my right leg itched and hurt like hell, even as it healed far too slowly. I watched Buell closely, but he was worse off than I was; he should have been dead. It was possible that the Order's chief scientist, Dr. Sebastian Porter, had given him some kind of synthetic Fangborn healing, derived from the Order's experiments. I didn't trust Buell as far as I could spit, not until I'd seen his head cut off and I'd buried him myself. Then put a big rock over him. Then nuked that, and jumped all over the little pieces.

Focus, Zoe . . .

I tried going to my mind-lab, the meta-space where I was doing research on the artifacts I'd accumulated. It looked like an archaeology lab, which was where I'd worked: black-topped work surfaces, desks, cabinets, a sink and hood. There were so many arti-facts now, it would take me several lifetimes to understand them and what they could do. But no sign of the lab, no matter how hard I tried, and no sound from Sean.

Buell moaned louder this time, crawling along the wall until he could stand upright. I took a certain fatigued satisfaction from his appearance; he was tall, dark, and tough as an old root, could do backwoodsman or "in New York to sell his first start-up" with equal ease, but now . . . he was bent over, limping still after I'd kicked his bad leg out from underneath him. His face was crusted with drying blood, his wavy hair matted. There was a wild mad-ness about him, added to the reek of evil and fear. As he reached the end of the alley, he found a discarded bottle. He leaned over, picked it up with some effort, and threw it at me, a noise of fury and frustration coming from deep within him. I automatically scrunched my eyes closed and raised my hand to protect my head. I was just trying to block it, but Buell vanished, as if he'd never been there.

Oh, shit, oh hell, where is he? I thought. *Where did I send him?*

Barbed wire sliced through every organ in my body. I passed out before I could scream.

When I woke, I don't know how much later, Buell was still gone from the alley. And it was raining even harder.

I didn't want to think I might have sent Buell where he'd do more damage. I had to hope I'd blasted him from the face of the planet.

But for now . . . I had only what was in my jacket pockets, which wasn't a lot. I'd gotten up this morning prepared to do battle—what time was it now? It was dark, but was it evening or actually morning with bad weather? Was it even still the same day? A quick check showed I had my wallet. I had some cash, some change, unhelpfully in Turkish lira, which I hadn't had time to convert at the airport, as well as some US currency. A couple of credit cards and a couple of phones—

The phone that Dmitri Parshin had given me worked internationally. But had it survived the Battle of Boston, intact and operable?

The screen had a new crack, but other than that, it seemed to be unharmed. I held my breath as I turned it on.

A sharp crackle. The screen fizzed and blurred a moment, and I thought all might be lost. I held my breath as it booted up.

It took longer than I thought possible, what felt like four or five years, but the logo screen came up and went through all its recognizable gymnastics. A moment later, I saw the home page.

One orange pip, the universal indicator of "Make it count, friend, 'cause you got just one shot."

I had no charger with me.

I wasn't exactly sure how to call the US, and rather than waste the power on talking to operators, decided to send a text. But to who?

I thought about it hard and quickly. The last friendly person I'd had communication with on this phone would be who I texted. I carefully pressed as few buttons as possible. Adam Nichols's name came up quickly.

Adam had been a friend to me and recently had been a good deal more than that. I had the silly notion that if he were here, everything would be all right. No, it wasn't silly. Adam had come to my rescue several times, was smart enough to figure out his own mind, and strong enough to live up to his ideals. It would have been a comfort to have dragged him here, instead of Buell, and we could have—

Was it my imagination or had the screen flickered again as my mind wandered?

With as little touch screen action as I could manage, I typed a message, short, sweet, and to the point: *SOS in kanazawa? japan? low batt. SOS!!!*

I would have added a few more exclamation points, but prudence prevailed over emotion, and I hit "Send."

The screen stayed, then seemed to send, then went black. I hoped my message made it through.

I'd done what I could. Now I needed shelter, food, and something dry to wear, maybe something that wasn't torn, bloody, and stained with gunpowder and demolition debris. I needed information.

I pulled my jacket tighter and prepared to find some place to regroup. I flipped my wet hair out of my eyes, which made my head ache anew.

The train station across the street had amazing modern arches, with columns made to look like drums. The posts in the uprights reminded me of a close-up of rope strands; over them was an elegantly curved roof with wafflelike recesses. It would provide shelter, a clock, a map, perhaps even an ATM that would take one of my cards. Vending machines. My "cousin" Danny had always raved about what was sold in Japanese vending machines, had a web page dedicated to it, because he thought it was an awesome idea to get noodles, beer, and bananas out of a machine, and because he is an enormous geek.

God, I missed him.

I tried to put that out of my mind as I navigated my way across the street, trying to pay attention to traffic coming the wrong way at me. The rain was now coming down in sheets and I thought I could smell the salt air of the ocean. It was just enough like home to make me feel even more miserable.

I pulled my hood up, kept my head down, and managed to make it to the shelter of the station. A clock there told me it was nearly ten at night, October 7, the same day it had been when I woke up in Boston. Even when I'm not brain-dead and hurt, I suck at figuring out time changes, but I eventually worked out that if I added a little time for being unconscious, I'd traveled across the planet in almost no time at all.

I hadn't stopped time, as I'd hoped to, as I'd done before. All I wanted to do was buy myself a few moments to get my friends out of a booby-trapped building and try and fix things so we could win the fight against the Order and the army of Fellborn they'd unleashed on Boston.

The only conclusion I could come to, based on years of reading science fiction at the library, was that I'd moved in space, rather than time.

I felt my knees give a little. A tremor went through me that I knew had nothing to do with trains rumbling beneath the surface of the station.

If I'd done that, what else might I have done? Is that what took my powers away, or was it that, um, discussion that went so poorly with the Makers? I'd learned about them through Quarrel, who was in communication with them. I'd hoped I might learn something about the Fangborn or my powers.

If I don't have my powers anymore, maybe I don't have to worry about all this stuff. Maybe I can just be Zoe, and leave all this mishegas *behind . . . politics, strife, dragons, crazy-assed powers, visions . . .*

As soon as I had the thought, I was ashamed of myself. People I loved were hurt, maybe dead. I owed them everything I could do to get back and help them.

Now what? Dedication and a good attitude were all well and good but wouldn't really count for much unless I could find a way to implement them.

I still felt woozy, but that made sense. Something major had happened, and I suspected I should feel a lot worse than I did. Ideas kept spinning around in my head about what I should do next, but the thing that kept coming back to me was: I need to get home. Now.

Right, I'd go to the nearest airport, get a ticket, maybe find a phone charger while I was waiting—

How are you going to do that with no passport, Zoe?

My heart sank as I realized I didn't have either the passport with my real name, or the fake one Adam Nichols had made up for me before we left for Denmark. I had been fighting the science head of the Order, Dr. Porter; I'd expected to be back at the Fangborn safe house, or dead, by the end of the day. I didn't expect to find myself on the other side of the planet, instantaneously. And now that I knew it was possible, well, this was going to have to be an object lesson. My brand new motto of "Never go anywhere without being prepared for everything" wouldn't help me at the moment.

I couldn't just go to the airport and hope they'd find a way to get me home. I couldn't just go to an embassy and hope no one would ask how I got into Japan without any documentation—tickets, passport, or visa or whatever. The best I could do was try to get some money, get my phone charged, and call for help. Hope no one took too much interest in me in the meantime.

And find something to eat. By all that was holy, I was *hungry*, as only a shapeshifter can be. While it hadn't been more than a few hours, as far as I knew, since my last meal, I felt utterly drained, depleted, stomach grumbling and gnawing.

That actually took me away from the edge of a teary meltdown. Where there's an appetite, there can be optimism.

I spied an ATM and flipped my hood back, wiping the rain from my face. I prayed I could make sense of the screens and make money appear, not necessarily in that order. I was fine with incomprehension as long as it got me cash.

I did some more praying during the long pause while my card was considered for its worthiness. Of course, I didn't know whether one hundred yen was a lot or a little money, but I figured I should get as much as I could. After a lifetime, I heard the reassuring clack-clack-clack that sounded like "three cherries, and here's your money!"

It was close enough to winning for me. I almost wept with gratitude. I stuffed the bills into my pocket before the ATM reconsidered and took them back.

I had cash, though I didn't know how much. Time to find a place to stay, for I didn't know how long, and food.

I pulled up my hood again, took a deep, ragged breath, and prepared to go out into the dark and pelting rain. To where, I didn't know—

I saw the sign and did a double take. Then a triple take.

I had to be dreaming. Or hallucinating.

I pinched myself. Ow—still awake, still here. Cautiously, I moved forward. The sign didn't change; it didn't appear to be a vision, which was a real possibility with me.

There were two people waiting in the center of the hallway leading out from under the massive roof. A young kid, maybe as old as eighteen, who looked like an American or European. With him was an older woman, Japanese. They held a sign.

The sign said, "Zoe Miller, Boston, USA."

Chapter Two

"I'm Zoe Miller," I said. My voice trembled, my throat sore. "Um, are you looking for me?"

The young man inclined his head to the very old woman, but his lips didn't seem to move. She burst out in laughter. "No, we're waiting for the *other* Zoe Miller," the kid said. He looked uncomfortable. "That's what she told me to say."

She hadn't spoken, not so far as I could see, but she was smiling; she'd made a joke. I noticed they were holding hands. Oracles, I guessed. Some oracles need physical contact to work their talents.

I didn't even have the energy to be pissed off at them for making fun of me. "I'm Zoe, and if you could give me some help, I would really, really appreciate it." I was too tired and too scared to worry that I might be kidnapped. Who knew I'd be here, after all? And they didn't look like kidnappers anyway.

The old woman nodded, serious now, and after glancing at the boy, he nodded. "Humor may help our situation, but now is not the time. My apologies. I am Akemi Okamura." Both bowed deeply from the waist.

"I'm Ash Dickson," the kid said. "We're Family. If you come with us, we can get you food, a place to rest." Then he added in an aside, "You should call her Okamura-san. Because she's so old and worthy of respect."

"Okay. Thank you, Ash and Okamura-san." I sagged with relief.

It was more than I could have wished for. "But . . . but first, is it really still October seventh?"

"Yes."

"So . . . what time does that make it in Boston? United States, the East Coast?"

Ash took out his phone, pulled up an app, and confirmed that I'd been correct.

The blood rushed from my face. There was still time! "I . . . I have to get back *immediately*. Do you know what is happening there?"

They both nodded. "We do," Ash said. "The fight is ongoing. We are in contact with Family there. We hope to hear more soon."

I shook my head. "I was *just* there and I need to get back there *now*."

"The only way to get back 'now' is to go the same way you came," Ash said. He continued hastily, probably seeing the anger I didn't bother to conceal from my features. "Okamura-san . . . I . . . we are serious. Unless you can teleport back—"

I spread my hands. "I . . . I have no idea how I—"

"Unless you can teleport back, you're stuck traveling the way the rest of us do. And that's going to take some doing," he said. "But for now, we both think it would be good to come with us."

"You don't understand," I said, a little too forcefully. We were starting to draw attention from the passers-by. "It's imperative I get home; I might be able to . . ." It suddenly occurred to me: Even if I could go back, what could I do? I felt nothing of the bracelet's power now. The Makers had stripped it from me, along with nearly all of the jewels I'd so painfully found and accumulated over the past months.

"You're tired, you're hungry, and you're scared. We can help. Come, now, it's not far."

It was eerie, hearing the cadence and rhythm of Ash's voice change as he switched from his own voice to communicating what Okamura-san silently conveyed to him. I nodded. "Okay, yes, you're right. Thank you."

We went around to the parking lot, and a car was waiting for us.

"Where are we going?" I asked as Okamura-san began to drive.

"Not very far. Just across town," Ash said. "We'll see my sisters there. Here."

He handed me a small lacquer box and a paper-wrapped set of chopsticks. I removed the top and found unidentifiable foods inside—amid the green wet stuff, the pinkish wet stuff, white stuff, and the lumpy brown stuff, the only thing I recognized was what I assumed was raw fish and rice. Didn't matter, though. It was all very pretty and beautifully arranged, but I demolished it, eating with a scary need. I didn't raise my head until I knew I'd eaten everything edible in the box and a few things that maybe were meant to be decorative only.

Remembering my manners way too late, I closed up the box and said, "Thank you. Um—"

The old woman laughed, and Ash said, "There'll be more at home. We want to get a vampire to look at you before you eat too much."

"Thank you," I repeated gratefully. Just taking the edge off my terrible hunger reminded me just how much more I wanted to eat, but it helped. I sagged into the car's seat, feeling so tired and sore I couldn't make one thought connect to another. I settled for simple questions.

"Where am I? How did I get here?"

"Kanazawa is the capital of Ishikawa Prefecture," Ash said. "I don't know how you got here."

"I mean, like, are we near Tokyo?"

"No, we're on the Japan Sea. The west coast, say, just opposite Tokyo. Very rainy, known for its seafood, to which I am allergic, and for its well-preserved samurai districts—"

I bit back my impatience; local commerce was all very good, but . . . "Yes, but . . . why would I be *here*? And, more importantly, how did *you* know I'd be here?"

"Rose saw you. She's been really antsy lately, so when she got a bead on it, we were all too ready to get on a series of planes and travel for about twenty-four hours. Why here, I'm not certain, but

Okamura-san tells me there is a tradition of strange happenings, in addition to shapeshifting *yōkai* and *kami*, associated with this place."

"Wait—what? Who's Rose?"

"Rose is my sister, and so is Ivy. We're the Dickson triplets—you've probably heard of us. We're from Milwaukee originally, but we're going to college in San Francisco."

Which told me exactly nothing. But by this point, I'd run out of coherent thoughts and found myself dozing. I hadn't realized how much of the trip I'd missed until the car jerked to a stop, waking me up.

I followed Ash and Okamura-san into the house, feeling more disoriented with every step. The past—well, I'd say it had been only four or five hours since I woke up in the States this morning—had been filled with fighting and death.

Another woman, younger than Okamura-san and dressed in a business suit, came to meet us at the doorway. She bowed, greeting me, and I managed to do something similar, I hoped polite, back. I moved to step in, and Ash said, "Shoes! Anywhere you see a change in the floor—going up or going down, but especially outdoors to indoors? That means you need special shoes. Or no shoes. You need to keep clean areas, uh, uncontaminated with shoes."

I followed his suit, exchanging my boots—laces knotted and broken, scuffed and scarred—for a pair of slippers that were lined up outside the door. They were just a hair too small for me. Ash's feet were laughably too large for his slippers.

Then the new woman got a good look at me and led me down a hallway, talking the entire time. Clearly, she was going to sort me out. Fine with me.

She pointed to a small room, and there were some clothes, neatly folded, on a futon on the floor. She said a few more words in Japanese and then cocked her head. "*Nǐ huì shuō pǔtōnghuà ma?*"

I shook my head when I realized she was asking if I spoke Chinese. "No, sorry. *Parla Italiano?*"

She shook her head. "*Govorite po-russki?*"

Where was Danny and his gift for languages when I needed him? "I'm sorry, no. *Sprechen sie Deutsch? Parlez-vous Francais?*"

Another shake of the head, and she held up a hand, bidding me wait. She called down the hallway, and Okamura-san and Ash came back.

Eventually, by talking to Okamura-san, who communicated silently with Ash, I found out that the woman's name was Kazumi-san and the room was mine. I should shower, dress, and there'd be a visit from a vampire to try to heal me before a late dinner if that was okay with me.

I nodded. As long as someone had a coherent plan that involved those things, I was good with it.

It took me a minute to figure out the shower knobs and the bottles I found there; I just used all the bottles of stuff on the caddy until I was clean. At the moment, I didn't care if I was washing with moisturizer or shampooing with body wash. I looked and smelled a whole lot better than I had.

There was still no trace of the constellation of jewels that had occasionally covered my body like flexible armor. They gave me powers that usually only vampires and oracles had, like the ability to nudge someone to do something or a kind of proximity sense. The jewels also provided me with painful visions that drove me to find more artifacts; if that was gone, I sure wouldn't miss it. The artifacts I found, ancient items that imparted Fangborn abilities, morphed into what looked like jewels and precious metals and became part of my body. While the bracelet, embedded in my wrist when I opened Pandora's Box, had once been several inches of gleaming, flat gemstones in every hue, it was now dull, lifeless. But it showed no sign that it was going to come away from my arm, and I could still barely make out the tracery of my veins beneath the clouded translucent stones. No more jewelry and armor had to mean that I'd lost whatever crazy powers I'd once had. I wasn't even certain still if I could Change, make the basic transformation from woman to wolf, which had become one of the principal joys in my life. I was healing, but so slowly I didn't dare try anything until I'd at least rested and eaten.

My new powers leaving me at exactly the time I needed them most was awful, but I could live with that for now. I hadn't mastered them, they were hugely and finally unreliable, and they still scared me silly. The emptiness I felt, however, at perhaps never being able to Change to either of my wolf forms again threatened to crush me. That ability to Change had given me answers about my history, a Family, and a sense of belonging for the first time in my life. It had also given me physical strength, and because of that, I dared to do more, be more myself. I couldn't bear to think that loss would be permanent and kept pushing it from my mind. I'd deal with the more immediate issues, then . . . then we'd see.

With a sigh, I found a towel and dried off. The clothes that were left for me were a T-shirt and sweats, socks with a separate compartment for my big toe, and the slippers. There was also a range of underthings in different sizes. I assumed there were a lot of guests who showed up here needing clean clothes in a hurry, the life of the Fangborn in the quest to fight evil.

A knock at the door; Okamura-san came in. She led me down the hall to a small room, where I saw a shrine. Several sticks of incense burned before it, and a middle-aged man, his head bowed, stood in front of it. He rang a little bell, made two bows, clapped, and bowed again, before he turned and gestured to me.

He bowed. "Hello, Zoe. I'm Kenichiro Mitani. Please call me Ken." He spoke English with an Australian accent; the way he said Ken was particularly striking. "I'll be looking after you if you don't mind. Please just wave the smoke over wherever you would like healed," he said. Then with a smile he said, "Or if you think you need more beauty, or more brains, wave some over your head."

At this point, I figured I needed to be smoked whole like a kipper if it was going to have any effect at all on me, purification- or healing-wise. But I waved smoke over my head, my wounded leg, and then, thinking of my friends at home, my weary heart.

I took a deep breath. My nose twitched, and I tried not to sneeze. The incense made my eyes water.

"If you would, perhaps start with a small prayer, or a moment of reflection?"

I bowed my head and thought, *Please get me out of this mess and back home.*

When I'd finished, he said, "Thank you. Now, may I?"

I nodded. Ken-san the vampire sniffed delicately, walking around me, and I was glad for his sake that I'd had a shower. He took my pulse and asked me where it hurt.

"Everywhere. But mostly, it's my right leg. I'm not healing as quickly as I should." The place where Buell had stabbed me still bothered me, having taken the better part of an hour to close up. Slow healing was disastrous for a werewolf used to fighting.

He nodded. "Anything else I should know?"

"Yeah. Last time a vampire bit me, she said my blood tasted funny." I told him about how my friend Claudia Steuben had determined that while my blood was odd, I wasn't evil. The word she used was *"predator."* I mentioned the bracelet and jewels, how I got them and how they had just vanished. "So, given that I unexpectedly found myself across the world an instant after I tried to stop time briefly, and may have had communication with a seriously powerful set of beings, you may want to brace yourself. Or avoid biting me altogether."

He smiled in a way that said he could handle it, that I was probably exaggerating, and then looked puzzled. "Beings? Do you know what they are?"

I shook my head. "I call them the Makers, because that's what Quarrel—he's a dragon—calls them. I assume they made him or made us Fangborn."

It took Ken-san a long time to speak. *"And . . .* you're in contact with a dragon?"

"Yep. Like I said: You may not want to bite me."

I shrugged and held out my wrist. "I'm just sayin'. God only knows what's happening inside me now. I might be radioactive or toxic or something. Your call."

Ken-san paused then. I wasn't joking. If I'd traveled through space and/or time, I might well have a new biology that would be dangerous to him. He took my wrist, though, and after a final, appreciative sniff, Changed.

Even now that I was used to seeing a man undergoing the half-Change into a bipedal snakelike creature, it still fascinated me. Kenichiro's dark hair shifted from brown to reddish, and his skin transmuted to scales of coral pink and yellow, with flecks of blue. His nose receded into his face and became a snout with small nostrils; his eyes grew wider and darker. The fangs were the weirdest, I think, watching his jaw change to accommodate them. I could feel the tug of his Change, like bubbles under my skin, and resisted my urge to follow suit. Soon, I promised myself.

His bite was barely perceptible, and I tried, as I had with Claudia, to alter my own blood profile to show him just how strange my blood was. When I tried, I got something like a migraine mushrooming between my eyes, as if someone was using a hand-cranked drill and bit on my forehead. I stopped immediately. When he pulled back after a moment, I felt a kind of relief. My headache faded somewhat, and while I felt a bit less desperate, I was still starving, still weak.

"I don't think there's anything I can do for you, beyond this simple healing. Your blood is indeed . . . complex. I must take time to consider it. But for now, eat, sleep, and perhaps a bath tomorrow."

"A bath?" I tried hard to keep the disbelief out of my voice, and failed.

"We have an excellent hot spring near here; this house is a retreat used by our kind in times of trouble, and so we have many more amenities than most houses."

I thought of the very nice shower I'd just had. I'd never had a prescription for a bath before. "A bath will help me, how?"

"It's very relaxing, good for the skin, excellent for your muscles, and helps fatigue. You should try it. Our American Cousins will be happy to show you how. The girls have become quite addicted." Almost a frown crossed his face. "Ash, not so much."

"That sounds lovely." My stomach rumbled, embarrassing us both.

Ken-san took the cue. "If you'll follow me, I think Okamura-san has prepared a proper meal for you."

"Thank you!" My heartfelt gratitude for the food reminded me of other manners. "And thank you for examining me. My Family—"

"If I understand correctly, they're still fighting. It will take some time to get news. Also, you would like to go home, but you have no papers? No entry stamps, no passport?"

"I don't."

Ken-san frowned with concern. "That is difficult but not insurmountable. As I say, time enough to arrange that. We will get you home very soon."

"Thank you." My relief could not have been greater.

Another man came in, nodded to me, and spoke quietly and rapidly to Ken-san. After a short exchange, he bowed and left.

Ken-san turned to me, his lips tight. "We've tried, repeatedly, to contact the Family in Boston but with no luck. It could be they are still engaged with the—what did you call them?"

"Fellborn. The Order."

"Yes, we know of the Order, of course. They've become very bold lately. And we heard from our Cousin Toshiharu Yamazaki-Campbell about the Fellborn—he's out there, too, correct? The Family may be following only local communication, too busy fighting and controlling the information about the existence of the Fangborn at the moment. In which case, it is only a matter of time before we hear from them."

One way or the other, I thought. Let's hope it isn't via the twenty-four-hour news networks.

"And now, if you are ready, there is food."

I tried not to actually drool as I followed him to the next room. The tiny little plates worried me at first, but they came in quantity. And quality—there were many types of seafood, mounds of rice, seaweed. I smelled vinegar, soy sauce, and a number of things I couldn't identify. It didn't matter—it was all delicious.

Ash was there and apparently so were the sisters he'd mentioned. As he'd said, they were triplets, and while Ash was similar looking to his sisters, if it hadn't been for the girls' radically different styles, it would have been impossible to tell the two of them apart.

They were nearly of a height, a few inches taller than me, maybe five eight, five nine. Brown hair, blue eyes, freckles, symmetrical features.

I only noticed now that I was fed that Ash was the picture of retro-prep: buttoned down, slicked back, and creased to within an inch of his life. It made me fidget just to look at him. I wanted to mess his hair or yank out his shirt so the tails hung outside his sweater vest.

The one I learned was named Rose was as gothy as they come. She wore drapey black with hints of jewel tones, which were a relief to the eye and yet somehow made the black all the darker. And speaking of eyes, if I'd had the money to buy stock in eyeliner and black nail polish, based on Rose alone, I'd make a killing. Her hair was dark black, but it was obviously the sort of home color job I used to do, because it wasn't exactly the right shade to go with her pale skin. It washed her out, which, come to think of it, might have been the point. But with the sapphire eyes she shared with her siblings, it was a striking combination.

Ivy looked to me to be the most normal of the lot. Which meant that she looked closest to how I usually dressed: jeans, layered tees under a jacket. Judging by the leather stains on her toes, she owned the boots I'd seen out front, nearly new. Her hair and Ash's matched, though hers was longer, pulled back into a sloppy, pretty knot.

The Trips talked nonstop while I took them in, which was nice, because it got me off the hook for having to join in the conversation.

"We were born at noon at the summer solstice," Ivy said.

"Well, you came at noon, and we shot out not too long after," Rose corrected. "Zip, boom, squish."

"We'll be twenty-one next year," Ash added.

"We always work together," said Ivy.

"But we can work with other oracles easily, which is kinda rare," Rose said.

"It's a real gift," Ash said. "We get a lot of work because of that."

"It's nice to meet you after focusing on you for so long," Ivy said.

"I've been seeing you for ages," Rose said.

"Like I said before, she nagged and nagged until we came here." Ash sighed.

"We usually wait until two of us have it, but this was different, somehow. So, *yeah*, I nagged."

"And it was a good thing, too." Ivy nodded. "It was the missing part to a puzzle the oracles had over here. They were expecting someone."

"It took them a while to realize that *we* weren't the ones they were expecting."

"Because we're totally famous."

I was starting to get the hang of them continuing each other's sentences, one complete thought shared among the three of them.

"Now, now," Ash said suddenly. His voice took on something of Okamura-san's quality, when I noticed her hand on his. "That's enough talk about you."

But the triplets had to have the last word. "Perhaps you've heard of us?" Rose said.

"Um, no," I said. "Sorry." Maybe it *was* a triplet thing, that finishing a sentence for each other, but I was willing to bet that like other oracles, they were completely weird. They were bright enough, but they certainly didn't act as though they were from our planet.

"She's a stray," Ivy explained.

"That's not a nice word!" Rose protested.

"*Baka!*" Ivy spat back.

"And that's a worse one!" Ash said. Then his voice changed. "I think that will be enough," Okamura-san via Ash said. "Now!"

"We're sorry," all three said.

"Well, it's true, I wasn't raised in the Family or with Fangborn culture. 'Stray' is as good as anything to describe me, I guess. Is there anything you can tell me about what you saw?" I said, setting my chopsticks down.

"I saw the mess in Boston coming," Ivy said. "That's why everyone thought we should be there."

"I saw the mess in Boston, too," Rose said, "but I saw *you*, and you weren't in Boston. You were here."

"So we hightailed it over here, having exchanged a few emails first."

"And nothing more about me?" I asked. "Or why I'm here?"

"No, nothing like that yet." Rose laughed.

"But we can do a reading tonight," Ash said.

Silence from the other side of the table.

Ash and Rose stood up. "Ivy?"

She'd dropped her chopsticks. Her eyes were blank, staring straight ahead.

"Ivy?" the other two said again.

Ivy screamed.

Chapter Three

Somewhere in an unoccupied part of my mind, I heard the crash and tinkle of breaking porcelain. It occurred to me that this was exactly how pottery entered the archaeological record, and I wondered briefly if it could be repaired.

The other 98 percent of my brain was riveted on Ivy's screams and the reactions from everyone around the table.

Rose and Ash pulled out soft gloves and put them onto Ivy's hands. Once that was done, they held her hands carefully. Ash stroked her head as she continued to scream. Rose dipped a napkin into some water and brushed her cheeks with it.

Okamura-san got a notebook, a pile of maps, and a pen.

Ivy's siblings joined hands and closed their eyes. Ivy gasped a bit longer, then began to speak. "One of us, in the dark. One of us, in new enemy hands. One of the enemy—how quickly he appeared!"

"How close?" Ash asked.

"Medium range," Rose said.

Ash kept his eyes closed; Okamura-san picked up the map, glanced at him, and then took a pair of dividers and found the scale. She put one point on a part of the map and turned the dividers in a small circle, no more than two inches across. She pointed at where the line intersected a fresh red mark and paused, staring intently, waiting for Ash's next unspoken communication.

"Ivy's telling us the Order has made an attack on one of our safe houses," Ash said, "which is not far away. They used one of our oracles to time it. They're fighting now. Somehow someone who shouldn't be there is."

A sick feeling began to well in my stomach. I was pretty sure I knew who it was.

"It came with you!" Rose said. "That new enemy! You brought it here."

"Please," Ivy pleaded. Her eyes were open now, tear streaks drying on her cheeks. "We need to get them out now. Who is this new guy?"

I nodded. "If it's what I think, it's a member of the Order named Jacob Buell. Somehow he got dragged along with me when I ended up here. I think I might have brought him here, trying to defend myself. Or maybe he contacted them or had a tracking device and they found him."

Okamura-san discussed something briefly with Ken-san, and they both nodded when she pointed to a place on the map. There seemed to be some disagreement after that, however.

"We should go immediately," Ash said, translating for Okamura-san.

"They'll be expecting us," Rose protested. "And if they have an oracle, it's possible they'll have noticed his connection with Ivy."

"We can't wait," Ivy said numbly. "We have to go now."

I agreed. One of our Family was in the hands of the Order and would be tortured for information or research.

Without a word, we began our preparations. I borrowed some gear and helped the others with theirs. It gave me direction I sorely needed and objectives I could meet. What kept me from begging off and pleading exhaustion, which wouldn't have been hard to argue, was the idea that the Order, and potentially the presence of evil among them, would be a test of my ability to Change. I needed to know if I could Change more than I needed sleep, and doing it among my own kind seemed like the safest way, even if it was in the middle of a fight.

A van was packed and a small car readied to follow. I was about to ask why we needed something so big when I saw the backboard and the medical kit go into the van. We had no idea how many of the Family were there and what shape they'd be in when we found them.

If we got there in time.

We drove north, along a cliff overlooking the ocean. The place we were looking for was meant to look like a family compound. We stopped partway down a long, winding drive that led to a high wall, plastered and painted. Two stone dogs with red cloth scarves stood outside of a small building near the gates, and I wondered if they were Fangborn signals or Japanese art. I realized with a shock that there were two trees near a small shrine in front; a rope was tied and suspended between them. Along the rope were carefully knotted pieces of paper. Ash explained those were prayers, but I had seen them before, in a vision at Ephesus. I'd thought I was seeing a tree covered in ghosts.

The Trips insisted on doing a reading. I became really apprehensive when they asked me to join them, not knowing what would happen if I tried to use my powers. I'd assumed they were doing a prognostication on the raid we were about to undertake. But no.

"We're still getting way too much interference from you," Rose said. "If we drain off those visions first, maybe we can check for the raid after."

I shrugged and made a corner to their square. It felt very silly to pause for any reason in the persisting rain. I could hear the ocean waves breaking on a beach somewhere beyond the cliff on which the house stood.

The Trips required physical contact to use their gift, and like many other oracles, they also used talismans to help them concentrate and align their power. Some oracles used crystal balls or stones to help them tune out the real world. Some used bones or trinkets they'd found. It was always a personal choice.

The Dickson Trips used smartphones.

Rose and Ash each took one of my hands. They linked arms with Ivy, who pulled up a *Tetris*-like game app.

"Old school," I said.

"It helps with concentration," Rose said.

"No storyline to distract us," Ash added.

Ivy said nothing, but she didn't need to. She turned her attention to the screen and stared, her thumbs jabbing the screen, slowly, and then picking up speed. Her eyes started to glaze over.

Plug in, turn on, tune out.

"Oh, boy," Ivy said. Her eyes rolled back in her head. Same with her siblings.

It took a lot for me not to pull away from them. They were nice kids, but this was just freaking me out. Sure as sin, it was no fake. Power came off them in waves. Somehow I felt I was completing the circuit, and what they shared was coursing through me. I saw fragments of their lives in a rush of impressions. I saw my shock mirrored in Rose's face.

"Hey, she isn't supposed to be able to do that!"

"Well, she is, so get back to work," Ash muttered, his eyes still closed. "We're nearly there."

Everyone who had been discussing our plan or checking gear looked up and waited.

"We're at a crossroads," Ivy said to no one in particular.

"You are the crossroads," Ash corrected, his head jerking toward me.

"Whatever comes next, you'll decide everything," Ivy said.

"The Family will never be the same again," Rose said.

"The world will never be the same again," Ash amplified.

"Go down, deep, into the ground."

"Climb up, high, among white stone pillars."

"Close the box you've opened. It will be a pity if you do."

"Drink Family blood, rend Family flesh."

"Splitter of worlds, binder of all."

"If you don't destroy us, we will perish."

The beeping that signified the end of the game broke the silence that followed, broke the spell over us. The Trips shook themselves and dropped hands with me, checking each other, reassuring themselves they were all safe and well.

"Yeah. Seriously," Ivy said to an unspoken comment. There was a shuffling among the non-oracle Cousins, and a cough. It had been as unsettling to watch as to participate, I guess.

"Sounds like you're pretty well screwed, whatever you do," Rose said.

"Thanks, guys," I said, shaking. "You couldn't give me anything more solid to go on?"

"Nope. But you can't afford to fuck it up," Rose said.

"Big help."

Rose shrugged. "At least you can stop worrying that you're evil."

I glanced around at the nervous adults around me and caught Kenichiro-san's eye. "See? Just like Claudia Steuben said."

"Yeah," Ivy said. "You're definitely gonna end the world, but we didn't get that you were actually *bad*."

"This should help quiet the Family buzz about that," Ash said. "That's a lot of bad reputation to be running around with."

My shoulders slumped. "Well, that's something, I guess. You guys gonna stay here with the vehicles?"

The three shared a look; all three shook their heads. "Not all of us."

"What do you mean?" I asked.

"One of us goes with you," Ash said.

"I think it's me," Rose and Ivy said at the same time. Perturbed, they looked at Ash, who shrugged.

"I can't see it," he said.

"I'm a better fighter," Ivy said.

"But I'm the one who saw Zoe coming—our paths are entwined," her sister replied. "I *feel* it, Ivy."

Once again, they looked to their brother. "We get to an impasse like this, we go by protocol," Ash said.

Rose and Ivy nodded, and then, at the same time, both held up a fist.

"Once, twice, thrice," they said together.

Rose's hand was flat; Ivy's was still bunched up.

"Rose," they said together.

They were deciding my fate and theirs with "Rock, Paper, Scissors."

⌣

The gate was unlocked, ajar, and we pulled it open to see a wooden building in what looked like a traditional style, emerging at the end of a short, winding garden pathway. At the end of the path, we saw that the building formed the right side of a courtyard; a second, similar building abutted the far end, forming an upside-down L, with the branches to our right and ahead of us. The courtyard was completed with the continuation of the wall on the left and the side through which we'd entered.

A battle was raging in the courtyard. I saw seven Family members: four werewolves half-Changed so that they resembled humans with fur, claws, and wolf-like visages, and three vampires with their even weirder snakelike heads and scaled, clawed hands. They were fighting maybe twenty members of the Order in their hateful black uniforms, and one of the Fellborn. I was glad it was one of the earlier Fellborn models, which was vicious and unthinking, and moved somewhat like apes, with loose skin covered with gray fur. The Mark Twos were nastier, smarter, and stronger, but even so, it took one vampire and one werewolf to keep this Mark One from doing more damage than it already had.

The remaining vampires and werewolves were using everything in their considerable arsenals to get past the Order's best weapon against us, after the Fellborn: their blasters. A combination of a compound that included a lot of black hellebore, which I knew had a horrible, sickening, disorienting effect on us, and electricity, which further scrambled our circuits and made us even more vulnerable to the hellebore. The vampires were slowly able to glamour or "suggest" that some of the Order assailants put their weapons down. Some were spitting venom. When one ran out of venom, I saw him emulate his werewolf kin and pick up a blaster and bash its owner over the head.

Somehow we needed to get past them to find the prisoner. The other werewolves and vampires who formed our party had already thrown themselves into the fight, evening up the numbers and giving heart to our besieged Family. I decided I had to risk the Change myself and hope that Ken-san's healing had helped patch me up.

To my vast relief, the Change came quickly, and as it always did, with a thrilling sensation of power and goodness and enough adrenaline or endorphins or pixie dust to blot out the rapid and radical metamorphosis of my bones and musculature. I was still upright, still dressed like Zoe, but now covered in a wolf's pelt, with upright ears and a jaw line that was more canine than human. I reveled in the feel of my claws lengthening and teeth growing, and the thought of a fight made me shiver with delight. For the past few hours, I'd been confused, scared, and weak. Now I felt like a purposeful demigod.

I gave into my baser instincts and howled, loving that I had a cause to fight for. I howled again, reveling in the way my war cry reverberated against the walled compound and was audible over the rain and wind and waves.

This also had the effect of attracting attention, which was all to the good. I dodged an overhand attack from an Order goon swinging a blaster; he'd probably run out of the chemicals they used to weaken us. On my way back upright, I slashed at his thigh and caught him across the femoral artery. Dark blood splashed against the already rain-soaked gravel and he went down screaming.

A shout from Rose. "In the back building, by the cliff! That's where our Cousin is!" She ducked a blow and slashed at the calf of the Order soldier who'd missed. He went down, and as he did so, a werewolf twisted his neck for him. The werewolf nodded her thanks to Rose and found another combatant. The Family redoubled its combined efforts to break through the Order ranks.

I circled around, hoping to find a hole in the ranks that I could sneak through. I managed to kick one Order soldier in the back, giving a vampire the chance to sink his teeth into the guy's neck. Then more shouts, and a scream. Rose was attacked by the Fellborn, who'd scrambled away from its assailants. She fought well with her knife, but the thing was single-minded in its brutality. I'd communicated with one of the Mark Twos briefly in Boston just . . . could it only have been hours ago? I learned that even they craved nothing but food and Fangborn corpses. I pulled it off her and bit deep into its neck. The blood was foul and black and, with the Fellborn weakened by its first attackers, soon stopped flowing.

Rose was bleeding badly. Oracles don't heal as quickly as shapeshifters and she could barely walk. I picked her up, slung her over my shoulder, and pelted back to the vehicles, the gravel crunching and shifting under my feet. I didn't dare try to heal Rose myself— that was a vampire power, not one werewolves ordinarily had. But her siblings, who apparently knew their share of battle first aid, were ready and waiting. They got to work on her.

"That was quick," Ivy said. "Told you I was a better fighter."

"But I found the captured oracle," Rose retorted. Then she grimaced as Ash began to clean the wound on her arm.

"And so that's why you were the one to go," he said, working steadily.

"You guys okay?" I asked.

Three nodded responses. I ran back to the gate. I decided to cut through the first building, hoping to find a way around the Order.

I'd vaguely been wondering why there were two Fangborn safe houses so close together, and now I knew. This wasn't a house at all so much as it was a museum.

I entered a long hall, the interior walls of which had traditional paper screens I recognized from samurai films as shoji. The light in the room was low but far better than the rainy night outside. Along the walls on both sides were tables covered in arms and armor from all over the world. Filing cabinets and notebooks and other recording information, even a photography stand, were scattered about in a makeshift lab space.

The weapons all had one thing in common: They were bladed. One in particular spoke to me—a long, slightly curved Japanese sword of Tamahagane steel on a table at the center of the wall.

That's what brought me here, I thought, these objects. Like the vision of the powerful Fangborn artifacts that had almost physically driven me to seek them out in Denmark and Turkey, these weapons had drawn me not only to this hall but away from the Battle of Boston. My oracle friend Vee Brooks had given my own power a boost, and my inexperienced attempt to stop time had supplied the energy while the artifacts provided the target, taking me away from where I was needed.

This time, however, there had been no visions, no terrible pain to make me desperate to find the artifacts. There had been . . . nothing. Were the artifacts now able to simply pull me to them, even from across the world?

A shout from outside woke me. The katana I'd been attracted to glowed violet, and I felt a hum through the air as I raced toward it. But something was badly wrong. My proximity sense flared a warning.

"Are you fucking kidding me?" A hateful drawl broke the silence.

I turned, growling before I saw him. Jacob Buell, his craggy face drawn with exhaustion, was limping and reaching for a pistol. His wavy hair was plastered flat, black with sweat and rain, and he still had burn marks on his hands and neck from where I'd hit him with an acid venom attack in Boston earlier this very strange day. Whereas I'd had the chance to shower, heal, and eat, I could see a long series of bruises and cuts ran up his face, and his head was hastily shaved and stitched, probably from where I'd bashed him into the floor before our sudden and instantaneous trip across the globe. If he still had a few burns on him, from the explosion he caused that destroyed the Museum of Salem, that was fine with me.

But there was not nearly enough damage. He was still upright.

"You can't go anywhere without taking me with you, can you, stray?" He limped a few steps closer, his bad left leg still fucked up from a rough landing in the alley, the gun pointed at me. "Why did you send me here?"

As I lunged for him, I realized that before I fainted in the alley, I had teleported him here trying to defend myself. That was what had knocked me out. But that wasn't uppermost on my mind.

Nothing else mattered, not the kidnapped Cousin, not the battle in Boston, not the rest of the world. Only Jacob Buell mattered. I wanted him to feel a little of the torture he'd put me through. I wanted him to know it was coming from me.

I landed on top of him as he pulled the trigger. I felt bullets slam into me and didn't care. I'd pay for it later, gladly, so long as I killed him first. When my knees hit his shoulders, he went over backward; I knew that unless I tore out his heart, now, forever, I was going to get shot again, at close range to way too many organs.

I felt more blows to my gut and dying suddenly seemed all too likely. I still wasn't healing fast enough and heard humming as a strange dizziness overtook me. It was as though I was losing control of my senses and my body. Why go for his heart, when his throat was right there?

Definitely dying, I thought bleakly. *But not before I take him on this one last journey with me—*

I shook my head, trying to quell the buzzing. I finally managed to stop digging through his rib cage—it felt almost as though I wasn't a werewolf at all, that I was a girl with a plastic ice cream spoon, trying to make a dent in Buell. With an effort, I raised my claw back, ready to tear his face off.

My hand brushed the table with the katana. The sword shifted slightly toward me and I grabbed it.

The long chamber's shojis and exterior walls vanished in a bank of flame that was gone almost as soon as it appeared, leaving the beams and posts untouched. We now could see everyone in the courtyard, and they us. Each of the other weapons and pieces of armor on the tables was glowing pale green, brighter and brighter, until each burst into a ghostly flame. Even while I felt life's blood leaving my body too fast, even while Jacob Buell was in my grasp, I could only stare.

The flames took on the distinct shapes of the pieces of armor themselves, and rose, sorting themselves out in anatomical order. The parts didn't match—the Incan helmet of wood and copper had no business hovering above the Mycenaean Dendra plate armor—but they created a nearly humanoid form.

They hovered briefly, and I had no sooner wondered what I should do next when all of the weapons flew into the katana I held, each slamming into the next—curvy bladed Indonesian kris, an improvised fauchard made of a scythe, an assegai with a long, leaf-shaped blade—until they formed a giant two-handed broadsword of green and violet flame in my hand. Each blow was like it had been made by a supernatural adversary, and I struggled to hold the changing weapon.

Before, when I'd assimilated artifacts, I'd been at least in decent shape. Mostly. Now I was pretty sure I had even less power than before, and was on the ragged edge of exhaustion, physically, and . . . magically. I wasn't sure I was going to survive this . . .

The green ghost of fiery, mismatched armor turned to me. The incandescence was blinding. I held up the flaming sword and braced for the inevitable. Pain and death.

I really hope this isn't the guardian of this collection, I thought. *Because if it challenges me, I'm in big troub—*

The buzzing increased, filling my head. A vision . . .

I moved toward the armored ghost, arms outstretched as if to embrace my own end . . .

No, not my end. There were craftsmen and technicians laboring over their wares. I needed to embrace the result of their skill, their ability to imbue the artifacts with power . . .

The ghostly artifacts winked out of existence and popped up less than a meter away from me. Somehow I managed to stand, found the strength to hold my arms out. I closed my eyes, not at all certain it was a good idea . . .

I felt the barrage of energy as the armor touched me, pressed itself onto every part of me, and . . . didn't stop. The armor melted into me, and it felt as though the energy was racing around inside my body, weaving bone and blood together with something else. Maybe this was what it was like to be electrocuted, I thought raggedly, or to be on acid while someone stuck knitting needles into random sections of your brain. This was what other people imagined it was to turn into a werewolf—a curse of bone stretching and crunching, muscles straining beyond human endurance, and the systematic ripping away of your humanity. The dizziness of reaching through time and space through Pandora's Box was a pony ride compared to this roller coaster. Just when I thought it could go on no longer, it found a way to get worse.

No, the ecstatic reward of the Change was the utter opposite of this.

But why were the artifacts still coming to me if I was depleted?

The armor had vanished, and I wondered if I was now burning with the pale green flame. I opened my eyes and saw the mystically born sword, still glowing violet in my hand. Then that slid out of my fist and up my arm and, like the armor, became a part of me.

I may have passed out, because I hardly noticed when it stopped, hardly noticed that I'd fallen down again. The only signal I had was that I could feel my heart racing so fast, it felt as if someone had set a drum machine for the bass drum at two hundred and forty beats per minute. When I registered the cool of the straw tatami floor under my cheek—how was it not burned?—I began to wonder if I'd become enmeshed with it, an integral part of the house. Then I felt my breath moving between my lips, which brought an unpleasant taste of rusty iron and bitter greens.

Buell struggled to his feet. Maybe it was some kind of "die in your boots" mentality, but he just stood there unsteadily, wobbling, not quite sure what to do with himself. His blank look told me he'd run out of mind to boggle. Outside, the battle was slowing down, as the Fangborn took the opportunity to disarm the Order soldiers who were staring at the spectacle of me melding with the hoard of arms and armor.

I was at least as beat up as Buell was, but I was still a werewolf and I was owed pain. I knew what to do, even though I could barely think with the images that were filling my brain, scenes of metalworking and leather curing and forges and workshops, showing me the Fangborn makers of these artifacts. Buell looked like a martial arts training dummy to me, and even if there were no magic on deck, I still had claws and fangs and a heart burning with the need for vengeance.

Slash across his chest—I'd finish what I began, tearing out his heart eventually. I wanted him to know that his death was here, in me. Another slash caught a corner of his eye and would have had all of it if he hadn't fallen back. I managed to tear the end off his nose, and the blood spurting out muffled his screams, which were music to me. His bad leg gave and he fell; his arm and face burns were still angry and red.

It was time to end it, before I couldn't. I needed time to acclimate to the rush of artifactual power, but all I required was just a second to kill him. One more slash to his throat and it would be done.

One, two, three shots. I went down, hard, my head spinning. I looked down. More blood poured from my abdomen. I didn't dare look further, afraid of what I might see.

"Zoe!" Ken-san called out. He had dispatched the shooter. There was no more threat. Just me and Buell.

Remarkably, Buell was still trying to crawl away. Whatever synthesized healing ability he'd had from Porter was still working. I rolled over onto my stomach and felt my insides slosh in ways I knew they shouldn't, but it was the only way I could move. I raised my hand, willing one last blast from it, one last bolt of power . . . *Just one more, please God, give me something to kill this monster . . .*

Nothing but a blinding, crushing headache, the sutures of my skull grinding against each other, bony plate against bony plate, with my brain a pool of lava compressed inside.

I tried dragging myself after Buell and managed to get to my knees. That was as far as I got. I reached into my pocket, hoping I'd find something I could throw at him. Nothing.

I tried once more to blast him, screaming, feeling the rage at the futility of it all, the blinding pain of pushing past depletion. He was *right* there . . .

"Hellbender, I am here!"

The roaring outside and within my head would have flattened me if I hadn't already been down. Quarrel, a vampire who'd grown so old he'd acquired the form of a dragon, had materialized in the courtyard as if out of nowhere. His sudden appearance and terrifying aspect had resulted in screams from the Order soldiers and more than a few from the Fangborn, to whom dragons were a thing of the distant past, if not myth. He raised himself up onto his great haunches, glittering black and silver in the rain, and spoke even louder, to make himself heard over the racket of his lesser kin and their enemies.

"Why do you assume that posture, Zoe Miller? It does not look like a fighting stance to me!"

Chapter Four

When Buell saw Quarrel, he did the only things possible. His jaw worked, he stared, and he dropped his empty gun, a dark stain spreading across his trousers. It is one thing to know, vaguely, that dragons exist and to understand something of their pedigree and powers. It is quite another to see one in real life: thirty feet long, a glittering bluish black, lizardlike body, with a red-gold belly; thick scales dotted with brighter jewels that looked similar to the ones I had on my body; foot-long teeth, and claws like polished daggers.

I was so happy to see Quarrel that I got to my feet. I nearly tore Buell's guts out with a slashing kick before I fell back to the floor, totally spent with that effort.

Buell and I stared at each other with impotent hatred. He looked at me blearily across the tatami as if to ask, "What are you doing? Don't you see this thing over here?"

Still, not quite dead. Whatever Porter had given him had been strong, and I was getting sick of it. There must be some way to counteract that. I must find out—

"Zoe Hellbender, why do you not finish with him? I have much news!"

I bet you do, dragon, I thought, *and even some answers for me, but I think I'm dying over here.* "Not doing so good, Quarrel."

I tried to push myself off the floor, but my arms were tingling like they'd been asleep, deprived of circulation, and I could barely feel them. Finally, I managed to sit up, my legs straight out in front of me. I heard shouts. I had to ignore those and Quarrel and get to killing Buell.

"It is no wonder I found you so easily! You are quite radiant with—" He used a word I didn't understand. "If I had been here sooner, perhaps there might have been some for me."

Reaching delicately through the standing members of the house, with no walls to impede his view or him, Quarrel nudged me with his snout, breathing small wisps of steam that added to the humidity. Being nudged by a dragon is a little like being nudged by a very dainty bus, even when you haven't been in a fight for your life, mystically transported, and shot repeatedly. I smelled a familiar aroma, bitter herbs, and felt my insides move sickeningly again, the pain from the gunshots and blood loss dizzying, as I settled back onto the mats. Maybe Quarrel was concerned; more possibly he wanted to see if there was any loose power left he could grab.

Quarrel had been a friend and ally, but I could never forget that he had once, on a hillside in Turkey, threatened to eat me and take my power as his own. This proximity and my weakness was not a good combination, as far as I was concerned. At least if it was Quarrel who killed me, it wouldn't be Buell.

"Oh, I understand. You have not—" He again used language I could not comprehend. He gave me a look of something like awe. "You are very weak."

I understood that okay. "Yeah."

"Pray, allow me."

He stretched out his claw daintily through the standing members of the house. I thought he was going to put me out of my misery and seize what power he could from me. This would be my obituary, I thought, as I felt the point of a claw dig ever so slightly into my flesh: *Zoe Miller, briefly an archaeologist, a werewolf for an even shorter period, leaving a trail of dead friends and chaos behind her, died finally by being dispatched by an ambitious dragon, Quarrel . . .*

Instead it was like lightning coursing through me, enveloping me. Somehow it was different from the artifacts' assault, controlled, like jumper cables being correctly applied, and oddly cooling. Then, way too cold; I felt myself go numb through and through. The big chill, the biggest . . .

Well, it was better than the bullets and fire and bruises, I thought sluggishly. My brain slowed and . . .

I gasped and sat bolt upright. I clutched at my stomach and felt my borrowed clothing soggy, heavy, and bright with fresh blood. Biting my lip, I probed further and then dared to lift up the hem of my shirt.

Wet, but not bleeding. I brushed at it. Nothing. No wounds, no blood, no bullet-churned guts spilling out . . .

I blinked, stared again, and then poked at the skin. Nope, all was well. Still no jewels, but . . .

I looked at Quarrel, who was eying Buell with an air of disgust. I made a noise of disbelief, and the dragon swung his head around to me. "Yes?"

Still incapable of speech, I raised my brows and spread out my hands to indicate, "Look, I'm alive!"

"Yes. Well, you know I was what you call 'vampire,' one of the healing warriors, before I grew into this form over the millennia. My skills have always been prodigious in that sphere."

"I'll say," I croaked.

"You were very weak, still adjusting to the assimilation of those . . . tools. I merely helped by employing"—he used unfamiliar language—"and by healing your body." The dragon cocked its head with concern. "You should eat. It's not good for one so young to go so long without food. Especially when there are many events unfolding."

I nodded dumbly. I could not agree more. "Thank you. Uh, for healing me."

"I am surprised you did not think to use that . . . foreign thing you have . . . on him." Quarrel's voice dripped with distaste.

I looked beside me and found a short sword, the one artifact that had not been transformed to the energy that was now a part of me. About three feet long, and iron; the blade looked sharp, but . . . primitive. Pre-Roman Celtic? The blade did not match the intricate red enameling that made me think of Anglo-Saxon art, or the later medieval reliquary that was set into its pommel. "I didn't even know it was there."

"You should pay more attention," Quarrel said tartly. "And now, Hellbender, do you wish to capture or kill that piece of refuse?"

Buell had information. As I watched him blubbering weakly, bloody bubbles popping at his ruined nose and mouth, his eye a ghoulish mess of jelly, I thought of how he tortured me, and still, I almost bade Quarrel hold. Then I remembered what he'd done to Toshi Yamazaki-Campbell's fiancé Sergio and Cousin Alexandra and the words were out of my mouth before I knew it.

"I'm done with him."

"Excellent! Stand well back!" he called. "Naserian, Yuan! Attend me, if you please!"

With that, two other dragons appeared out of nowhere. Naserian was dark garnet red and twice the size of Quarrel; Yuan was young-grass green and smaller than Quarrel, though quite a bit thicker around the middle. The remaining Fangborn were slack-jawed with awe. The members of the Order had fallen on their faces, covering their heads against the sight.

Even when you knew that dragons existed, it was pretty shocking to see one. Never mind three.

Quarrel reached through and snagged Buell on one claw. He dragged him outside to the gravel courtyard, leaving a glistening red smear on the straw mats.

"Prepare yourselves, my very young Cousins!" he cried out in our minds. "Your ears are ridiculously fragile!"

The dragons bellowed and thundered. Their bodies shuddered under the effort, jeweled plates sparkling in the moonlight, and the dragons dug their claws into the ground to brace themselves. The noise penetrated our covered ears and seemed capable of liquefying our brains.

Jets of pale blue liquid shot from their dagger-filled mouths as if from fire hoses and hit Buell with a terrible impact.

Buell screamed as the force of the blast pushed him along the gravel a short distance. I smelled burning flesh, a barbecue gone badly wrong.

Two more short blasts and steam rose in larger and larger clouds. The venom began to eat through his head and hands. Flesh burned back, peeling and cracking black as it did. Muscle and bone exposed, and the last thing he saw, before his eyes evaporated, was me holding the short sword I'd taken across my shoulders.

What had been Buell collapsed on itself. The dragons raked through the still-burning parts, better to finish the job. Soon, all that was left was a puddle on the broken ground and tiles. I thought about my earlier wish—to nuke him and salt the earth— and decided this would do nicely.

"It will cease being corrosive in an hour or so," Quarrel said with some pride. "And there will be no trace of him. He has effectively returned to the earth, though she would not wish his stain upon her. But I didn't summon Naserian and Yuan merely to deal with one so small. Now we must go."

"Where?"

"To continue your inspection with the Makers." I had just enough time to wonder about the timing, why they would show up at exactly the wrong moment, when we were in the void I associated with the Makers.

I'd first experienced that cosmic nothingness when I opened Pandora's Box and was flooded with images and ideas too big to comprehend. Several occasions since then, I'd only felt the void.

The thing that was different this time was that I could see the dragons. It was less empty and, therefore, less terrible.

I tried holding my hands out in front of me; I could see them, too. My foot was paler, more translucent, than the rest of me, and I could see stars through it. I wondered whether my head was visible, too. I didn't have a mirror to check.

Interesting.

After a moment—which could have been a year long, in that place—I saw Quarrel go rigid. The other dragons did as well.

I was about to ask what was going on, when they turned to me expectantly.

"Zoe?" Quarrel prompted.

"Yeah?"

"The Makers await your response."

"What did they say?" I craned to look around me. "Where are they?"

"They are eager to hear from you. Can you not perceive them? With any of your senses?"

I felt a kind of shiver, but that was probably adrenaline. I shook my head and then remembered to speak. "Nope."

The dragons conferred among themselves. Quarrel leaned toward me. "Naserian suggests you do not have your full eyes yet. The Makers can hear you, but because your voice is still strange to them, I shall communicate between you."

"Okay. Um, what did they ask?"

"They want to know how your war to subjugate the population goes."

"What? What war, what . . . population are you talking about?" I began shaking as if I was in one of those nightmares where I'd forgotten all the lines to the play I was about to do.

"You were preparing to invoke the powers of war. They want to know how you fare and why you took on this task." Quarrel was also surprised. "I am also curious to know what war you will commence."

The idea that I was going to war, that I was trying to subjugate anyone, just about knocked me on my ass. "Wha . . . huh . . . no, that's not what I'm doing at all! I mean, fighting yes. Subjugating, no." I thought about it a bit more, tried to gather my thoughts.

"*Tell them,*" I said, trembling, "*we are fighting to stay alive and safe, against enemies who wish us dead or in cages. I'm fighting for my kind, for survival.*"

There was a long pause, from my point of view, before Yuan responded this time, his voice piping and reedy compared to Quarrel's, which was deep and dark as old oak. "*They express curiosity and concern, Hellbender. If you are so attacked, why do you consider anything but eradication and subjugation? It is your purpose.*"

"*Say what?*"

"*It is your purpose,*" *Yuan piped up.* "*They say it is why the—you say 'Fangborn'—were created. To be the predators who rule a world. The Makers do not understand . . .*" *He—she?—paused a moment.* "*I think you would say, they do not understand your . . . 'half measures.' This is all very surprising to me.*"

It was surprising to me, too. "*Half measures?*"

"*You have it in you to destroy the less-evolved humans. If you are threatened, you have no choice. They want to know why don't you?*"

There was more conferring among the dragons.

I held up my hands. "*Whoa, whoa! This is crazy talk! So crazy, I don't know where to begin. I don't have that kind of power. I don't even have everything I started out with today. And why the scorched-earth policy? That's just for starters. I'll come up with other questions once my head stops spinning.*"

Quarrel was silent for a while, perhaps still in communication with the Makers. I did not expect his next response.

"*Huh. I never imagined that was the case,*" *he said.*

"*What? What's the case?*"

"*Zoe, we've never discussed these objectives, these plans, our purposes with the Makers before. When we exceeded our natural lifespans and were not killed in the pursuit of evil, we withdrew from the world of man for ages. We've been so retiring, so inactive in the world, that . . . this talk of 'subjugation' never came up. But you, with your similar adornments, the tools, are still a part of the affairs of men. I believe this* is why you've attracted the Makers' attention and the reason for these confusing statements and questions on both sides."

"What do you mean?" I asked. "What purpose? What . . . affairs of men?"

"Age has made us sluggish, and most of our powers were acquired after we withdrew from the world, by our musings and communication with the Makers. So . . ." If it was possible for a dragon to sound sheepish, Quarrel did. "What we were meant to become, what the Makers intended for us, never came up. At least for us, and—" Quarrel glanced at the others, who went blank for a moment, and then seemed to agree. "And for those others of our kind, we are aware of. This is . . ." He paused again. "This is not the first time this matter has arisen, but the latest in a very long time."

"When was the last time?"

There was another conference. "Long before any of us. Perhaps when those intrusive Latin types began overrunning their bounds."

"Hey, I was married to one of 'those intrusive Latin types,'" Yuan protested. "Some time after the glory of the empire, however."

Quarrel ignored him.

"Okay," I said, "so if you'd been in this situation, with a terrific threat to the Fangborn, you would have been expected to go to war with, what, humanity?"

"Yes, that is something like that word: humanity. And yes, we are told now that we would have been compelled to destroy those who threatened us."

"Why? Why not try to find some way to live with the aggressors, those who threatened you? Why such a drastic response?"

Another pause, and an exchange of glances suggested a communication among the dragons I couldn't read. "There is no other response from the Makers than, 'It is what we are made to do.'"

I went cold all the way to my marrow. "You're made to destroy humanity?"

"The Makers use a word and you have one similar: We are made to *be predators. Predators do not negotiate. Predators find their way to a place of dominance and maintain their place and order beneath them."*

I didn't think I could get any colder, but I did. "Is that what the Makers intended for us, the Fangborn?"

"As necessary."

"So, we're meant to prey on humans? On those who threaten us?" That didn't make sense, I thought. Everything I'd encountered in the Fangborn I'd met all across the world had some variation on the idea that Fangborn were meant to be benevolent, protectors. This was a giant step away from that. Somehow the message must have gotten garbled, as it was told in Fangborn folktales through the years. This couldn't be right.

A tiny part of me said, It has the ring of truth. You always worried there was something too convenient about these rationalizations and tales. And now you're getting to the heart of it.

The dragons were silently communicating again, and this time I had the distinct impression that they were worried about something. The only time I'd seen Quarrel worried before was during the Battle of Boston, and shortly after that I found myself transported across the world, apparently stripped of my powers. "What? What is it?"

"The Makers have conferred. They have agreed that reviewing our history—"

"Our history?"

"Our history, going back tens of thousands of years, that our behavior does not conform with what they anticipated." Quarrel did the dragon equivalent of gnawing on his lip.

"Okay. What does that mean?"

"They have determined that we are broken. They are considering what to do with us. This will take some time."

Suddenly I was back in the courtyard of the house outside Kanazawa.

Little or no time had passed here. Somewhere in the distance, Rose screamed. There was so much anguish that it wasn't something we heard in our ears but in our hearts and minds.

Okamura-san, Ken-san, and I ran down the path to the driveway and the Trips. Rose was bleeding still but standing with her knife—still clean—in her hand. Ivy was holding Ash's head in her lap; a long hunting knife, smeared from killing work, was beside her. Ash's chest wasn't moving.

I had a flash of a vision.

An Order guard had come across the Trips and shot Ash in the back. Rose had rolled out of the way and Ivy in turn had cut the killer's throat.

"Quarrel, Naserian! Can't you do something?" I shouted. "Yuan?"

The dragons appeared out of nowhere. "It is beyond our skill, Hellbender," Naserian said. Her voice was even rougher than Quarrel's, like shifting old stones rather than oak, and heavily accented. If her scales were dark garnet, her eyes were bloodred. "Even we have no power to raise the dead."

"Perhaps you?" Yuan suggested. His voice was surprisingly high-pitched and youthful, considering his girth. "With all your glorious energies, perhaps it is not beyond you."

I tried and felt . . . something.

Not enough, not nearly enough to heal Ash, much less raise him from the dead, but it infused me with a joy that I couldn't have imagined.

I wasn't done. My powers were still there. They hadn't been stripped away by the Makers. They'd seemed burned out of me because I'd overextended myself.

But that moment of exultation and realization was short-lived. I tried one more time, but it was like the solenoid clicking on a car's ignition. The parts were there, but I needed a jump or a tune-up.

Rose stood bloody handed, staring silently at her brother. Ivy was shouting incomprehensible words perhaps only her siblings would have understood.

Without thinking, I ran over and grabbed their hands.

Why I thought they'd need me, I didn't know. In the instant between me extending my hands and each of them taking one, I realized what I was trying to do. It was a wild-ass guess, but they held on to me like they were drowning, and briefly, oh so briefly, I saw Ash's eyes flutter and felt his hand twitch in mine. And I knew I was right.

Ash's life had left his body, but a charge like static on rippling silk went through me, following a fine scarlet line that connected him and his sisters. Rose slumped forward. The sensation passed, and as the other two came out of their brief confusion, I realized what had happened.

Something in me had acted as a conduit, funneling something of Ash into his siblings. What I'd felt reminded me of the sensation that accompanied the upload of a dead person's mind—usually someone whose blood was literally or figuratively on my hands— into my mind-lab, but this was different. Cleaner, smoother. When I'd taken their hands before the fight, and seen their lives, it was a jumble. This was me taking some of those memories and weaving them together with what they knew, retracing and reinforcing their bonds of kinship and psychic ability.

I hoped they would forgive me this ill-conceived, clumsy, and fumbling invasion of their privacy. My hope was that this connection with their brother would fill in the gap his death left in them.

Appalled at what I'd just presumed, I began to apologize.

The sisters exchanged a look and then took my hands again, gently, insistently.

I felt their grief, blinding and soul wrenching, as they guided me along that thread. I felt their fears, that if one perished, all three would, the gaping hole left behind spilling their wills and energies until those remaining siblings were husks. They knew this as well as each knew herself and the other. But now there was the faintest rose-colored line that bound up the rough edges of where Ash's . . . soul . . . had been ripped from theirs. Fainter strands like weaving silk maintained a connection that, absent, would have torn the other two asunder as well.

I fled their minds. The pain of loss doubled, tripled, was too awful, but I was left with the clear idea that I had made it possible for Ivy and Rose to survive.

"Thank you," they said in tandem, their voices harsh. "Thank you for Ash's last, impossible gift."

My throat closed. It could have been so much worse, I understood now. I thought about what it would be like to lose Danny, the closest thing I had to a brother, or Adam. Or Will. The hole in my guts that any of those losses would mean. The welter of emotions I felt so acutely was mingled with pleasure at finding my powers restored.

Everyone was a little stunned.

But there was work to do. I hauled myself unsteadily to my feet and turned to the captured Order soldiers. They'd seen the appearance of the dragons, their final removal of Jacob Buell from the face of the earth, and me channel Ash's spirit into his sisters.

"We need answers about your assault on this place, how you knew to come here, where your headquarters are." I pointed to the bubbling stain that had been Jacob Buell. "I suggest you talk. I think Quarrel and his friends are hungry after all that. And I'm not feeling very patient."

The Order soldiers erupted in a chorus of breathless and anxious voices, all competing to be heard. After a moment, I was forced to say, "One at a time, please!"

Finally, we sorted out translations and began to get information about the Order in Japan. The oracle they'd captured had died under torture, trying to resist giving his captors any more information about Family locations and movements in Kanazawa. This group had become bold with their information and acted on it immediately, with the knowledge that around the world, other branches of the Order of Nicomedia were launching its massive crusade to end the Fangborn.

The ride home was quietly traumatic. Ken-san administered sedative bites to both of the remaining Trips to ease their grief enough to rest. There was more mourning for the dead oracle, and the wounded needed tending. The dragons had vanished and everyone had questions.

I didn't care. My brain and heart were full, but I'd reached the limits of even werewolf stamina and pushed beyond. Despite the crazy blast of healing that Quarrel, Naserian, and Yuan had given me and the rest of the Family, I was exhausted. I stopped only to take off my shoes and wash my face before I went to the room I'd been assigned, fell flat on my face, and went to sleep.

Later, I learned I'd slept for close to thirty-six hours straight.

When I woke, it took several worrying moments to remember where I was and to convince myself that I hadn't vanished from where I thought I'd be again. Although Quarrel had reassured me that I was entirely healed and that I might use whatever powers I had, those powers still weren't under control. If I could teleport before, it meant I could do that again. Without knowing how, I had no desire to find myself some place unintentionally. That meant my investigation of whatever the new artifacts might do would have to be postponed. I had to focus on what I had already and solve the riddles of my unpredictable power before something worse than teleportation happened to me or those around me.

I knew, after opening Pandora's Box in Ephesus, that there were four more artifacts that contained huge power in the world. In searching for those four, I'd found there were even more than I'd anticipated, and when I found them, sometimes there was a contest with another Fangborn to acquire their power. Whoever was strongest "won," but in every case, the more artifacts I found, the more other relics called to me.

There was no one-to-one connection between any of the artifacts and a single, specific power. It was as though I got a bit of a boost in several different abilities, or a hint of a new one. I did know that the more artifacts that I assumed, the more I was able to control and direct those new powers.

Each time I'd acquired a new piece, it had been added to the original bracelet on my wrist. Sometimes this was in the form of a new row of stones on my right arm, but recently, the small jeweled plates began appearing on my back, my ankles, my collarbone. More than that, a fine, almost invisible net of gold began to cover my limbs, dotted with tiny round diamonds. So while I still thought of those artifacts melded with me as "the bracelet," it had become much larger and more complicated than that. I had to hope that those elements would return, as they seemed to have vanished on my sudden trip to Japan, and I had a suspicion I'd need all the power I could get in the days to come.

I ate without paying attention to the food I was shoveling into my mouth. Too much to think about, and more besides. Ivy and Rose had arranged to go home on the first available plane. I longed to go with them, but without papers, it was impossible, for the moment. The Fangborn who usually handled the fake passports and papers had been killed by the Order in the raid. I knew I had brought the Dicksons, by my actions, to this sad state, but so far, all they could do was thank me.

"There's something there in us now," Ivy said, her eyes red and swollen.

"That wasn't before," Rose said.

There was a brief, heartbreaking pause when they both instinctively waited for Ash to say his part, and then both rushed to fill the void.

"I hope it helps," I said.

"Yes. If we decide to foretell again," Ivy said.

"It won't feel so . . . broken with just the two of us," said Rose.

"Then take care, you guys."

I hugged them before they left, and while Ken-san was working on finding me a way home, I took the dreaded bath.

"Look, I'm not sure I'm all that into public nudity," I said. "I'm sure it's relaxing and all, but . . ."

He gave me a look that spoke of disappointment and disapproval; I reconciled myself to doing it.

He told me the many steps of preparation, and the do's and don'ts—where to leave my clothes, how to wash off the little stool on which I would sit before bathing, how it was important to not let my washcloth or any soap get into the water of the spring itself. That left me even more nervous about flubbing those and insulting my hosts with some inappropriate or contaminating behavior.

"Don't sweat it," he said in his Australian accent. "Okamura-san and Kazumi-san will help you. They'll tell you what to do. Remember, they don't want their bath ruined by you any more than you want to ruin it."

I was still skeptical but realized I wasn't going to get out of it. Their house, their rules.

I stepped into a small changing room, very plain with lots of wood, trying to keep track of putting on the "toilet" slippers to use the loo, then stepping out of them and leaving them in the correct space after I washed my hands. I moved to another space where I could undress and left my clothing in a small basket.

As I undressed, I was able to see that the bracelet was still on my wrist but looked flat and lifeless, despite the dragons' ministrations. There was still no sign of the other jeweled armor that had been gradually covering me. A distant part of me liked the idea of feeling in some way normal again, but the loss of the powers along with the jewels was a grievous one at the same time. I was disappointed not to see anything new from the burning broadsword and armor at the safe house.

I was left feeling very vulnerable in a way that had nothing to do with having nothing but a small washcloth for a cover-up. The cloth would only go as far as the washing-up area of the bathing room itself and must never touch the bathwater, as I'd use it to scrub myself before I entered the bath proper. So many rules . . .

I stepped into the washing area, which was paved with stone. Along one wooden wall there were several faucets and hand sprayers, each with a small wooden stool and bucket in front of it. I filled the little bucket, rinsed off the stool, and began to wash, using the little cloth to soap up and the bucket to rinse myself off. Okamura-san came in, naked as the day she was born, and nodded to me, saying something I didn't know besides "Zoe-san."

"*Kon'nichiwa*, Okamura-san," I said. "Hello" was the total extent of my Japanese.

She laughed and replied with the same, very gravely. She followed the same procedure I had, and suddenly it occurred to me: She wasn't judging my body. This wasn't a smirking contest. This was a shared time and I immediately felt more comfortable. If she'd been nervous or hesitant, I would have been paralyzed. Daring greatly, I tried to use the hand sprayer to get my back. I turned the wrong knob, and suddenly Okamura-san squawked with surprise, as I accidentally hosed her down with water.

I grabbed at the sprayer and turned it away from her, apologizing; she gestured to the correct knob. Finally, I was deemed clean enough and went to leave.

Okamura-san said something sharply, and I turned around. More gestures; I needed to rinse off the seat I'd used. I thanked her again.

In spite of gradually turning up the temperature of my shower, the heat of the water was still a shock. Once I gave into it, it became better. Then it became amazing. Not a joint in my body remained knotted and I felt muscles relax for the first time in months.

Okamura-san climbed in without hesitation. Kazumi-san soon

joined us. A short conversation followed, and when I saw Oka-mura-san mimic me wrestling with the sprayer, I nodded ruefully. Both women laughed. Some things transcend language.

I smiled, closed my eyes, and let the water leach away my care . . .

"Zoe-san!"

I heard a short exclamation, then a frenetic exchange between the two older women. I opened my eyes; the cave-like room was lit up like a disco, lights swirling and reflecting off the ripples of the water. Pretty—

Both women had their eyes wide open, staring at me.

I looked down. The lights were coming from me.

"Whoa!" I yelled, almost jumping backward out of the pool. Then I saw it.

The bracelet was alive again. The fine mesh of what looked like a net of gold thread and tiny diamonds was back, as were the stones that I'd accumulated around my ankle and shoulders. There were new ones, too, a rank around my left ankle and fine mesh that ran up both legs. The new additions were clearly from the ghostly weapons and armor that were kept at the other Family house.

The light show was getting even more frenetic, a blaze of white and gold speckled with all the colors of the rainbow dancing across the gray stone surfaces and reflecting crazily off the water. Desperately, I tried concentrating on the stones to see if I could get them to calm down.

They went away completely. The bracelet still retained its renewed bright luster, however. The stones of the bracelet never seemed to vanish, a result of either a broken part of Pandora's Box or my tampered-with blood.

Daring greatly, I tried bringing the jewelry of my body back. They reappeared.

I disappeared them again. And settled back into the water. "Sorry, Okamura-san, Kazumi-san. I didn't mean to startle you."

The contrition on my face must have shown through my relief. If the stones were back, then maybe so were my powers. And now, apparently, I had the ability to camouflage most of my armor.

Maybe I'd run out of juice during my mishap in trying to stop time in Boston; it wouldn't be the first time I'd overextended myself. And that's why I hurt so much for so long. But this was exciting . . . I could regulate the glow of the bracelet enough to appear . . . Normal. Human.

When I began to feel sleepy, I got out of the water; curling up for a nap in the spring was not an option unless I grew gills. I took my time exiting the bath, pouring cool water over me until some of my lassitude departed.

After I dressed, I looked for Kenichiro-san. His eyes were red from sadness about the dead Cousin, but he was researching the one weapon that had not assimilated into my body and consciousness, the Anglo-Saxon decorated sword. He called me aside, with a strange look on his face.

"Zoe-san, your father is Richard Klein?"

I blinked. I'd only just learned his real name a short time ago, along with the fact that he *hadn't* died shortly after my birth as I'd believed. "Yes . . . I think so. That's one of the things I've been told."

"You do know . . . I'm sorry, I may have difficult news for you. He died here, several years ago."

I wasn't sure what to feel. I was surprised, a little stricken, but had no reason to be. I'd never met the man, but . . . I guess I thought someday I might.

"Please come with me," he said. "I'll tell you what I know."

Ken-san led the way to a small cemetery.

I looked at the square grave marker, very simple, stone carved with a set of initials and two dates. By my calculations, he'd been about seventy-five when he'd met my mother and conceived me, an adult Fangborn who, to human eyes, looked only about to enter middle age. The emblem on the marker was one I'd never seen before, or rather, it had elements I'd seen before, but never in this combination. A serpent swallowing its own tail, the symbol of eternity and the world, the Ourobouros, the world serpent. Inside the circle of its coil was an oval, which in turn encapsulated a wolf's head.

"Your father was old fashioned, it seemed," Ken-san said. "These days, you more often see just the snake and the wolf left. The eye, the symbol of the oracles, was more prominent once, the center of the piece. Lately, it's been left out. He wanted all three elements combined, as it used to be."

I nodded. I recalled what Vee said about the lack of political power that oracles had these days. It wasn't common for symbols to change form through the centuries, and the current mood was reflected in the current omission of the eye.

"We didn't know what faith he followed. Like you, he arrived suddenly, though not by teleportation. He brought the item he was entrusted with to us, and then was killed in action, helping us save a family from a fire. He perished in the burning house." Ken-san shrugged. "It happens too often, with our kind. You meet and get to know a distant Cousin, only to have him die by your side the next day."

I knew all too well, I realized with a pang: I was thinking of Ash. "I'm sorry. This is fine, thank you. This is lovely." I made a mental note to have something like that put on my mother's headstone if I could, when I got home. If I got home.

I don't know why I was thanking Ken-san. I didn't know my father's tastes and preferences; I didn't know what he wanted for a funeral. But I was grateful someone had looked after him, had been with him at the end. We walked back to the house in silence.

So now I knew I was truly an orphan. I didn't believe I really expected to ever meet my father, but somewhere in the back of my mind there must have been a flicker of hope, waiting, hoping, nourished only by the fact that I hadn't found proof of his death yet. I found myself surprisingly sad, when I stopped to think about it. I hadn't been sad about not having a father present for a very long time. Maybe it was because now I knew he wasn't part of a gang of vigilantes, at least not with the sense my mother had suggested, not knowing he was Fangborn, and not knowing she was, either. Maybe it was because I finally knew what I was, that I wasn't crazy, a killer, and that I wouldn't have been ashamed of myself when we finally met, which I guess I was still hoping to do.

Back in the room with the sword, I brushed the tears away with the back of my hand and cleared my throat a couple of times.

Ken-san put a glass of water near my hand, and I nodded thanks, drinking thirstily.

"We have a plan underway to get you home," he said. "And I have a time set up for you to call the Family in Boston. They know you are alive—"

I'd forgotten trying to call home. "How . . . are they okay? Is—"

"Losses and confusion, but so far, we're still a secret. Barely, from what I can tell—there was a lot of chaos. Explosions, buildings on fire, reports of gas leaks and sewer breaks."

"Do you know how many were . . . lost?" I tried not to think that the worst had befallen my human and Fangborn families, but the battle had been brutal and covered a large area near downtown Boston. Was it possible that I might have sensed something if anything had happened to one of them?

He shook his head. "The details are coming in, only slowly. The main emphasis right now is to make up a most plausible explanation and keep the Family out of the media for as long as possible."

"Yeah, but . . ." To me, knowing who was alive and who was dead was more important than the secret, but there was more than my needs at stake. If we could contain the battle, we'd gain some time in trying to ready ourselves for I-Day.

The Order was making that increasingly difficult. "If you find out anything, will you—"

"Yes, of course."

He shrugged and slid a file across the table. "But for now, you should look at these."

There were three documents in the file; he left me alone to read them: a Fangborn will; a copy of my father's will for the state of New York, where he had a legal residence; and a note—for me. Zoe Miller, by that name.

My mother had run away as soon as she knew she was pregnant with me. He wasn't supposed to know I existed. We both spent a lot of energy and heartache making sure he didn't find us, because she didn't know he was Fangborn, and she was, too. Her early life had been spent at an "asylum" where her blood had been altered intentionally, to hide her identity from herself. Senator Knight had collaborated with Porter, the man who'd done the experiments, in the name of aiding the war effort, but eventually killed him when he went too far. The Order of Nicomedia, however, flourished with the research of his son, Sebastian Porter. In many ways, Senator Knight was my enemy long before I was born.

The New York will said that if I could be located, I was his heir. If not, whatever he had should go to the kitty to fund Fangborn activity. It wasn't a lot of money—his cover job as an insurance claims adjuster didn't pay well—but he did declare me as part of his family, which I understood gave me, not rights within the Fangborn society, but . . . standing.

So, not entirely a stray. I had a family within the Family, and maybe even close Cousins, if I wanted to look them up. Maybe I would.

The letter cleared up many of the mysteries the first two documents presented me. I came very close to trying out a little oracular push to see if I could get anything else—an idea of my father's voice or personality or intent—from the document, but caught myself in time. I just couldn't bring myself to try out my "extra" powers just yet.

Dear Zoe,

You don't know me, and if you're reading this, well . . . I'm sorry, is all I can say. This is not what I wanted for you or for us, but if my choices kept you safe, then that's okay by me. I'm just a werewolf, working in the Family business. Nothing special about me, until you came along, and with you, a whole bunch of mysteries I hope I'll get to solve one day.

Your mother and I . . . that was complicated. I was drawn to her, right away, and she to me, but she had this odd shyness about her. She struck me as . . . different, and at first, I thought she was a Normal. Then I kept thinking she wasn't, but it didn't matter, because I loved her. After I caught a scent of her a few times while I was out on Family business, I began to wonder, and when she vanished . . . I didn't know what to think.

I began to look into the story about her past, the "orphans asylum," and began to wonder if she hadn't been a member of the Order, and then I began to wonder if she hadn't once been a subject of theirs. I found her trail easily enough, but gave her the space to think herself hidden from me, until I could find out more.

He'd known my mother was pregnant, I realized. He knew of me, knew my name, had seen me. He'd kept our secrets.

Once I discovered she didn't know what she was, that she truly believed she was a Normal human, I knew if she was so driven to hide from me and the Family, it would be dangerous for me to try to stop her. She had the knack of knowing when I got too close, so it took time to find exactly the right distance. That's when I figured out some of the story of her past—and if I live to write the next version of this letter, I'll have the proof I need and share it—and determined that she was an oracle, who had been subjected to some kind of tests by the government's secret agency, the TRG, for Theodore Roundtree Group. Later, many of those left the TRG to join the Order of Nicomedia. The TRG's goal was to conceal her Fangborn identity from her but keep her powers viable until they were needed. But I was there, Zoe, trying to watch you and trying to keep your life as little complicated as I could.

Now I had a letter from my mother and my father, filling in some of the blanks of my history. I folded the print out of his and would keep it with the well-creased note she'd left in a cemetery in Cambridge, Massachusetts. Two parents, two letters. Two communications from beyond the grave.

I sucked up my courage to read the last page.

Zoe, there's this sword. I was charged with transporting it from London to the research facility in Japan. I felt something I couldn't explain when I handled it and I wanted to keep it. I wanted to keep it and stare at it and study it all the days of my life. But I brought it where it would do our people the most good, and didn't think about it after. I wanted you to have it. Zoe, if you have the chance, if you should find this, if you should ever see this letter, try and go to Kanazawa, in Japan. They told me the sword was two thousand years old, a mishmash of styles with some kind of medieval jewelry set into the end of it. It's not mine to give you, but if I had one wish, besides meeting you, it's that you have it. I feel certain you'll see what I mean when, if, you ever have the chance. There's just . . . something special about it.

*Wishing I'd had the chance to meet you, and knowing
I would have loved you as soon as I did, Richard Klein.*

I looked over at the sword on the table, which had to be the one he described. While I certainly felt an affinity for it, it hadn't joined the other artifacts in assimilating into me. Something was up with it. Someone had made a sheath for it, probably more to protect it than to use it, but it would do for the time being.

"Do you mind if I take this?" I asked Ken-san. "I mean, I know this is part of a reference collection, and you don't just take things from it, but if it's at all possible . . ."

Ken-san raised an eyebrow. I remembered the overturned tables, the blood-smeared floor mats, and the general destruction of the place left when the flurry of artifacts had abruptly raced for me. Then the sudden vaporization of the walls of the structure when the artifacts found me. "Whatever the collection once was, it is no longer. You might as well take the sword."

"Thank you," I said. "I know it's an odd request, but—"

"Zoe-san," Ken-san said gently. "After what we saw yesterday—dragons dissolving men, all kinds of unearthly shit? If you wanted it, how exactly do you imagine we could keep it from you?"

Chapter Five

I tried the Skype number again and finally got hold of Gerry Steuben, who had acted as my mentor in a crash course in how to be a werewolf, when he and his sister Claudia Steuben, a vampire, had tracked me down. I didn't recognize him for a second, because last time I'd seen Gerry, right before we went into battle, he wouldn't look me in the eye. With my rapid gain of power and knowledge from the artifacts, I'd been challenging a lot of his core beliefs about the Fangborn and their purity of purpose. It was unlikely that I'd be doing anything different in the near future, but he did count as my oldest friend among the Family.

But his face lit up when he saw it was me; that unconscious, unspoken friendliness was wonderful. He still looked haggard as he had before the battle, two days ago, but now there was some color in his cheeks, and he had shaved sometime recently. His brown hair hadn't seen a comb in a day or so, though. While he still had to do laundry, there was a definite improvement in Gerry's demeanor, a lift to his broad shoulders. Action agreed with him.

"Holy shit, you *are* alive!" he said. "I had no idea what to make of the news. And you're *where*?"

"Yep. Alive. Kanazawa. I don't know how. How are *you*? How are Danny and Will and Adam and Vee and Claudia—"

He laughed. "Yes, alive, and all doing good! Thanks to you, is what I understand. Vee said that you slowed time enough for her to get the others out before Porter's building blew up. Zoe, what in the blue blazes are you getting up to these days? Healing people from a distance, flying across the world on a broomstick?"

I laughed back; it felt as strange as it felt good after so much sadness and anger. "I sure don't know, Gerry, but we can hash that out when I see you in person," I said. "And I'm hoping that will be soon. Did we . . . How many Family were killed? Were we able to contain the battle?"

When I'd left Boston, the Fangborn were trying to drive the Order soldiers and Fellborn to an evacuated section of the waterfront. The Order's goal had been to incite the Fellborn to wreak havoc and death on the city, making it look as though the Fangborn were responsible. The Family's goal had been to contain them. Last I saw, there was a terrible battle on the streets of the waterfront. It was Quarrel's arrival, churning through the sewers and destroying them, that had largely tipped the scales in our favor. You've never seen anything until you've seen a dragon peel the top off a step van and eat the men inside.

"We lost about fifty Family, but not nearly as many as we could have," Gerry said. "Normal losses were nil. Part of that was that our surprise attack worked out better than we'd hoped. And the initial news reports are muddled, which is good. What with the explosions in Salem and the destruction of the Museum of Salem just a few days ago, and then Porter's building exploding, people were saying it was all part of a terrorist plot. For the moment, it's being treated officially as a perfect storm: decrepit infrastructure being overwhelmed by a small earthquake and electrical problems caused by a movie shoot. We have a cousin in the office that licenses such things, so we have 'retroactive paperwork' put into place. But if that works, we'll be on the road to maybe—maybe—being okay."

"Okay." There wasn't much else I could say; I had no way of doing anything about any of that. And even if I could, I was still half a world away. "What's the bad?"

Gerry was worried. "There's two brands of bad. The first is that we've lost some close friends among the casualties, including Justine Nash." Gerry cleared his throat and looked away briefly. "Justine has . . . had a family."

"How many kids?"

"Three. It is . . . was so unusual." Gerry took a deep breath, his eyes glassy. "I still refuse to believe that. I mean, first time the Fangborn population is growing in generations, and then we take a hit like Boston."

"I'm sorry." I digested that. If we had close to three hundred Family members gathered in Boston, that was a loss of close to 20 percent of that number, a terrible blow for the Fangborn.

"The good thing is we've been running scenarios on this for a while. Hang on a sec?" Gerry turned away to answer another text, and then a phone call. There was still a lot of mopping up going on. It had only been a couple of days since I'd actually been in Boston.

"Sorry about that." He picked up another phone, frowned at it, and slammed it facedown. "Like I said earlier, dealing a lot with containment. For now, via public channels, we're holding, but that won't last. There were news helicopters, and well, shit, anyone with a cell phone—and that is everyone, today—had their cameras out. And we had a dragon rampaging out there! Right now, people are upset by the lack of answers and what looks like a bureaucratic screwup; it's flimsy, but at least they're not talking about werewolves!"

"And the other bad?"

"There were an awful lot of people out there, Zoe. More than we'd hoped would be. And that leads me to the oddest thing. No one's talking."

"What do you mean?"

"I mean, we have some rough counts of how many civilian planes, helicopters, boats, and cars were anywhere nearby. Some we've been able to discount, and some we've had the vampire squads on, with good effect—they'll believe the new story. But there are a lot of others, too many, and . . . there's nothing out there on the rumor mills. No conspiracy-nut websites blowing up, no nothing."

I shook my head. "And this is bad because?"

"It's not the ones we can find. The vampires can handle them. It's the ones we *can't* find, Family and Normal, I'm worried about."

"Well . . . were they really there to begin with? What if they had to go away on business, right after, or go on vacation? Are you sure you had the right names and plates and numbers?"

He nodded. "We were very careful, used the best software, were super careful about covering our hacks into social media sites. There were a higher number than usual occurrences of violent crimes associated with the folks we identified as possibly having seen too much in the area. Much higher, much more concentrated than ordinary. Some of them we think were the Order's retreating troops. A few of them, twenty-five or so, got away and we're tracking them. But that leaves still too many, and it's slow going, trying to find out whether the police have taken them, arrested them, or finding out details about anything at the crime scenes."

"Hmmm." I bit my lip, trying to come up with something and failing.

Gerry also looked unconvinced. "There is the possibility of a clue. Some people were found to have seen the battle and were questioned by the vampires before they were given the forget-me venom. Nearly all of them refused to talk about what they'd seen, at first, which is in itself significant. Of those, some of them had a weird flavor, according to Claudia and the other vampires, and the same trend occurred elsewhere. Under much more active questioning and with the help of some truth venom, it turns out that these folks had been injected with something they were told was an antidote to side effects from the gas explosion causing all the damage and confusion."

"Wait, that doesn't even make sense. Who was giving it to them?"

"That's the thing. Some said they were police officers, some said ambulance medics, some said it was the army, and some said it was the CDC."

"And I can assume it wasn't any of those."

Gerry shot me a look. "Uh, no. They most certainly do *not* have that kind of technology. We are the only Men in Black around here. Until now." He shook his head. "What I think we're seeing is that there was someone else on the ground, who knew about the battle, who is keeping a lid on the information, keeping the actual news channels shut down. And we really need to find out what they want. Especially if they're getting more victims for the Order to use in their Fellborn experiments."

I thought about that. The Order used Fangborn and their Normal allies to try and reproduce the various healing and fighting abilities of werewolves and vampires. So far, the Fellborn Mark Twos represented their "best" success. But the Order didn't have the pull to keep *everything* quiet. "Who could it be?"

"We don't know, but it's got to be someone with juice. A lot of power, a lot of resources. We haven't ruled out other national entities yet."

"Who has that kind of technology and that kind of force on the ground? Inside the US?"

Gerry looked tired and grim. "That's what we'd like to know. There are too many Family members missing, out of touch, unaccounted for. I don't like it."

"You know," I said, "if I didn't know better, I'd say someone was copying our tactics. No chance it *is* Fangborn, is it, behind these things? Like some kind of I-Day evangelists?"

Some factions within the Family were more than ready to Identify themselves to the Normal population, and I suspected that if any of them were going to act, it would be now.

Gerry shook his head. "Too amateurish. They wouldn't bother leaving a trail; they'd just go to the nearest television station and blurt it out. But I suspect the senator is keeping a lid on them."

Senator Knight was a vampire and one of the major proponents of Identification. He'd caused me a world of heartache and physical pain, and was massively pissed off at me for having opened Pandora's Box when he felt he was supposed to. At the moment, we were fighting the Order on the same side. Barely.

I thought a minute. "Were there any traces of evil, where the crime scenes were?" True evil has its own putrid scent, which is impossible for most Fangborn to resist tracking. Some very old Fangborn were not so affected, and I'd recently been able to ignore the call to track evil down if I had to.

"In most of the cases," he said, "it was the killer who was evil, not the victim."

Ah, jeez. "Okay, so someone's doing their best to cover their tracks in a remarkably Fangborn-like fashion, changing memories, making witnesses disappear."

Though when we did it, it was on the side of good, there was no permanent damage, and if we killed, it was because someone was irredeemably evil. I wasn't thrilled about that, but what Gerry described was a whole lot less selective.

Gerry ran a hand through his hair. "It's possible the Order is working with someone, but we've got other problems. Right now, we're working on I-Day, how to keep folks from panicking and turning Identification into a nine-eleven scenario with everyone going mental with conflicting stories."

"If you can do that, I'll be impressed."

"Well, we're deciding right now. I-Day is on us, Zoe."

I digested that. And that reminded me to ask something else that I'd been worried about. "Hey, Gerry? Is everything okay there? I mean, not the battle, but have there been any . . . I dunno. Weird temporal shifts? No flying giant shrimp? Hitler's descendants aren't the rulers of Europe?"

Gerry stared into the camera, frowning. "Zoe? You okay?"

"Yeah, I just worried that . . . I might have done something, when I was trying to freeze time. Screwed up the time–space continuum, something like that."

"Not as far as I know," he said, still doubting my sanity. "But then . . . would I even recognize it if you had?"

Another uncomfortable question. "Beats me. Okay, well, thanks. Is it okay to call again? Maybe when I get a plan for finding my way home?"

"Oh, right—hey, we're going to have to smuggle you in, aren't we?"

"Well, yeah, but don't worry about it. I think we have it solved on this end."

"Good. We're stretched as thin as we can be here. But sure, call. If you get through, I can give you an update. But right now . . ." Gerry gave me a weary grin. "Keeping in contact with you is the least of our worries."

"I hear ya. But Gerry, damn. It's good to see you. Please give everyone my best, okay? Tell them I'm coming home soon."

"Anyone in particular?"

He was asking if I wanted to send a message to Will or Adam. Will, my first love, who betrayed me to the TRG believing I'd turned evil, and Adam, my recent ally and . . . confidant. Both Normals, both extraordinary people.

I colored. "Just . . . give everyone my love, okay?"

He paused and gave me a look that asked, "Isn't that why you're caught in that little triangle right now?" But instead he said, "Will do."

"Thanks, Gerry."

I hit the off button and closed the program.

⌣

Ken-san had contacted a Cousin with a spare US passport and had it doctored up appropriately. "It's rough," he said, "but with a vampire's assistance convincing the airport officials, it should get you out of the country."

"Thank you. And I'm so sorry for all the trouble I've brought you."

"Zoe, trouble was already here," he said simply. "The attack would have happened without you or Buell, perhaps with a different, even worse outcome."

I wasn't so sure.

"Before you go, would you please join Okamura-san in her room? She'd like . . ." He smiled. "She'd like a word."

I raised my eyebrows. He knew I now had about three words in Japanese. "Okay."

Okamura-san was in the middle of the floor, surrounded by paper and brushes. She was on her knees, both hands together, rubbing a stone against another stone. For a moment, I thought she was using a stone mano and metate, but then realized that she was grinding a block of something solid and black against a stone. She was making ink.

"Please come sit next to Okamura-san, on your knees if you can."

Once I was arranged, Ken-san said, "Okamura-san would like to do a reading. And in order to do that, she will do a writing."

Another secret smile, and this time, I got the joke. Okamura-san did her readings with calligraphy.

What "word" she'd find for me, I was very curious to learn.

When the ink was prepared, she sat back and stared at the paper. Sunlight flooded the whole room, and as hard as I tried to concentrate and be patient, I felt myself dozing off.

"If you would very lightly place your hand on Okamura-san's," Ken-san said quietly. "She is ready to begin."

Okamura-san had picked up a brush and was poised to work. Her eyes were glassy and unfocused, and when I reached over, I was very careful to place my hand on hers without adding undue pressure.

Her brush suddenly flew across the paper, and as she worked almost effortlessly, I felt another flowing between us, similar to what I'd shared the first time I'd worked with the Trips. This was a fainter connection, possibly because it was just the two of us, but it was there, and my hand moved with hers over the paper, gliding like a planchette across a Ouija board.

The brush left the paper several times to finish characters, and once for more ink. The ink was beginning to thin as we made the last flourish, and Okamura-san sat back with satisfaction, placing the brush neatly beside her.

Okamura-san studied the calligraphy and then began discussing it with Ken-san. They both looked at me, and then Okamura-san shook her head.

"When you arrive in Boston," Ken-san said at last, "please let us know. I will email you Okamura-san's reading then."

"Uhhh, but I'm right here now?"

"It will make more sense once you are home," he said.

He was lying and I knew it. I was about to protest again, but instead nodded. No sense telling him I could detect lies, and no doubt, they had their reasons. "*Dōmo arigatō gozaimasu*, Okamura-san." I bowed deeply and she returned it. I struggled to get back to my feet. My legs had gone to sleep.

I didn't press Ken-san because I was horribly afraid he'd tell me how hard a time I was going to have getting home. I had enough bad luck without looking for more.

The ride to the airport was quiet. Our good-byes were muted, and my newfound Family rushed off once I was at the airport, because there was a lot of work to do in the next few days. They'd handed me off to a vampire named Viktor Denisov, who escorted me, easing my way through immigration with some pheromones that convinced the guards that I wasn't worth noticing, and a few gentle, persuasive nudges suggesting my papers were perfectly in order.

Only once we were through did I realize we were not going to the commercial airlines.

I was expecting a cargo plane of some sort and was surprised to see a sleek private jet. "That's *us*?"

Viktor laughed. "Yes, that's us. Welcome to Fangborn Air's prize Gulfstream. As far as my Normal colleagues know, I cater to businessmen and the wealthy who aren't rich enough to own their own jet. This will get us to San Francisco, and then we'll refuel and change pilots."

I sat by myself; another Fangborn was sitting in the back, working furiously on a computer and phone. She waved and then ignored me, which was fine with me. I pulled out the phone and new earplugs Kazumi-san had thoughtfully provided for me to replace my battered ones. She'd even added my sim card, so I could settle down and listen to music, a pleasure I'd been denied for . . . I couldn't remember how long.

Viktor went through his pilot checklist. We took off, and I watched the cityscapes and cargo ships fall away beneath us. When we left the fascinating coastline behind, I slept.

"Hellbender! Where do you go?"

I sat bolt upright. I could not see Quarrel when he contacted me like this, but even when he spoke in my head, muted to keep from scrambling my fragile werewolf brain, it was a shock to hear the dragon's voice come from nowhere. I looked around. The werewolf on the computer was still busily at work crunching numbers or writing press statements or playing *Angry Birds*.

"Uh, home?" I said quietly.

"You left in such haste. Naserian recalled something to tell you, but I cannot understand it. She asked if she might communicate directly with you, as we are now."

"Uh . . . sure?"

As soon as I'd given my consent, an image blasted into my head—one of my visions from Ephesus, of a cave in a desert and a scorpion, coming back hard and vivid. The last time I'd had this vision, I was in the middle of a raging gunfight, in addition to opening Pandora's Box and feeling the bracelet driven into my flesh for the first time. Now I had time to pay attention to the details.

The cave I'd seen was actually a tomb overlooking a small village on the Nile. The blues and greens of the river and its banks stood out starkly against the sere brown of the hilly desert that stretched out beyond.

It had just dawned on me that Naserian was telling me I had to go to Egypt. The urge to get the artifact that was in that place was distressing.

Before I had time to panic, to worry that I might suddenly wish myself to nineteenth-century Egypt, more images flooded my brain, this time somewhat more familiar.

A young woman, in a smart 1940s suit, walking down a runway with a small square suitcase in her hand. She was clutching a ticket that said "Kuskokwim" and hurrying from a small prop plane to a log cabin with red shutters.

The artifact was in the Alaskan bush. I had to get it.

Naserian was gone as soon as I'd had that thought. I felt a vague sense of satisfaction from her, as if I'd successfully understood her meaning.

"Quarrel?"

"Hellbender?"

I chose my words carefully, knowing how dragons could be about objects of power. "Why did Naserian give me that information?" I was curious about why Naserian didn't try to seize it for herself, but didn't want to tip off Quarrel if I didn't have to. I would not want to fight him over such power, especially because he seemed so much more vigorous than our first meeting when he considered eating me.

"She says she pledges herself to you."

"Ah." Which meant exactly nothing to me.

"She claims there's power to be had by following you." Quarrel didn't seem convinced yet. "She is terribly learned among our kind, but she is so old she sometimes forgets how to communicate, with you, with us . . ." He continued in what I think was meant to be a whisper, but would have put the jet's engines to shame for volume. "I think she may be losing grasp on her human memories entirely."

"Well, convey my thanks."

"What did she say, Hellbender?"

"I didn't understand most of it. Mostly it felt like . . . best wishes. That sort of thing." I decided if she wasn't sharing her conversation with Quarrel, I wouldn't, either. I changed the subject quickly. "Quarrel, why do you call me that? Hellbender?"

"It is what you are," he said, a bit puzzled. "It is very unusual in one so young as you, especially with your incomplete—" Quarrel often became incomprehensible when speaking in terms only a dragon could understand.

"Well, thank you." I thought a moment. "What are you up to now?"

"Up to?"

"How do you occupy yourself when I don't see you?"

"I am often resting. Moving about as I do takes much energy."

"I can imagine."

"But sometimes I am in communication with the Makers."

That reminded me of something I'd prefer stayed buried in memory. "Quarrel . . . how greatly did my speech, my manner, offend the Makers?"

"They were curious as to why you left so abruptly. They found that . . . worrying."

"I left? They didn't . . . send me away from them? How did I get to Japan, then?"

"That was all of your doing. If you do not yet comprehend your powers, as you seem not to, you must study them as I do."

The dragon's rebuke was as stern as it was silly to me. If I'd had a chance to catch my breath, I'd be studying those powers very closely indeed.

"Perhaps I could speak with the Makers directly? I have many questions, especially about how we are considered to be broken. And what does 'broken' mean?" I recalled my own issues and the mishap that landed me in Japan. "What do *they* think we *should* look like?"

"I shall see if we may speak with them. And I shall ask your questions." The dragon's attention was suddenly elsewhere.

There was a long pause that worried me increasingly as it continued. At least Quarrel seemed relieved when he disengaged from the conversation and returned to me. "Ah, much is made clear."

I tried not to be impatient. What was clear to dragons wasn't necessarily clear to the rest of us. "Okay."

"I have explained what most of us born to the Fang and the Talent perceive as our function. The Makers expressed great surprise at this, which is only partially what their intent was. Not at all what they expected to find here."

"And what did they expect to find?"

Naserian picked up here; she could speak more easily now. Her voice was like iron, ringing against stone, with the weight of years and authority. "They anticipated, with some logic, to find, once we had grown sufficiently in power to communicate with them, that we would rule wherever we went."

The dragons, believing their tasks completed, vanished.

———

I rested my head against the window, the vibration rattling my brain almost as much as my thoughts were. I'm as open-minded as a girl who's a werewolf fighting an evil mutant army can be, but understanding dragons was beyond me. It made me worry about meeting something even more inscrutable than they were.

When Viktor came out to chat, I told him about my change in plans. "I guess I'm getting out in San Francisco. I'll find my way to Anchorage, and maybe someone will be able to help me find Kuskokwim."

"I've never heard of the place, and I have close Family in Alaska," Viktor admitted. "But let me see what I can do to help."

At least I had that much flexibility, though I didn't like the idea of anything that took me away from going home. "Thank you."

"I'll let the folks in Boston know, too. Try to get some rest." Viktor looked at me appraisingly. "You're going to need it."

Eventually, I managed to sleep, but my dreams were full of bloodshed and overdue library books.

Chapter Six

Viktor managed to arrange it so that a California Cousin, Hal, who was one of the western American partners in "Fangborn Air," picked me up and flew me to Anchorage. From there, Hal gave me instructions on how to get to McGrath. I discovered that I'd have to travel on a small prop plane that only carried about a dozen passengers, which made me much more nervous than the very sleek and quiet jets Viktor and Hal had flown. We flew for about an hour into the bush to McGrath, a very small town where I'd get an even smaller plane to Kuskokwim. It was in there my luck ran out. The weather had turned; a nasty front was predicted. The sky was already dark and the clouds loomed.

I called Cousin Hal back in Anchorage. "I really need to get to Kuskokwim."

He said, "You can need all you want, but if the pilot doesn't think it's safe, she's not going to go. And the airfield isn't going to let her."

"I don't suppose there's a train? Or a rental car?"

His silence told me how fond a hope those were. "The only way in there is by plane. You could get there by boat, but only from somewhere else you'd have to get to by plane."

I paused. He said, "There's still a chance, but even if you get to Kuskokwim, you might not be able to get out again."

"Can't you fly over and take me?"

"Zoe, even if I could, if the weather is bad . . ."

"I can pay you," I said. "Whatever you want." The Family in Japan had set me up with emergency funds and credit cards. There were advantages to being Fangborn, and apparently, one of them was a platinum card.

"It's not that. For one thing, I'm on my way to shore up the front in the northeast. Some Family there is threatening to go public, and we're hoping to talk them out of it. For another, I wouldn't fly in that weather, either. For a third, my plane is too big. The airfield at Kuskokwim can't handle it—too short, too narrow."

I remembered his plane, which was actually pretty darned small to my eyes. I was getting a real education in small aircraft, hitherto a mystery to me, if you didn't count the airplane ride outside the Kmart when I was a kid. If his plane was too large . . .

"Okay, I guess I'll take my chances."

"It's not only your chances you'd be taking. Ms. Whitbeck's gonna take you. There are old pilots, and bold pilots, but not both. She's got enough mileage on her that you'll be safe. She's not one of us, but she's good people and I trust her. It's not up to you, unless you can Change into a wolverine and run all the way there."

I had been about to snap at him when I glanced over my shoulder.

"Hal, uh, I think my ride may be here."

"All right, Zoe. Good luck."

I sighed. "Thanks. You, too."

I turned off my phone, took a breath, and focused on my ride.

If her plane was anything like her car, I was in a whole new world of trouble.

The station wagon was at least twenty years old. The windshield was cracked in three places. A bungee cord was holding one of the back doors closed, because there was no handle. The number of scrapes, dents, and broken trim on the outside suggested it had been driven blindfolded and drunk.

The passenger-side window was rolled down—check that. It was missing entirely.

"I'm Luanne Whitbeck." She had the same drawl and aviator sunglasses every other pilot I'd met today had, with what sounded a little like a Northeast accent, but definitely not Massachusetts. "You Zoe Miller?"

Seeing her car, I thought about denying it, but I'd come this far . . . "Yeah." At least her name checked out.

"Get on in. We have a very small window for getting out of here, and I understand time is of the essence."

I nodded and got in. The inside was no better than the outside. The upholstery was cracked in places, missing entirely in others. Duct tape abounded. I could see glimpses of tarmac through the floorboards on my side and made sure to keep my feet along the edges that seemed intact. The odometer said "65,094" on it, and I was pretty sure next time it turned over would be its third, not first time.

The pilot was dark haired, tall, and slender; better, she radiated confidence of age and experience. A little weather-beaten around the eyes, she gave me the impression she could handle whatever aviation and Alaska could throw at her. She shook my hand, and we were off before I could shut the door.

It took three more slams for the door to shut. I looked over at Luanne, wondering if she would chastise me for being too rough on her car.

"There you go," she said, nodding. "You show that door who's boss."

I nodded, my heart sinking.

"Now, we're going to take a left turn up here. The door's going to open again. Just slam it again." She caught me looking around. "No, there isn't a seat belt, sorry. But I know you'll do the right thing."

The right thing was apparently jamming my heels under the seat and clutching the ragged upholstery with one hand while I reached out to slam the door again with the other.

"There you go. Won't happen again."

"The fourth time's the charm?"

"No more turns until the other side of the airport."

It took five minutes and we were there. A fleet of small planes of various colors and shapes greeted me. I looked for the worst one, convinced it would be my ride.

"We're over there, on the end."

I saw three sleek little planes, all in what looked like perfect shape. Any of them looked up to the job.

I may have exhaled my relief. All Luanne's money went into her fleet, not her ground transportation. I could live with that. "Have you always been a pilot?"

"Past fifteen years. I was a geologist for ages. But now I like seeing the earth from the air. A new perspective."

"Oh. I'm an archaeologist." I thought about "used to be," and decided, no, fuck that. No matter what happened, I was still me. Falling off my feet with fatigue, I handed her my bag to stow, and climbed into the cabin. I found the safety belts—yay, safety belts!—and strapped in. After being on small planes for the past day, I knew the "in the event of an emergency in Alaska guns and survival gear" drill.

Luanne gave a slightly different version of the drill than I'd heard before. "Okay, there's a flare and supplies in back if we decide to go camping. There's a gun up here if we want to go hunting. And if I pass out from too much partying, there's a radio here, and in back, in case you want to take over the DJ'ing. You got it?"

I blinked, and it was the first time I'd smiled all day. "Yeah, I got it."

"You know, I don't like the looks of the weather. I think it's coming faster than I expect, I'm going to ground us. I'm not going to get us killed."

I thought about giving her a vampiric nudge, about making her forget the weather and just going. I could have done it. But I didn't know anything about planes, and Cousin Hal trusted her. I'd seen what it took to fly, today, and I didn't have it. So it was her expertise, and my skin, and I wouldn't do anyone any favors by being dead. Alive, there were always more options.

"It's really important I get to Kuskokwim today. But I don't want to be killed."

"Anything you can tell me about?" She was assessing me but didn't ask why it was so important. "Maybe I can find you another solution."

I shrugged. The smartest people I knew, with the most on the line, hadn't been able to come up with another solution.

She waited for an answer. "Hal has some very strange friends." She cocked her head at me. "But this is Alaska. My friends are all strange, too."

I shrugged again.

"Okay, let's get going while we can."

She called back to the tower, got a satisfactory response, and we were up before I could have another thought.

The light faded dangerously fast. The clouds moved in. My time was running out. Never had thirty minutes seemed to drag so slowly.

"You'll want to hang on here," Luanne shouted over the noise of the engine, almost deafening in the small cockpit. That was the most she'd said about anything since my instructions on boarding, and even the Chuck Yeager drawl every pilot affects couldn't conceal the fact that it was getting hairy.

Suddenly, through the clouds, as if out of nowhere, a ridge appeared directly in front of us. I saw what looked like a line segment of a dirt road on top of a mountain, no houses in sight.

I realized: *Fuck me, that's where we're supposed to land . . .*

"I can do this, but watch your lunch. Here we go."

Another direct reference that I didn't like. I hung on.

We went into a steep climb, followed by an equally steep descent, our only chance of hitting an airstrip barely worth the name. Clouds had rolled in again, and I couldn't see a damn thing.

Luanne Whitbeck couldn't see a damn thing, either. She pulled up. Hard.

"We'd be better off heading back to McGrath," she said. She looked at me, trying to decide.

I didn't think I'd used any pheromones on her, but she sighed and turned around.

"Okay. One more try."

Another realization: *Today, Luanne's gonna have to be an old, bold pilot, the kind that don't exist.*

Luanne sat up on top of the windscreen, peering out. Then she glanced at the controls.

She finished the loop. "Gonna be close."

"Gonna be close" meant we may end up smeared on that little dirt line segment.

"Here we go."

We made the descent. For a critical thirty seconds, we could see the landing strip. It seemed smaller than a football field, impossibly narrow. But it had a light and it was clear, for the moment.

"Hang on."

We hit with a bump and immediately started decelerating. I hoped it wasn't skidding I felt . . .

As the trees slid past us, I reviewed the scant emergency procedures I was given at the beginning of the flight before I figured out that there wouldn't be any need for them if we went over the side. According to the maps I'd looked at in McGrath, the drop off the strip was close to seventy feet.

Luanne pulled up hard.

We stopped, finally, ten feet from the edge.

Every single muscle in my body was tensed for falling, crashing, dying. I tried to relax them, with varying degrees of success.

"That's closer than the manual recommends," she announced after taking a breath.

I was inclined to agree. Breathing unnecessarily would, it seemed to me, tip us over the edge. "Mmm . . ." I finally took a deep breath, rotated my shoulders. "Thanks."

She understood I meant "Thanks for the ride, for not killing us, for getting me here."

"No problem. Who are you going to visit?"

"I'm not sure." I'd been so busy finding my way here and making connections that I had no idea of how I'd find the house on the hillside. We'd landed on a small mountain, and there were foothills and mountains all around us. "I'm looking for a log cabin–styled house, red shutters, on the side of a hill?"

"You want Fatima Breitbarth's house." Luanne paused, opened her mouth, and then shut it again. "I'm sorry. It's just kind of unusual to come to Kuskokwim if you don't have a pretty good reason."

"I have a good reason," I said. "Just not a lot of details. Can you point me toward it?"

"Sure."

We said good-bye and I saw Luanne batten down her plane for the night. The weather was turning bad indeed. I pulled up my hood and followed the pilot's directions, keenly aware that every eye in the village was on me. Curtains twitched in the windows of the tiny, weather-beaten single-story houses that clustered by the river along a dirt road. Another road wound around the base of the mountain we'd just landed on. Gas tanks were behind every house—*How did the fuel get here?* I wondered—and a few of the more ramshackle places looked as though they still utilized outhouses. I nodded and greeted the five people I met on the road, which was probably about a tenth of the population, telling them I was heading to Fatima's house and asking, was she in?

"Maybe," one of the kids on a three-wheeler said. "Sometimes she takes off into the bush."

My heart sank, and I thanked him. He tore off down the road toward the one large, modern building, which I assumed was a community center or school.

While it was possible I could track her down in my wolfself, I couldn't handle another detour. I really needed Fatima Breitbarth, whoever she was, to be at home right now. Among other things, it had started to rain, and in Alaska, October feels more like winter than autumn.

By the time I finished the hike up the hill, it was pouring down, and it was cold. Any colder and the snow would have been flying. In my borrowed and mended clothing, I was not dressed for the coming winter.

I knocked. A light at the back of the house gave me hope, and when I felt the vibrations of an interior door opening, I couldn't help myself. I started to cry quietly.

Fatima Breitbarth was very old indeed, with bone-white hair piled up on top of her head in a style that seemed appropriate to the nineteenth century. The skin of her face was brown and fine and paper thin, her sharp features reminding me of the Moorish trader I'd seen in a vision once. She wore wool trousers that were getting rubbed thin at the knees and a sweater I'd seen in an L.L.Bean ad.

"You're Zoe Miller, aren't you?" Her accent was a mix of Arabic and German. "Please come in."

"What? How the hell do you know that?" I said, crying harder now. "How do you all keep knowing when I'll arrive before I know I'm going myself?"

She smiled and guided me into the house, and waited until I had controlled my sniffling before helping me with my coat. "Even if I didn't know the sound of Luanne's plane arriving off her usual schedule, even if I didn't have the airstrip in McGrath calling this morning to let me know someone was on the way, even if it wasn't for Viktor Denisov tracking down Family in Alaska to find the one closest to Kuskokwim and let me know, even if everyone in the village didn't know, for perfectly mundane reasons . . ." She shrugged. "I could feel it in my bones. It's always been my private theory that the older we get, a little bit more of the oracle takes over to make up for the lack of speed, the dullness of tooth. If we're not killed outright before now. It's just a shift in roles, an easing out."

I wondered if that wasn't in part why older Fangborn didn't react to evil the same as we younger folk did. The way I used to. A dulling of the senses, an easing out, as she said.

"Okay," I said, feeling abashed. "It was oracles who greeted me in Japan, even before I knew I was there."

She nodded. "I have dinner ready."

I was grateful for anything that helped someone anticipate making a meal.

As we ate, I told her about my visions. "The original one showed me what looked like Egypt. The most recent showed me this place, too. You coming here, with the village's name on your ticket." I pushed my empty dessert plate back, having declined, barely, thirds. "It's a long way from Cairo, isn't it?"

"The longest possible way."

"So, why?"

"It is quiet. Exquisitely quiet, and I have earned the rest. The cities I've visited, the crowd of bodies, the crowd of minds . . . After a hundred and fifty years of that riot, with another fifty of wandering before? About seventy-five souls seems just right." She smiled. "I can do my job here—oh, it's still not as easy as being an oracle, when one can telecommute sometimes if necessary. But I can protect the artifact, and this village is the best protected in the world, while I have teeth in my gums. Besides, there's not much use these days for a werewolf so broken down, so useless. I'm almost outstripped by the technology."

I swallowed, trying to figure out how I must bring up my mission.

She put her coffee mug down. "It's okay. I know why you're here. It's fine."

"You know why I'm here?"

"Of course. For the one reason *I'm* here." She tilted her head toward the back of the house. "Just because I moved, doesn't change my job description. Also, it's why I chose this place. No one gets here without a lot of effort, and you don't need to be an oracle to know when someone new is on the way. So *ja*, I knew you were on your way, and why. And it's fine."

I breathed a sigh of relief. It would be more like Ariana and Ben in Venice than Roskilde, then. "So, you're going to help me?"

"We'll talk about it in the morning," she said, pouring more coffee for herself. "For now, rest."

"Do you mind if I . . . There are a few people at home I'd like to talk to, if I can."

"Use my computer," she offered. "I'll get you set up."

When it was Will's face I saw on the screen, the honest face, the cowlicked brown hair, I squeaked with joy. "You look good! *So* good! When I last saw you—" When I'd last seen him, I'd pulled him back from the brink of death. At least I'd done that much right. I never would have forgiven myself if Will had died.

His warm laugh was part happiness to see me and part disbelief; his perennial look of skepticism, one eyebrow often raised, was a wonderful thing to see. "I haven't shaved in two days. I need a shower, but there's so much work to do. It seems like five minutes is a luxury. I'm so glad to see you! It's like being back in the field again. I'm so glad . . . you're okay."

Last time he'd seen me I'd vanished to Japan, via thin air. Our relationship had moved from awkward, when he was my TA in college and refused to date me, to torrid, when we moved in together, to nonexistent, when, worried that I was a psychotic killer, I dumped him. It became complicated when we met again, when I discovered he knew I was a werewolf before I did, and then ended again when he was convinced to believe that I'd been corrupted by my new powers and he tried to turn me in. Our time together had not been boring, to say the least.

I nodded. "I haven't got much time. I'm about to fall asleep where I stand. But I wanted to see a familiar face. A friendly face," I conceded. Maybe asked.

"More than friendly, I hope." Will shook his head. "Never forget that, whatever else we need to sort out, Zoe, I love you. We have history between us."

"And some prehistory, too," I said, smiling as I finished our private joke. One of the most wonderful moments we'd ever shared was after we were reunited in Greece. It had always been our dream to visit ancient sites together. That we'd spent more time fighting the kidnapper Dmitri Parshin and government agents than touring ruins didn't matter. We'd rekindled our love on a yacht under Aegean moonlight . . .

I caught myself in the intimate memory and blushed. "And I wanted to say that I'm coming back to Boston, as fast as I can. I just have something I have to do here first."

He raised the eyebrow. "Okay. Be . . . be careful. God, it sounds so dumb, but I couldn't not say it."

"I'm right there with you." I gave him Fatima's name and contact information and then wished him good night. "I'll see you soon!"

"Zoe, I love you."

I hesitated no more than a fraction of a second. "And I love you." It was the truth, but I wasn't sure what it meant between us now.

I signed off before things went any further. I was so confused about our relationship. I still seemed to have feelings for Adam, who was there when Will had misguidedly betrayed me. I simply had no idea what to do about it and for now had decided to keep affairs of the heart on the back burner. There were bigger problems at hand.

Almost immediately, a request from Vee Brooks. I answered happily. "Lookit *you*! All alive and teleporting!" Her face was broken by a huge smile, her Cleopatra curls pulled back into a knot. "Jesus, Zoe, you had us worried!"

I knew "us" meant her and Danny, my cousin. Vee had returned to the Family after keeping her distance for some time, making a living in high tech. An oracle, she wasn't thrilled that her precognition and her vast talent at amplifying another's power were always in demand. The exertions left her depleted. She'd only rejoined the Fangborn efforts when I'd found her, triggering a vision of Danny. They were a new couple, and the intensity of our plight would test their relationship.

Vee looked exhausted. Her eyes were tired and her dark face was drawn, so I gave her the short version of my doings.

"There was one weird thing." I told her about the sword that I'd felt an attraction to but had not assimilated. "It's weird, like pieces that were added over the centuries to form one piece made by three different artisans. You got any clues?"

She laughed. "Uh, *no*. That's way out of my wheelhouse. So far out, I can't even suggest where to start looking." She tapped at the keyboard. "What you need is someone who already knows all this stuff and isn't going to be hand-waving and referencing *Star Trek*, Warren Ellis, or Heinlein. You need someone with real, hard science skills."

"I need someone who knows this stuff and the Order's experiments and isn't afraid of hacking."

"Well, how about someone from the Order?" She tapped some more, brought up some files that flashed by in a blur.

"Yeah, right." I sat on the counter. "That'll work. Half of them are on the lam—"

"You did *not* just say 'on the lam'—"

"Half are dead, half are in prison, and at least a quarter of the rest are just plain uncooperative."

"Dan was right; you really can't do math."

"But you take my point."

"I do. And because I am just a demon with a search engine, I have what you want."

"How?"

"I'm pretty sure most of it is genetic—my parents were pretty smart, too—but lots and lots of study. Practice, to embellish talent."

"Ha. Ha. No, I mean, how did you find such a person?"

"Like I said—the Order. I searched who we have in custody, or who we can locate—who isn't dead, etcetera. Then I checked the reports and interviews the Fangborn have for their contacts with any Order personnel, especially in the science branches. That leaves very few, but there is one within five hundred miles. She's not been *super*-cooperative, but I bet we can find some leverage."

"Not so much leverage that she goes squealing to the press or does something even more drastic," I said. I didn't like the idea now that it was a possibility.

Vee shook her head. "The vampires say she's reasonably trust-worthy, and you'll be able to tell, won't you? She just has a problem dealing with us being 'vigilantes.' If you can reason with her, maybe we can get somewhere."

"I think you should reason with her. I'm not going to be the one who can talk her into it."

"Why me?"

"Because you can speak at least a little of her language and appeal to her sense of scientific curiosity. Or just offer to pay her a lot of money. Tell her she'd be doing her country a service—all of these things will work. Do anything, but I need help, fast, Vee." I worried a hangnail, still not liking the idea, but I didn't have a choice. "I'm in way over my head, and things are getting out of my hands way too easy."

"I'll see what I can do."

"Thanks, Vee. Give Danny a hug from me, okay?"

She smiled. "I'll give him a hug from me and say you said hello."

"That will do. Talk to you soon."

I ended that session.

"Is there anything else I can get you?" Fatima asked. "Otherwise, you should probably get some sleep."

I wanted to stay up and talk to her, about her role in the Family and life in Egypt, but fatigue took over as soon as she mentioned it. I gratefully accepted her offer of a nightgown, though flowered flannel was as far from my taste as you could get. It felt . . . reassuring. The light was still on in the kitchen as my eyes sagged. I fell asleep on the couch, listening to the clicking of the computer keyboard and the soft patter of rain on the roof.

The next morning, I woke quickly and smelled coffee in the kitchen.

We ate in silence, and when Fatima set her plate aside, I remembered with regret my real purpose in being here.

"So . . . ," I began.

"Zoe, as I said last night. I know why you're here, and it's perfectly all right. You can do what you came to do."

"You can let me have . . . whatever it is?"

She shook her head vigorously. "Oh, no. You have to take what you came for, and I have to stop you. It's the only way."

I needed that artifact. I needed its power. I couldn't let her keep it. I remembered the fight I'd had with Toshi Yamazaki-Campbell and how, half-dead already, he'd almost killed me. I'd almost killed *him*, driven by the artifacts to demonstrate our potential.

No.

She tried to stand up, reached for me. I hurried to support her, and she clamped on to my arm and stood up, with tottering difficulty. "Ouf . . . It takes me a long while for the joints to warm up in the morning."

My throat closed and I felt myself slump. I had to kill this old woman? I knew she'd fight to the death to protect her charge.

"Come on, no point in waiting. Let's get started."

I'd reached my limit. "No! This is enough. This is bullshit! I'm *not* going to do this. The other stuff . . . Buell? Turkey? I was trying to defend myself. I'm not going to do *this.*"

"Zoe, you have to. It's been written."

"Fuck written! I don't *buy* written!"

One disapproving look almost stopped me.

"I won't do it," I insisted. But as soon as I said it, I knew how childish I sounded. "Fatima. I *can't.*"

"Zoe. You must." She shook my arm. "We don't have a lot of time. Help me through the door. I've been waiting for this, thinking about this, for a century. I knew it would come, someday. Please."

This was as fucked up as anything I could think of. After so much sacrifice, I had to—

Fatima patted me on the arm, but that only made it worse.

"You're going to make me angry, Zoe," Fatima said in a moment. "You wouldn't like me when I'm angry."

She caught me in a hitching breath as I stared at her.

"Yeah, I know Bruce Banner. I've been around since before comic books." She gestured to a stack of DVDs and a player next to a screen and satellite equipment. "And I have a lot of time to watch movies. Let's get this over with. Help me in."

I gave her my arm. What else could I do? My thoughts raced: Maybe I could keep her talking, slip some sleeping pills into her coffee? Maybe I didn't have to—maybe I could just lock her in her room or something?

She went to the kitchen, rummaged behind the cupboard, and I heard a switch click.

"Okay, I've got the alarm off, and the traps have been disarmed. It's out back."

"What?"

"Walk about twenty steps directly back of the house. You'll see what I mean."

Miserable, I nodded, still trying to find a way out of this. Though it was only October, it was very cold, and a few bitter flakes of snow contrasted with the tall dark trees, adding to my sense of desperation.

I started counting, but just past a few low-hanging branches I saw what she meant. An old outhouse was back there, the door nailed shut and the little moon eaten away at the edges by wind and insects and weathering age. To one side, a nice shed with expensive equipment nearby; no one would go for the outhouse with that shed or electronics in the house so obviously sitting there.

My nose wrinkling automatically, I slowed as I approached. My wolfy senses, however, told me there was no odor. I unknotted the twine with the sign that said "Caution" and saw the boards across the door only appeared to be nailed down. I pulled on the rope handle, and the door swung open, cosmetic barriers and all.

Still, I hesitated. My eyes adjusted to the light gradually, and while there was an even layer of dirt and cobwebs over everything, I realized the bench that had once housed a seat was made of much newer wood than the rest of the structure. I bent over and shoved it, feeling it solid until I pressed a knot in the panel. A click, and the panel slid around, revealing a space. The front of the bench had been made of three planks meticulously cut into panels. It rolled like it was on bearings, and when I slid the panel frame back, I saw what I'd come for.

I was not expecting the crude glass case. The glass was dark blue, barely translucent, and the waviness—it was remarkably free of bubbles—suggested that it was made in the sixteen hundreds, carefully crafted to protect what was inside. My bracelet flared, filling the small chamber with golden light. I knew I had to have whatever was in the box.

Moving as smoothly as I could, I pulled the case loose. The morning light showed another puzzle: inside the glass box, a rounded oblong about a foot long, were several glass pillars, filled with a dark liquid. In the center of the case, the most clear panels revealed the contents, which I knew was what I was after. It was a scrap of paper, the ink faint and illegible but still visible.

It was in very good shape, and I knew that if I could get this into the hands of an expert, we'd get a rare and valuable glimpse into the Fangborn past. The liquidity of the ink in the pillars, the fineness of the glass, and the preservation of the paper were all so improbable that I knew some mastery approaching magic had created this.

The burning need became even stronger, and the urge to hold the paper, to smell it, to feel the ink strokes on the rough surface of the paper—papyrus?—was irresistible. I could not wait for experts. It did not matter that I could not read the text. I needed it.

My pulse was pounding as if the bracelet was communicating its desire for the paper directly into my heart. I was sweating in the cold air as I tried to figure out what to do. If I broke the glass, the ink would splash the text, making it illegible. If I didn't open it, I'd go mad.

The glass began to dissolve, and when the glass began to flake away, disintegrating before my eyes, I saw the aqua glow of a light inside that reminded me of Claros.

It was either use my powers or lose the gift of Naserian.

I half-Changed and pushed my hand through the glass without shattering it. Again, I was reminded of the rubbery resistance of the "stone" at Claros and even more of my use of the artifact catalog in the lab bench. As my fingertips brushed the uneven edge of the papyrus, the outhouse disappeared.

Chapter Seven

A whoosh, a roaring in my ears, and the sense of vertigo that accompanied many of my visions or transportation to some . . . otherwise. This had happened since the bracelet had claimed me, and I was getting used to the disembodiment, the confusion. I was getting better at these transitions—whether they were in my head or some alternate universe—less panicky in the experience and stronger in my recovery. They were a part of my life now.

So I was unsurprised when I found myself in the middle of a vast space, clutching the fragment.

I hastily uncurled my hand, carefully smoothing out the piece without rubbing it. I heard the shuffling of human feet, the small noises of people standing quietly nearby, and saw that I was in a short line. I craned around and saw that there was a desk with several people ahead of me.

The space around me flickered and changed. At first, I thought I saw marble and sandstone columns, with racks of baskets in niches on the walls, filled with scrolls. Another flicker, and then it was as though I was in a busy newsroom, filled with blinking screens, the light reflecting from the readers' faces like the glow from a microfiche reader. But the "screens" were actually bright columns of text in midair, and there were no visible computers or keyboards. I hadn't had time to try to analyze the language on the screens when the scene shifted again. This time, I found myself in a library, like that of a university or research center. The other patrons were dressed in clothing similar to me. I could have been on any campus in the United States.

I get it, *I thought. It was another attempt to communicate with what was familiar to me. The librarian sat at a wooden desk with a lovely modern computer. She wore a blue sweater, jean skirt, and glasses; she had the cliché of her hair in a bun.*

I saw the librarian's lips move and heard the sound of her voice speaking in twenty different languages inside my head.

"Uh . . . come again?"

"American English?" *she said with some amusement.* "I said, 'May I have your credentials please?'"

I thought rapidly and handed her the papyrus fragment.

She took it, glanced at it, and nodded brusquely. "Yes, yes, perhaps. But I must have your bona fides first. A request like this . . ." *She raised her eyebrows to indicate the fragment.* "It requires quite specific credentials to access this."

I was pretty sure she didn't mean my Boston Public Library card, or my BU alumni card. I needed desperately to see whatever that papyrus got me. Now that I knew it led to something else, my desire turned toward the unknown thing it might bring.

I wanted it so badly that my instincts gave me inspiration. I had something that the other patrons might have, or they might not; as far as I knew, it was my only currency in this meta-realm. Remembering the trick I learned in the bath, I dimmed the camouflage that concealed the jewels and armor I'd acquired from the artifacts.

I flashed them once, very bright. I figured, if they meant anything to the librarian, she'd get it all at once. If not, maybe I'd dazzle her into giving me what I craved.

She blinked, a little surprised perhaps. "Very well. Forgive me for asking, but you will appreciate our need to check. We can't let just anyone ask for anything in here."

I was about to say, "But isn't that what libraries are for?" *but didn't. This felt more like an academic library than a public library.* "Thank you."

"Do you require a translation?"

"A translation from what?"

She sighed heavily. "A translation to . . . whatever language will be most . . . accessible to you?"

"Um, yes, please?"

"The trade-off is that it will be approximate. You'll understand the gist of it but will lose a lot of subtle resolution."

I figured, better to get some straight answers and lose the subtlety, just this once. "Let's go with the translation."

She flickered in and out and said, "You may look at it in the last cubicle on the left."

I followed her directions and pulled back a curtain. I didn't see a carrel, as I expected. It was more like the rooms where you open a safe-deposit box. I saw a very plain bent metal chair and industrial desk. There was a box on top.

"Okay, okay," I muttered. "What happened to the 'I caught it, I got it' school of artifact assault, when the power came automatically and became another part of the armor and bracelet? What's with all the boxes and chits and credentials?"

I opened the box and a gray mist filled the cubicle.

I found myself in my mind-lab.

"Sean!" I hollered. "What's going on?"

If the last time I'd been in the lab I'd thought it crowded, now it was barely possible to move through it. The spaces around the benches, in the hallways, and on the counters were filled with the artifact boxes from the Museum of Salem and the ceremonial mask I'd taken from Porter just before Toshi had killed him at the Battle of Boston. On top of these were more boxes from the artifact onslaught in Kanazawa. Now books bound in ancient, deteriorating leather were stacked next to my computer.

"Zoe, we got another upload of data," he said, mopping his brow. He edged sideways through the labyrinth of boxes, barely able to squeeze his big frame through. His sandy-reddish hair, Van Dyke beard, T-shirt, and jeans were all smeared with sweat and dust. "The undergrads and interns? You know, the imaginary students we cobbled up to sort all these artifacts? They and I are on it, but we'll never get through it all and make sense unless we get more resources—time, bodies, money."

All of which I knew was a metaphor, but I got what he was saying. We needed to spend some energy focusing on these additions with our full attention. "Okay, okay, I'll see what I can do about getting in here to help you. But it's got to be later."

A burning smell, a crash, and shouts from the coffee room. The door to the lab slammed open; a tall, dark-skinned black man with a graying beard, glasses, and a tweed jacket and corduroys stood there. I'd never seen him before.

"Who are you?" we asked at the same time.

"I'm Dr. Geoffrey Osborne," he said. His voice reminded me of London, educated, but overlying something else. Like when my friend Jenny got mad and her posh accent slipped. "What are you doing here?" He looked around. "What am I doing here? Where *is* here? You really must tell me what's going on."

"Well . . ." I decided it was better to rip the bandage off quickly. "Generally, everyone in here is dead. Those guys you just surprised in the coffee room? Most of them are mercenaries who were working for Dmitri Parshin when I killed them, but some of them worked for the Order, maybe a couple of government agencies, and some are just generally bad people. Sean here was—is—my friend, and he died in my arms."

Sean nodded. "I did. I am dead."

"So for the most part, folks who died near me. But you? Best I can think of, you came in with the information I had from the librarian. She had offered me a translation, so maybe she meant you'd be here to help me out."

"So . . . that's it. I'm dead." He sunk down. "That explains a lot."

"I'm sorry. Yes, that's how everyone gets here. Do you remember anything?"

"The last thing I remember . . . I was doing some work on understanding the physics of Fang—" He looked at me suddenly. "Ah . . . you wouldn't happen to be Family, would you?"

"If you're talking fangs and fur and not Cosa Nostra, then yeah. You can speak freely with me." I glanced at Sean. "With anyone here."

Professor Osborne gave me a sour look. "Fangs and fur—figures. The bitey ones always seem to forget about those of us with the sight. Well, I'm an oracle. My work was finding an explanation in advanced physics for Fang-born abilities. The last thing I remember was a lot of shouting, a lot of hard men in black uniforms raiding my lab . . ." He trailed off. "And a lot of pain. Then . . . nothing. I need to . . . Where's my wife?"

"I don't know. If you tell me her name, I'll try and find out. She thinks you're dead?"

"Well, I expect since I *am* dead, she knows about it if she isn't dead herself. But I'd like to let her know I'm . . . okay."

"I'll see what I can do. But for now . . ." I gestured around the lab. "This is my place."

His eyebrows were raised and furrowed at the same time. "It's a bit of a tip, isn't it?"

"It's an archaeology lab. Not an operating theater." I frowned. It looked pretty damn tidy for an archaeology lab. Which I suppose meant that it looked pretty grubby if you were used to environments with no dust, highly sensitive scientific equipment, clean suits, that kind of thing. Still, it stung, and I made a note to get the undergrads on it. Wouldn't hurt to push a broom around the place, run a cloth over the counters now and then, once we got them cleared off. "A lot's been going on. And I'm new to all this, so it's taking me even longer to get used to it than you might expect."

"Wait . . . are *you* still alive?"

"Yep."

It took fully five beats for him to realize that meant he was inside my consciousness . . . or somewhere not . . . exactly normal. I had a hard enough time figuring out the mind-lab for myself, never mind explaining it to someone else.

"Okay. Okay. Okay, I'm going to need some space . . . a little time." Hysterical laughter went on a little too long for me but seemed cathartic for him. "We need to work together on this, you and I, correct? If there's a corner I could have to do some work, and computers . . ."

He stopped, suddenly wondering how that might be possible.

"Think about your lab," I said suddenly. "Or your favorite classroom or your study or whatever. Think about it hard."

"All right."

I felt an itch at the edge of my consciousness; a space had come with his memory. A bit of discomfort—I was doing a lot weirder, more complex stunts without really knowing all the ramifications. It was getting easier and easier to control, though. "Okay, down the hall is . . . let's make it a pedestrian walkway. It leads to your lab. You need any more space, resources, I'll see what I can do."

"*My* lab."

I reached out to see what I'd reeled in. Looked like an academic office. Lots of books, lots of whiteboards, lots of computers. It wasn't so much cleaner than mine, but the equipment room next door certainly was spotless. "I think so. Go have a look."

He ran down the hallway and came walking back, looking stunned, a few moments later. "How did you . . . maybe I . . . I need to sit down."

"Okay, you take a minute, collect yourself. Sean, do we have any coffee—oh, great, thanks." I handed it to Dr. Osborne. "Sean will look after you. I have to pop out for a bit, but I'll check in later."

"Wait! Wait!" Geoffrey Osborne was out of his chair, clutching my arm. "What if . . . what if when you go, I go? I mean, I'd rather not . . . if I am dead, I wouldn't mind working out a few problems I never had the chance to address. It'll be . . . quiet."

I shrugged. "I don't know. But tell you what—I'll go out, then pop back. You tell me what happens."

Before he could protest, or I could second-guess myself that I was about to kill him even deader than he was, I slipped back to the here and now and the outhouse.

Then back to the lab.

All was well. Geoffrey Osborne hadn't seemed to move since I left. "What did you see?"

"You . . . flickered. Just a few . . . you . . . wavered." He sat down, heavily, staring at me. "Bloody hell. A parallel universe?"

I shrugged. "All I know is, my lab, my rules. So make yourself at home, collect yourself, and I'll see you later." A thought struck me. "Here. Could you have a look at the papyrus while I'm gone? Do something . . . physics-y with it, find out what makes it special?"

"I don't do work on anything big enough to see with an SEM," he said, somewhat huffily. Then the idea seemed to strike him. "Why not? It'll let me test out the equipment in the other lab."

"Great, thanks. I gotta jam."

I was back in the here and now, outside the outhouse, shivering, the papyrus now a part of the lab. I needed to figure out what to do with Fatima.

My footsteps slowed as I returned to the house. My plan was to try and subdue Fatima without hurting her, if I possibly could. Even that plan was filled with problems: She was well past the prime of her strength and deep into her decline.

She was waiting for me in the living room.

"Stop!"

Her sudden command halted me instantly. Dreading this moment, I gathered myself and turned.

"Okay. You can keep going. Go straight out the front door. Don't stop until you're out. Then we'll see. I've been thinking about this forever. The prophecy says I 'will stop you.' It doesn't say for how long."

Everything in me rebelled at her direction and what I perceived to be her lack of logic. I didn't believe that prophecies were word games, and I didn't believe they were riddles. It was absurd to think of them as living things, capable of being fooled. While I still had serious doubts about prophecies originating with the Makers to be communicated to the oracles, I didn't think the Makers would be intentionally cryptic and I didn't think they'd be so easy to logically outwit.

Unless they were just messing with us. In that case, eventually, I was going to have a word with the Makers.

I went out the door, shivering. I kept my mouth shut and my thoughts to myself. I left the house, the slamming of the door behind me startling and . . . welcomely mundane. Having walked a good twenty steps away, I turned and looked around. Fatima had followed me out of the house, closing the door quietly behind her.

She was shaking, though, gray around her eyes. She looked another hundred years older.

I figured it out. "You didn't know if that would work, did you? You were taking a dreadful chance."

"A dreadful chance is better than none at all; remember that."

I didn't dare go back into the house, for fear something would command me to . . . do something terrible.

Fatima said, "I spoke to Luanne last night. She's going to take us to Canada, and from there, we'll cross the border in wolf form. Easier to avoid detection that way. And depending where we end up crossing, we can hook you up with Family to get you to Boston, if that's where you need to go."

I'd be that much closer to getting home. "I don't know what to say. Thank you!"

"No, I'm grateful. You've released me. For the first time in many decades, I'm free to do what I want! I can leave the village— well, not permanently, but I can do so without guilt that I'm leaving my charge untended. I'm coming with you!"

She returned in five minutes. She'd obviously kept a bag packed, as I was learning I needed to do, no matter what. Until I got the hang of resisting the Makers or controlling my own power, it could be lifesaving. Fatima handed my small bag to me, and then another bag similar to hers. I frowned; it looked like a kind of saddlebag.

"It's got a few standard supplies," she explained. "Specially made for Fangborn survival."

Leaving her driveway, we followed a well-worn path to the airstrip. Luanne was waiting.

I kept my eyes shut as we took off, but opened them again, not willing to let fear rob me of the view below. The weather had cleared; I'd never seen any place so utterly without the mark of humans upon it, the scrubby brush in reds and browns in tangles, with occasional open spaces of dead grass and bushes. The river cut through, dark blue, reflecting the sky. It only took a half hour again to get back to McGrath, and I found myself wishing the trip had been longer. The quiet had been . . . lovely.

In McGrath, Luanne handed us off to our next flight. She mentioned that folks had been asking questions in the village about me, and while that was no surprise, it was concerning her that some strangers had been calling and asking around, too.

I nodded, worried. Maybe it was the Family, checking in on me. But why not call Fatima? More likely, it was the Order. One reassuring thing was that Luanne spoke to the pilot herself, basically saying he'd answer to her if anything happened to us. He assured us that all it would be was several smooth hops to the border.

"We'll cross the border in our wolfselves," Fatima explained out of earshot of the Normal pilot. "We want to keep as low a profile as we can for you, and using a passport with your name on it might set off alarms."

Our goal was a small private airport near the Washington State border. When we arrived, we took a shuttle to a nearby national forest and ate lunch there.

We hiked out on the trails and left them, making sure we were alone. Without a moment's hesitation, and with none of the Normal prudery I'd been raised with, Fatima stripped down, packed her clothes and boots into the pack, and settled it on her shoulders, snapping belts and straps that I'd never seen on a backpack.

It was a custom job.

She Changed fully. I felt the thrill and a Call to Change myself when I saw a large white wolf, with violet eyes. With her teeth she tugged one last strap that helped her settle the pack to her wolfish form. It now looked like the kind of packs I'd seen working dogs wearing.

She barked at me, her tail wagging with the anticipation of centuries, the stiffness of her ancient joints all but vanished.

"Okay, okay," I said. I followed her example and stripped down, packing my meager possessions into the new bag, shivering as the cold air hit bare skin and goose bumps. It occurred to me that this time spent with the Family was starting to make me more comfortable in nothing but my own skin. I strapped the sword I'd taken from Kanazawa to my pack. Fatima paced impatiently and then paused so I could observe how she arranged the straps. After a moment, I'd done well enough to please her and feel comfortable in the rig.

I Changed.

We ran.

Fatima never led me astray. I felt like we were lost in the woods, only our tracks showing that anyone or anything had passed, which wasn't such a bad thing. She'd done this before and her senses were more attuned to direction than mine. While she was fast and smart with maps and GPS, which she Changed to check every so often, she also sniffed the air for clues as to the best direction to take, and no doubt knew the northwestern plants well enough to take cues from the change in vegetation as well.

The weather grew gradually warmer, and with that, more of Fatima's physical vitality seemed to return. Part of it had to be the relief of her long custodianship being over, her duty discharged. Still, while she always took the lead eagerly, she had to slow and rest long before I needed to. This gave me a chance to study how she chose her movements as a wolf. I hadn't spent much time as my wolfself in the wild, and there was an art to paw placement and choice of gait in getting through the wilderness quietly and quickly. My nose became attuned to the smells of wind and weather, and I was pleased when I identified the presence of a bird before I startled it from the bush. Fatima had mentioned during one of our rest breaks that she had preferred life in the bush to the heat of Cairo. Now she reveled in the cool temperatures and wooded terrain.

We spent one night in the woods and I had the chance to ask her about her life in Egypt. From that we moved on to a discussion of werewolves in general, and how she believed that the man-beast Enkidu was a very early variation on the Fangborn story, dating back perhaps more than five thousand years. Enkidu was a creature made to protect other beasts and people from a predator, in this case Gilgamesh, who later learns to behave responsibly. Enkidu was not human, but molded in clay by the goddess of creation, with attributes of the sky and war gods; he eventually learned the ways of beasts and men. I was sold. Immediately resolving to do more research on this myth, I added Enkidu to my list of potential Fangborn origin stories.

"I'd read something about Enkidu going to the underworld to recover some lost artifacts," I said. "Do you know—"

"Enough!" She laughed. "That's enough for one night. I need rest if I'm going to—"

She was interrupted by the howling of wolves.

"What do we do?" I asked anxiously. "Are we supposed to answer back?"

"No. We try to leave true wolves be. We're not wolves, Zoe, though we take that form. We're not here to contest territory or mates with them. The less we interfere, the better for them."

I fell asleep next to the dying fire, listening to the howling in the distance.

If we were not real wolves, we were much faster than them. The next morning, we broke camp, reassumed our packs, and Changed to our wolfselves. We ate up the distance as blurs across the rough terrain.

As soon as we crossed the United States border, I felt better. We left the national forest in Washington and continued on private lands, the trees becoming thinner, the smells of nearby towns coming more frequently.

A whirring noise appeared that I felt before I heard. Helicopters. Then . . . rifle shots.

Someone was hunting wolves. Or maybe they were hunting us.

It gave me some indication of just how old Fatima was when I realized that she didn't hear it right away. I yipped, and tore ahead, faster than I knew I could run.

She followed me.

The helicopters followed us both, gaining on us. It was as if the ground was shaking, with the number of bullets thud-thud-thudding around us.

The cover of the tree line was too far away. We weren't going to make it. Fatima's eyes had been bright with exertion and her tongue hanging out even before we started to run.

I stopped and Changed back to my skinself.

The shots continued.

If they're shooting at a wolf, and then keep shooting as it turns into a naked woman, then they're Order.

I was going to stop them. I hauled back and punched the sky.

A bolt of energy and an explosion, a crash, and flames and fireworks shot from my hand, power coursing through me straight into one of the craft.

One down.

A yelp. I turned my head back and watched Fatima stumble and hit the ground, blood streaming over her pelt.

I ran to her, my bare feet getting torn up by the cold, rocky ground and biting plants.

Quarrel appeared. He announced himself in my head, careful to keep his volume to just below organ-shattering loudness. "Zoe Miller, the Makers would speak with you."

I stumbled and tried to concentrate on where I was going as I answered. "I can't—I have to—wait! Quarrel, you must help me heal my friend!"

"The Makers do not wait. They brook no resistance, particularly after your last inspection. We must go!"

"Quarrel, no!" But with a crack that seemed to split the air, we were gone.

Chapter Eight

For a moment, I thought that I'd messed up again, unintentionally transporting myself back to Boston. Boston University, to be precise, just outside the archaeology department. Not at all what was necessary . . .

Until I realized there was no traffic. No cars at all. No trains, no tracks. No people.

Boston without traffic, without pedestrians or half the student population circling like vultures looking for a parking space wasn't right, not in any dimension. It beggared imagination. And without the MBTA trains clacking along Commonwealth Avenue, clanging their warning bells, it was wholly surreal.

There was a kind of traffic, I realized, as my eyes adjusted and the vertigo passed. There were flashes of green, blue, and purple light about ten feet over my head, as if things were whizzing by in midair, too quickly to be identified. Another meta-realm, perhaps one where I could communicate directly with the Makers.

There was a drabness to the landscape, which, added to the silence, further reassured me that the place wasn't real. It was a bit like looking at a sepia-toned photograph, with the color of the stones and bricks so washed out as to be practically monotone. The only place that wasn't washed out, that was nearly as I recognized it, in full Technicolor glory—and then some—was the Castle, which among other things, housed the graduate and faculty pub. A big Tudor-revival mansion with steep roofs, windows of diamond-shaped glass panes bound with lead, and stone walls covered in ivy, it stood on Bay State Road, away from the busyness and traffic of Commonwealth Avenue, and felt like a step back in time. The basement housed the pub, and I'd always found the gloom comforting.

Okay. If the Makers wanted me to go to the pub, I would.

The door was red-painted wood set against aged dark gray stone. The doorknob and knocker glowed gold. No sooner did I put my hand on it than it swung in. I stepped down into the familiar near-dark and paused. Something was wrong. I remembered I had been naked save for a backpack, but looking down in a panic, I saw that I was wearing something approximating my usual street clothes. But the feeling of something wrong persisted.

I sniffed the air and got nothing. I sniffed again and smiled.

When does a bar not smell like a bar? There was no odor of beer and popcorn in the carpet. I couldn't detect any trace of the cracked leather of the seats or the polish and dust on the dark wainscoting. There was a light at the bar, however, so I went to the other end of the room.

No one was there. There was, however, a small tray. Two beers, my usual brand, in the bottle. Two short, chilled glasses—vodka, no doubt. Two joints, neatly rolled, sat next to a lighter.

Someone knew my tastes. I decided it would be churlish to refuse hospitality, so I took the bottle of beer. After a moment, I pocketed the two joints and the lighter, too. I didn't think anyone would try to poison me, not when they had such power at their command; I wondered briefly if the "beer" was something to help me adjust to my surroundings, or if the Makers were just being courteous.

I took a swig, and saw the lights flicker on, leading to what I assumed was the office of the pub. I'd never been back there before.

Instead of an office, I found myself upstairs in the main lobby of the Castle. I'd only ever been in there twice, when I was at BU, for a reception for some visiting lecturer. Needless to say, I was only there in the least possible way to schmooze; that was left to the faculty and ABDs.

No, both times I'd spent with the rest of the graduate students, making a meal of the crackers and cheese cubes, gulping down the free wine.

Why here? I wondered. I mean, I get that it's familiar, but frankly, there's something much more unnerving about seeing a place you know that isn't entirely . . . right. And yes, yes, I can read the symbolism. It's a place of authority—the Castle had been the home of the president of BU and now housed offices and was used for receptions and other functions.

I followed the lights as they moved through offices, which I'd never seen, and I started to see people I'd never met.

They didn't go out of their way to notice me, or ignore me. When I paused to get my bearings, one smiled and pointed. "Just down the hall. You can't miss it."

I followed her directions and found another administrator behind a desk. "Good morning, Miss Miller. If you'd just sign in, just here."

She proffered a paper, with text I couldn't make out, and a pen, silver, heavy. I signed where she pointed, not bothering to read the fine print because I suddenly knew it didn't matter.

The pen bit me.

Like the door knocker in Roskilde and the artifact in Claros, I knew they were identifying me, testing my blood. Why, I didn't know; maybe to make sure there were no tricks in store. I would have asked for ID, too, if I'd been in their shoes.

She indicated a seat, and I felt a warm sort of glow, like I was sitting under a heating lamp. I glanced up and saw nothing but office lighting, but I assumed I was being scanned.

"You can go in now," she said, nodding at the door behind her.

I paused by her desk, trying something stupid that had just popped into my brain. "Did you know my mother? Nancy Miller? She used to work over in the dean of students' office?"

The administrator blinked, so slowly I had the impression she was searching files behind her eyes. "I know of her. Never met her."

"Can you tell me anything about her?"

"She's no longer relevant."

Okay, yeah, Ma was dead, but that wasn't a nice way of putting it. "I meant, her origins?"

"She's no longer relevant. You can go in now."

Okay, lady. I get the message.

"Thanks for your help."

"You can go in now."

"Yeah, gotcha."

I don't know who I was expecting to see behind the desk, but it sure as shit wasn't this guy.

Like all the other denizens of the Castle, he was unknown to me. Tall, pale, thin, going to thickness about the waist, with glasses that had been out of date before I was born. His hair was slicked back over an oblong of a head; I had the impression of jowls beginning to form. He reminded me of a long-ago German teacher I'd had: cautious, particular, self-contained, and restrained. There was a certain bureaucratic smugness about him, though I didn't feel his demeanor was unkind.

"Good morning, Miss Miller."

I didn't tell him how good a morning I didn't think it was, with a good friend bleeding to death in the snow and me caught up here. I kept quiet. I couldn't afford to offend him, not with this kind of power. I'd try after a bit.

"Good morning." *I swallowed.* "Er, how should I address you?"

"I'm just an administrator. You can call me that."

"Thank you."

We sat uneasily for a few moments, and I swigged my beer. Finally, I said, "You've . . . you've been trying to communicate with me. Via the dragons."

He sighed, deeply. "Yes, there have been so many attempts. We're not sure what's gone wrong. When we can sense you most easily, you're inevitably using your powers in a quite desperate situation or your emotions are running high. That may be the distraction that is keeping you from giving us your full attention. We were also so surprised to find you could not communicate with us. Ordinarily, at the stage you've reached, you'd be capable of perceiving and understanding us both."

Distraction? I felt my temper flare. "Speaking of distraction, my friend back there is dying—"

He totally ignored my concern. "We don't have much time; this connection is weakening. What do you want to know?"

The enormity of that question left me at a loss. I went with the first thing that came to mind, as he said time was short. "The dragons said you thought we, the Fangborn, were broken?"

"That is a harsh word, but . . ." He trailed off. "We were . . . um, taken aback, is the closest way I have of expressing it, to find not only were you in hiding from the other creatures around you, but also that you imagined you were somehow in their service."

"He also mentioned the word 'subjugation.' So we were meant to be, what? A spearhead? An advance army? You're going to swoop in and take control? Of who?"

"Oh, no," the Administrator said hastily. "No, the word we use is not unlike your 'ambassador.' And not take control, only . . . well, organize and keep in reserve. If there were resources or technology that developed since we scattered your—" Here the Administrator said a word I could not understand. "We would take them into account and catalog them against our future need.

"Your genetic material is human. We changed some of that, to accommodate the ability we find useful. For some reason, it did not grow as it ordinarily would, and rather than being dedicated to our purposes—"

I nodded. "The Fangborn thought we were dedicated to protecting humans."

"Yes, exactly!" The Administrator leaned back.

"Wait—what about the dragons? Aren't they more . . . advanced than I am? Why am I suddenly the center of all this attention?"

"The dragons are too old, too distant from their humanity. You're the closest to our ideal, within our perception, and your power makes you available to us." He actually began to tidy files. "We must decide *how to proceed. And do not worry. We can give you some assistance with your people. We don't want to cause any trouble, either of precedence or misunderstanding. We will sort it all out. Thank you, Miss Miller. That will be all for now."*

"Wait! No! My friend—"

But I found myself dismissed and was slammed back into the here and now. Which was not a particularly good place to be. While I'd had my attention drawn away by the Administrator, for even just a fraction of a second here, I found myself in my skinself, confused. I sat down, naked, on the hard ground, my backpack still on my back, the bullets still flying. A fine mist was descending over the area, and it seemed to be coming down from the remaining helicopter.

I didn't smell hellebore, one of the few things harmful to the Fangborn. I could only assume it was my journey back from wherever I'd "met" the Administrator that made me so powerless.

The big bird landed, and a statuesque blonde right out of a recruitment ad for Valkyries hopped out. She held a rifle on me, approaching cautiously.

"Stay down, bitch." As she got closer, I heard her laugh. She raised her goggles and relaxed slightly. "I've never seen the like. Running around, naked as a jaybird with a pack—and a sword? You really are some kind of freak, aren't you?"

I gazed up blearily to see the rifle barrel as it met with my forehead.

———⌣———

I woke up later, feeling seven kinds of hung over. I was wearing what looked like medical scrubs and dumped in a chair. "Rise and shine, Sleeping Beauty. There you go, sweetheart. I got you some water. Sit up easy now . . ."

I'd barely made sense of the words when an ice-cold blast hit me in the head. I screamed with the pain and surprise, sputtering and choking with the water up my nose.

A barking laugh was my only response. Taking a big, gasping breath, I managed to wipe my face on the coarse fabric of my shoulder. My hands were cuffed in front of me. I still had no ability to focus—tried to summon the Change and couldn't.

"Time for a little trip, kiddo." It was the Valkyrie who'd smashed my head in.

"Fatima?" My question came out as a croak.

"That mangy old thing? Dead. We burned the body, too. Right there on the ground." The woman—I could see a name badge that said "P. Halle" on her uniform—shook her head with mock sadness. "I *love* a flame thrower. You know, it's possible she was just coming around when the flames really got going. The bullets and the gas might not have been enough to kill her. That's sad to imagine, isn't it?" She wuffed and coughed as if she were Fatima suffocating.

I lunged for her and fell to my knees. I felt a jarring bolt of a Taser and the prick of a needle.

"Oh, save it for someone who cares. You and me, we're gonna go see the big guns." She pressed her face down into mine as I sank into unconsciousness again. "You're getting a treat. Not everyone gets to meet Carolina Perez-Smith in person."

Carolina—"Leena" to those very few who knew her well—was only in her early fifties and already a one-name celebrity, but one who most certainly didn't crave the spotlight. There was a great deal of mystery and mystique around this woman, with her trademark flaming red hair, alabaster, almost translucent skin, and rectangular glasses, so much mystique that I was surprised to see how petite she was, no taller than me, and chicly thin. Asked yesterday, I would have said I had as much chance of meeting Carolina as I did meeting the queen of England.

She had the eyes and ears of billions of people and her Rolodex might be the envy of the NSA. Industrialists craved her attention and fortune and feared them. With ten houses and a fleet of personal jets, she had a net worth that was conservatively estimated to be equal to the GNP of a not-so-small country—much bigger than Belize, but smaller, probably, than Jamaica. While her own fortune was rooted in real estate and industry, she married into communications. Information gathering was now something of a passion of hers. That marriage was short and tragic, and after the death of her husband, her army of lawyers made certain that the children of his first wife never saw anything like the fortune they should have received. So now Carolina had newspapers and television stations and satellites of her very own. She hired people to create a compelling image for her.

Recently, she had been developing an interest in politics, which was reciprocated eagerly. In an age where airtime means elections, there was no part of Carolina's wealth and influence that was not attractive. Websites were devoted to demonizing her as a modern-day robber baron or praising her as a model of the American dream.

A temporary office had been set up; this place had to be an Order facility. I knew most of Carolina's office real estate was back east. She glanced up, her eyes flicking over me. She seemed disappointed in what she saw, and I couldn't blame her.

Though the stuff she'd doped me with was strong and new to me, I was feeling better than before. Okay, maybe I'd find out something by letting her think I was weaker than I was.

"It's as simple as this," she said, making no introductions. "You're useful to me, for a while. You creatures quite possibly represent the next step in evolution. Even if the rest of us have to wait for ten thousand, fifty thousand years before we see any new physical, evolutionary developments, what your powers represent is certainly the next renaissance. What we apply from studying you to medicine, technology, exploration will be the heart of that renaissance. Sebastian Porter was making tremendous strides when he was killed.

"Even if we only use observation and testing, we'll gain in one year the same amount of ground we've covered in the past thousand. Imagine what we can do with vivisection." She smiled. "Cooperation would be more efficient, of course."

It made sense now. "You're part of the Order."

"I funded Porter's research; I'm the financial foundation of the Order. And with his death, I'm seeing a vacuum, so I'm stepping into his place. For my investment, I have in my hands the chance to control that next leap, to make sure that it benefits the right people."

"You and your friends."

"I mean, our country and her allies. And yes, it would be disingenuous if I said I didn't think I'd be able to make a fair bit of money off the process, too." She paused, then gave into curiosity. "I was on my way back from LA when I got the call you'd been captured. I had to see you for myself. People like you . . . Do you even know what you are?"

"A woman. An American. An archaeologist. A werewolf and Fangborn. Not always in that order."

"You're a threat. If you're the next evolutionary step, then you're gunning for *Homo sapiens sapiens*."

Look at La Leena, busting out the Latin and anthropology, however misinformed. "That's simply not true."

"If you are a mutant strain of humanity, you threaten to overrun us, like kudzu. And if you're not human, you're a threat."

"Where's the logic to that?" I said. "We've been here forever, unseen and contributing to society." It was very important I watch my words now. "Sacrificing ourselves for it."

"And what happened at Boston? Was that contributing to society?"

"It was. We were asked to help with a situation that was directed at us and threatened the general population."

"Humans were killed," she said. "Because of you."

"On both sides. And don't forget: Porter and the Order started it. We were—are—trying to protect ourselves. And for the record, we consider ourselves human." I had no idea if that's how most Fangborn thought, but I knew I sure thought of myself as human.

"I have no interest in what you think. I'm interested in the threat you people pose, and I mean to mitigate it."

I've been "you people" to a lot of folks through my life, and it is possibly my least favorite insult. It dismisses with no discretion, it lumps, it ignores, it diminishes.

I bit my tongue and kept my cool. I had to find a way out of this. "What threat?"

I felt her annoyance like a slap. "You know the stories; you yourself have *made* the stories. Murder, breaking and entering, theft, in your case alone. You killed Sebastian Porter."

"I don't know what you mean." My friend Toshi had in fact killed Porter, but I could have, just as easily. I of course knew what she meant, but she wasn't the police and she wasn't a jury. More than that, I reminded myself: Even now, even with me drugged and cuffed, she wasn't the boss of me.

"I have proof on every aspect of Fangborn life. I intend to reveal it."

"You can't! It would be catastrophic." I began to worry. She was the one behind the missing Fangborn and Normals in Boston. She had been in on the plan to set the Fellborn loose on Boston and blame their carnage on the Fangborn.

"All evolution, all revolution is ultimately catastrophic. It doesn't matter to me, as long as I'm the one controlling it. And it seems I am. Things are moving apace, Ms. Miller, and I'll need you only long enough to finalize my own plans. In the end, shortly, you'll be irrelevant." She turned back to her keyboard. A door opened, Ms. Halle and another guard entered, and I was escorted back down the hallway. Carolina was done.

"Time for another shot," Halle announced. Her exquisite model's face was gleeful, and I realized, that's why she was here. She was a sadist.

"Shot?" her colleague said. "Jesus, Penny, you said nothing about another dose."

"We need that. This one—" She tripped me, let me fall on my face, and then hauled me back up. I thought about busting loose and going to town on her, but I wanted to hear this conversation. "She's a priority. Keep her alive, keep her locked up, but give her the injections."

"The prep suites and cells are full since we started the major push," the other guard said. "This place was never made to hold this many . . . subjects. And we're not going to get another delivery of the serum until later today." The other guard was visibly nervous; the idea of failing Carolina scared him.

I could make that work for me, I thought woozily. I tried to summon up some vampiric influence. "You should just let me go. Anything you do should be about setting me free."

"Jesus, will you ever stop!" Halle slammed me into a wall. The blood flowed freely from my head. My healing was slowed. I felt three hard punches to my stomach. She pulled out a small canister, and I braced myself for pepper spray.

Instead, I felt my muzzy-headedness return threefold. Again, there was no smell of black hellebore—just the same strong reaction as to the mist that was sprayed by the helicopter.

"I love this stuff," Halle said. "Gonna be available at every corner store, come the day. Better living through chemistry."

"What is it?"

"Some new stuff from R and D," she said, dragging me along. "Labs were going mental when her nibs came back from London. Some old book sale she found had her creaming her panties."

"You shouldn't talk like that."

"Why? You gonna tell on me? Anyway, it's stronger than the old stuff, much more efficient, and even better when it's injected. We can just use the aerosol until the new doses arrive."

"Fine, but where are we going to put her? We can't just leave her out here, and we're beyond capacity."

"I have a plan, don't you worry your pretty little head about it," she said to the other guard. When we entered an elevator, Penny Halle opened a panel and typed in a code. She shut the door with a smirk.

"Jesus, Penny, we can't do that. We have to keep her safe. That thing in there . . . Do you know how many men he put in the hospital?"

"I know he's making my life even harder with a staffing shortage, and I'm gonna give him some eggs for that." She patted a billy club on her hip. "We'll dope 'em both up, make everyone's life easier."

"I hope you're right."

"Don't worry, princess," she mocked. "It's all on me."

I could smell the wrongness of one of the Fellborn before the door opened. My heart shriveled with fear. Helpless against one of those unthinking killing machines . . . It had been very bad, fighting them in Boston.

I heard a growl, and a snarl, then a hiss and a thud. Halle had gassed the other occupant of the room. It was pepper spray, though; he wasn't Fangborn, of course. More thuds followed, and I assumed that the "eggs" she'd promised the Fellborn for making her life difficult were being administered.

Footsteps, and she grabbed my arm. Not content with the beating she'd just administered to me, Halle and the other guard picked me up and threw me to the floor. I turned my head to avoid eating cement and losing my teeth but still felt a couple of layers of skin rubbed from my face as they were left on the dirty floor.

They were going to leave me here, defenseless against the Fellborn.

The door clanged shut and I struggled to get up.

Far on the other side of the holding area was movement. The smell grew stronger, and I strained to make my body work. My head ached inside and out, and whatever that stuff was they gave me kept me from healing, kept me from being able to Change, kept me from being able to defend myself. I couldn't shift my bonds, and just sitting up cost me a lot of pain.

Soft padding across the dimly lit room. I could hear the claws *tack-tack-tack*ing on the floor, in that peculiar half-upright gait of the Fellborn. In a moment, he'd be tearing into me.

I couldn't quite bring myself to close my eyes. That would come soon enough. I turned my head away.

The steps paused about ten feet away from me. I could practically feel its muscles tensing, bunching up, preparing to pounce on me.

A wheezing cough came. Gasping breaths, and clearing of a rough throat. Lots of phlegm.

"So, kid. What are you in for?

Chapter Nine

If I'd had any more screams left in me, I would have used them then. That thing had just *talked* to me?

I must be hallucinating. That happened sometimes, like when—

"Hey! Cat got your tongue? I said, how'd they get you?"

Growling, rasping, like a four-pack-a-day habit, but unmistakably human speech. The pain I was in was enough to convince me that I was conscious; the hallucination made it clear I was still suffering the effect of the aerosol.

"Got caught trying to impersonate a wolf," I said, playing along.

"Sweet. Nice to know I'm not locked up with a killer or anything."

"Well, I've done that, too."

"Shit. Well, don't try anything with me. You're not in any shape, by the look of you, and while I'm not at my best, either, I could cross some ethical boundaries of my own."

"Um, okay." I tried the obvious. "You're really talking to me, aren't you?"

"No, I'm an elaborate hand puppet and Miss Penny out there is a really good ventriloquist. Of course I'm—say. What do you mean? You seem surprised."

"Well, yeah. Last time I met something—someone like you, it attacked me. Actually, every time I've met something like you, it's been a fight to the death."

"Jeez, you must have some serious temper."

"No, I mean it was coming after me. Relentlessly, powerfully, lethally." It dawned on me. Must be the drugs slowing me down.

"Yeah, kid, I'm just teasing you. Tell me there are no more like me out there, could you? You know, good looking, thoughtful, capable of speech."

"Trust me when I tell you: I've never seen anything like you. You're different. You can talk, you're not . . . vicious."

A short barking laugh. "I wouldn't say that. They said I was slated to be the next model, Mark Three. They kept more brains and this time, unfortunately, got more ethics as well." He coughed again. "First time I've disappointed someone for being smart. When they found out I'm not one of those hyped-up, meth-head wolf wannabes, that I was protesting what they told me to do, they chucked me in here."

"Maybe you could do something about these ropes?"

"Yeah, sure."

The creature stepped closer, and I could see him now—upright, bipedal, same gray skin as the Fellborn, but his skin was less baggy and his lupine face had far more humanity than theirs. A tightening, briefly, a pinch where claws caught my flesh, and then my arms fell uselessly to my sides, limp with lack of proper circulation. "Thanks."

There was a long pause before he spoke again. "You know that's the first time I've found something useful about this form. I ought to thank you."

It occurred to me that I was thinking of *it* as a *him*. "What's your name?"

"Max."

"I'm Zoe."

He sniffed the air, a rough, wuffing sort of noise. "Zoe, I have two important questions for you."

"Shoot."

"You're Fangborn of some sort, aren't you? An oracle, maybe?"

That took me by surprise, but it shouldn't have. Of course he knew about the Fangborn. "Werewolf. With some . . . alterations."

That struck a chord with him. "Your 'alterations' come from *them*?" He jerked his head toward the door.

"No. Mine are . . . complicated. I was trying to find out more about them when I ended up here." I remembered my manners. "And you?"

"Oh, a human. Born and bred," he said, with another one of those hoarse laughs. "I was with the TRG. Just a security guard, but I saw some stuff. When the organization was dissolved, I had a friend who said I could come along with him, get a job with the Order. I didn't like what I saw, but it was too late, and when I tried to bail, they said I would be the next guinea pig. But let's face it, Zoe, you gotta use the past tense. Whatever I once was, this is what I am now."

The desolation of his voice was so great, I felt as if I were looking over an open grave. "Maybe not. Maybe there's a way to reverse it."

I knew it was stupid as soon as I'd said it. The report on the fragmented information we'd taken from the lab we'd raided in Istanbul had told us there didn't seem to be any way to reverse or undo the effects. And now Porter, the man behind it all, was dead, and all his secrets with him.

"What's your other question?" I asked when the pause between us grew too uncomfortable.

"I would give ten years of my life for a cigarette. You don't smoke, do you?"

I almost laughed at the pathetic look in his eyes but remembered how hard it had been for Sean to quit. "No. Sorry."

"I should have known. They wouldn't let you keep them anyway." Max stood up and dusted himself off. It was surprising to see such a human gesture from the sort of—well, I couldn't well call Max a Fellborn—a creature I'd thought of as a mindless, wanton killer.

"Well, there's only one thing for it," he said.

"What's that?"

"You and me are going to bust out of here, soon as you can walk and fight."

I looked around; I wouldn't tell him that it wouldn't take long for me to be up. Not yet, anyway. "The door is steel, locked, and I assume, guarded by assholes with clubs, some kind of amped-up gas that works miracles against me. *Lots* of guns. There is one window that I can see, and that's barred. And whatever shit they injected into me earlier is still really fucking with my head."

He loped over and tried the window. "It's barred, but it feels like there's a little movement to it. I think with the two of us, we might be able to pull it off."

I raised myself up cautiously, feeling like someone had dropped an ax between my eyes. My legs weren't all that cooperative, but I hobbled over. When I saw what he was talking about, I knew my new friend believed in fairy tales.

"You're crazy. Even if we could move the grate, we'd never fit through it. It's what, like a foot square? And just how high up are we, anyway?"

"I figure four stories. So . . ."

"So not necessarily fatal. Possibly just massively and painfully maiming."

"Yeah, okay. But there's still a way to use it."

"I'm listening."

"Take off your pants."

My horror returned, only to be replaced by doubt as he told me his plan.

⌣

"Hey!" I shouted. "Hey, anybody out there?"

"Shut up in there!"

"Hey, if you're going to keep me in here, you might give me something to eat. Or a bucket to pee in or something."

"I said shut up! I'm warning you!"

"And a blanket! It's fucking cold in here, what with the window open and all."

"What?"

"Ever since that hairy monstrosity jumped out the window—"

"Bullshit."

But then I heard scratches at the door and knew Halle'd got the keys out. I braced myself, knowing what would come next.

I wasn't wrong. The first thing that happened when the door opened was that when I tried to grab her, I got a jolt of Taser. "That's for being a pain in the ass. Again. You'll get worse when I find out you're—"

I fell, but as we'd hoped, Halle's eyes were drawn to the open window. Blood was spattered around the floor. It was only for a moment, but it was long enough to slow her reflexes when Max stepped from around the door.

Max grabbed her by the back of the neck, claws extended. He ripped down and it was like a class introduction to the musculature and bones of the back. Her head lolled around, not quite detached, as the rest of her body collapsed. The weapon fell with a clatter.

He picked it up, hefted it. "Can you walk?"

"Yes. Get her keys, her cards—"

"I'm on it." He rifled the corpse's pockets and then scooped me up with his other arm, helping me walk.

Up close, it was strange. I didn't have the urge to attack him, nor he me, apparently. I'd never been so close to one of his kind without being in fear for my life. Fangborn were drawn to their evil scent, synthesized by the Order to lure us in.

Instead, Max smelled like a wet dog had rolled around in salami, as well as the metallic smell of the blood he'd drawn from his body to create the illusion that he'd forced himself out the window. My eyes were watering, but to be fair, I was pretty sure I didn't smell like lilacs, either. Captivity hadn't been kind to either of us, and our joint exertions in removing the bars—my rust-stained scrubs gave us a little extra grip and leverage—hadn't helped.

We didn't meet any resistance, but we weren't convinced our luck would hold. Eventually, my strength came back, and I was able to keep up with Max's pace. It was like moving out of a fog, my vision clearing, my brain working better with each step.

A little opposition came up suddenly, and we took care of them swiftly. So far, we'd managed to avoid raising a wider alarm.

Max paused outside one door. "Hang on a sec."

"We don't have time for this!" I hissed.

"They had me in here when I came in. They took my phone. I need it back."

"Your phone?" I shook my head incredulously. "They'll have destroyed it, long ago."

"Yeah, but not before I made a copy of it. Trust me. You're going to want it, Zoe."

Well, he'd gotten me this far.

The late Penny Halle's magnetic card worked and the doorknob turned easily enough, so I didn't have much hope he'd find what he was looking for. I gave Max a look, but he dodged in. After a minute's cursing under my breath and pacing, I slipped in after him.

He'd hidden his copy of his phone on a DVD of security records. A duplicate with a date in different ink.

"Ha! Knew they wouldn't check their own files!" He looked around, patted himself. "It has pics I took of their operation here and a copy of their files for this facility. Just a little taste of how they've been kidnapping people—Normals and Fangborn—and experimenting on them." He paused. "Uh . . . I seem to have lost my pockets. Help a brother out, Zoe?"

I would have stopped to marvel if we had time: I had the Order's undoing in my hands. I found my pack and sword tossed carelessly onto a shelf until it could be examined. I stashed the DVD away in my bag.

"Wait!" I said, remembering. "There are other people here!"

"Zoe, like you said, we haven't got much time, and if we go looking for them, we'll raise the alarm faster!"

"I can't go without trying! Where would they be kept?"

"They could be anywhere, but most of the regular holding areas are down the hall."

"Two minutes," I said. "That's all we'll need."

Max fum-fuhhed before relenting and then grabbed a handful of key cards. "One minute."

We tore down the hall. Max stayed behind the door so as not to startle anyone while I opened it. "We're busting out of here," I yelled, and tossed key cards to the three startled inmates. "Take these; let anyone out you can find! Run fast, and be quiet!"

I repeated the process twice more before Max finally insisted we leave. The alarm would be raised at any moment.

We left the building, following the routes Max knew would keep us out of sight. We hit the door and ran for cover. I still had a killer headache, thanks to that guard's blast, but all I had to do was remember Jacob Buell torturing me and what my prize would do to people like him. The mere thought of it gave me wings.

Max seemed to recover, too; he'd had no fun being cooped up. It occurred to me: The Fangborn couldn't be the only enemies the Order had.

We were almost to the gate, and I began to let myself believe we might get out without an incident. A car was pulling up and presented the perfect opportunity to get out without having to find a weaker spot in the high walls.

Max stopped entirely, as if he'd run into an invisible wall. I grabbed his arm and pulled him behind a parked car before anyone could see us. We were so close . . .

"What's wrong with you?" I whispered. "This is our chance. As soon as the gates open—"

"That's . . . my car," he said. "My friend, the one who got me the job, is driving. Bastard never even tried to spring me, never tried to stop them. I'll kill him," he growled. He made as if to stand, and I yanked him down.

"No, we can't risk that now. I know what it feels like when you think you've been betrayed. But we've got to get out of here."

He opened his mouth to disagree and I hurried on. "This is a chance here. We gotta go. Okay, Max?"

His hesitation was too long. "Okay?" I repeated.

He nodded, and I shook his arm. "Okay, then. When the gate opens, we're going to . . ."

I filled him in on the rest of the plan as we sneaked closer to the gate.

"It's too risky," he said. Good, at least his mind was back on the immediate business of getting away. "Why won't they just—"

"Because as soon as we're clear, their way will be blocked, and once we make the tree line, we'll be closer to the public and have a better chance to escape." I didn't want to tell him I might be able to blast the guard shack, because I didn't want to get his hopes up.

He shook his head but got ready. "Don't know what the public will make of me."

"Doesn't matter now. Count of three, we go."

The guard went back into the booth. The "friend" rolled up his window.

I didn't have a chance to say "Three!" Alarms began to wail. The facility would be kicking into overdrive any moment.

We exploded from cover like we were startled quail. We hugged the wall as long as we could, until our two observers were convinced their business as usual was concluded, and then we bolted out.

Straight up and over the rail, onto the car and right down the back of it.

The railing was going up, but our presence startled the driver so that he didn't move. His car blocked the way of the guy in the guardhouse. And before they knew what was happening, we slid and clattered over the roof and down the hood. It wasn't the most graceful exit—cars are meant to be slippery and aerodynamic and not for running over—but it was surprising, and that worked for us.

My muscles found release in exercise. It felt so good, I ran faster, which was a fine idea, because I heard the telltale noises that let me know that the bullets had started flying.

I turned my head just enough to sniff and make sure Max was right behind me. I shouldn't have done it. He was so hot on my heels, we nearly tripped each other up.

"Whatever you do, Max, don't stop running!" I shouted. "It's gonna get noisy here!"

I turned, paused briefly, and blasted the guardhouse. That would keep them wondering for a while.

"Holy shit!" Max yelled, and ran faster, as if he'd been goosed.

I'd thought that we'd be safe once we were outside the walls and under the natural cover of the trees. I was only partially correct; as we huddled under a large pine tree, I realized I should have anticipated that there would be unmarked SUVs in the area.

I also should have anticipated there would be helicopters. Fucking drugs. Sirens sounded in the distance.

"Pick your spot, Zoe." Max was huffing, out of breath. "You figure out where you want to make a break for it, and I'll distract them."

"Max, we're both getting out of here. I probably have a few more blasts left in me—"

"Don't risk it. I'm going to look like this forever, Zoe. If one of us can get away from these sick fucks, I'll count that a victory."

Suddenly an anger like a firestorm blew up inside me. If he'd been wearing a shirt I could grab, I might actually have laid aggressive hands on him, but fortunately, his rough gray coat prevented me. "This isn't the time for that. How about we try a little harder first, before we go to dramatic sacrifices? That time may come soon enough, but for now, we're both going to—wait!"

My proximity sense kicked in; I had tuned into who was on the chopper. "Follow me—make for that open area! Run!"

The helicopter found us. That *whmmp-whmmp* noise was worse than an enemy's footsteps drawing closer. It was like thunder, especially made to bear down and crack the sky over my head.

But it was our copter, and I knew the people on it.

"Zoe! Get your ass over here!"

I looked up. My ears didn't lie. Adam Nichols was in the helicopter, his shoulders making a wall in the doorway, his light blue eyes intense. The wind from the copter barely moved his short blond hair.

I waved as I ran, extra glad I hadn't Changed. "Max! Take my hand."

He picked up his speed and grabbed my hand. He gave me a look but didn't slow down. I liked that. No questions about what I'd asked him to do.

The helicopter hovered, then set down. The racket was still unbelievable, but now that I knew it was on my side, I wished it a thousand times louder.

Adam hesitated when he saw Max, but he gave a signal, and I saw shadows within the helicopter shift and move. I wondered how many guns had been trained on Max, convinced he was a Fellborn chasing me.

Just to confirm the point, I shoved Max into the doorway first. Adam had no option but to help him inside if he wanted to get me inside quickly, too.

I grabbed his hand and jumped in. Adam kissed me, and I kissed him back hard, loving his strong arms around me, not caring what I looked or smelled like, or who was watching. With Adam here, I suddenly felt like I could take on the world.

A barked order from someone I couldn't see, and Adam broke the kiss, not entirely releasing me. I didn't want him to, but we had an audience. He pressed something into my hands, out of sight of the others. "Jean Leigh sends her regards. She's particularly pleased with the work she did on the Japanese landing sticker and the exit stamp."

I realized he'd pressed my real passport—now made somewhat less authentic by the forger I'd met with Adam—into my hands. I furrowed my brow but stowed it away. Time for questions later.

"Start talking, Zoe," he said. "What have we got here?"

"Max is, uh, a friend. We escaped together."

"How you doin'?" Max said. "You wouldn't happen to have a cigarette would you?"

"There's no smoking in here," Adam said automatically. Then a pause. "You spoke."

"Yep."

"And your name . . ."

"Is Max DiSilvio. Used to be with the TRG."

"Sure . . ." Adam still wasn't sure what to do with the information. Not only was Max *not* automatically attacking us, he could talk. Pretty good, too.

Adam looked at me. So did all the other guys—uh, troops with guns. One woman looked as though she'd happily shoot me as well as Max. There were a few Fangborn on board, too; one with some kind of headdress sat in the shadows.

I nodded. "He was another prisoner. They threw me into his cell—"

"Hoping I'd attack and eat her or something," Max added helpfully. "Or at least keep her too busy to escape."

"But we did escape," I said, "and there's a whole bunch of others trying to get away as well, spillover from her research joints back east. If you could let someone know to look for them—"

More barked orders.

"And the faster we get out of here, the better," Max said. "It'd be just like these bastards to have a rocket launcher and use it."

But we were already airborne and making fast progress. The speed with which we moved startled me. The ride was smooth, if noisy. As if reading my mind, and there was no reason to believe she didn't, the female trooper handed me some earphones. After a pause, and a meaningful look from me, she handed some to Max, too.

"Thank you." I nodded at Max, who seemed happier without the racket in his ears, which were probably even more sensitive than mine at the moment. But I noticed there were lots of eyes making contact and silent communication. There were a lot of looks cast back at Max by someone with a radio as well.

I don't know how much ground—air—we covered, but it seemed like no time before I recognized the features of the landscape below me.

We were nearing a Fangborn compound outside Chicago. I was about to be debriefed.

As soon as we landed, things went wrong. A team of former TRG members were waiting for us, guns at the ready. A couple of werewolves were half-Changed and poised to attack, and one vampire, too.

I decided to take matters into my own hands and jumped out as soon as the door was open, squeezing past Adam, which was its own reward. I jumped out and held up my hands, creating a shield between the welcoming committee and Max.

Of course, everyone in the helicopter was armed and on edge, too. So mine was an empty little gesture, but it had to be made.

I yelled as loud as I could over the dying noise of the helicopter engine. "No, no, nope, we're not going to do this! Max was a prisoner, like me, and I'm sure you have questions for him. But you know, I think we'd all be happier without adding more guns and suspicion to the mix." Finally the engine switched off, and it was a relief to everyone. "So put them down or . . . or . . . I will do something cataclysmic!"

They'd all heard the stories.

Max hopped out beside me. Guns bristled, werewolves growled, vampires hissed.

"I mean it!"

"Zoe, don't bother." Max put a hand on my shoulder. "Hey, anyone got a cigarette? I haven't had one in a dog's age." He caught himself and snorted at the joke. "Yeah, maybe a little longer than that, too, at least since I was a human, which was probably a couple of weeks now. But since then, I figure, I'm aging seven times as fast as the rest of you. Anyone? C'mon, help a brother out. I'm dying over here."

Someone from the helicopter team nudged him on the shoulder, handed him a packet and a book of matches. "Ah, jeez, thanks, friend. I cannot tell you how much I . . ." Before he could finish, he'd lit up. His eyes rolled back, and it seemed his anticipation in no way lived up to the act itself. I thought the next couple of puffs would bring the ash down to the filter, but he finally sighed. "Thanks. Zoe, don't worry about it. You don't know if I was put there to feed you false information, to help bust you out, or whatever. These guys are gonna have to find out for themselves. They can start by pulling the file on me from the TRG, Max DiSilvio. Then we can answer all the questions. Hey—hey, is that Eliot Thompson over there? ET, it's me!"

"Jesus, Max?!" Thompson stepped forward. "What happened?"

"Long story. You vouch for me?"

"He's okay." Thompson shrugged. "Don't know about what else might have changed, along with his new haircut, but he was a decent guy, for what it's worth."

One trooper relented. "We'll still have to hold you until we verify—"

"No problem at all, friend," Max said. "Just as long as I can get a shower and something to eat." He sniffed. "Better make it a big bottle of shampoo."

Finally, someone with a lot of stripes on his sleeve started shouting orders. Everyone seemed relieved to have procedure to fall back on. Max was whisked away, but I wasn't worried now he'd found a friendly face among the new ones. Plus, I'd made eye contact with the shouting leader. He knew I'd remember him if anything happened to Max.

"Come on, Zoe," Adam said. "We gotta get you cleaned up and to a meeting."

"I have a meeting?" I looked at my torn scrubs, covered in rust, blood, and ash.

"We're going to downtown Chicago before we go back to Boston." Adam's face was carefully unemotional. "I'm going to take you to meet my mother."

Chapter Ten

We ended up in a bland office building in Chicago, in a suite of borrowed rooms. There was only time for a quick shower and change into a borrowed uniform, which was way too big for me. Still, it was a chance to catch up with Adam, even if for just a few minutes.

"Two minutes," I said as I finished a sandwich, then tied the laces of my loaner boots. "You first."

"After you . . . left Boston, it took us a while to realize that you weren't coming back immediately, so we were really concerned about what had happened. Eventually, we figured out we'd better start the mopping up. It was looking grim until that . . ."

"Dragon," I prompted.

Adam still didn't seem to believe what he'd seen. "Yeah, dragon showed up. We had a lot more cooperation with our prisoners and many more surrenders because of . . . him?"

"Him, yes, Quarrel."

"Since then, I've been helping look for the missing Fangborn and Normals." Adam hugged me suddenly. "I was so glad when I got your text from Japan. That you were all right."

His lips brushed mine and we used the last thirty seconds of his two minutes in a kiss that was warm and passionate. I was almost willing to bet that Adam's kiss might be the antidote to the Order's new brand of mace.

His watch alarm went off. "Time to go." He paused. "Just so you know. I told my mother that you're . . . important to me. That should help a little."

"Help, why?"

"Because she's still pissed about the trouble you got me into in Venice."

Adam had once worked for Senator Knight. He hadn't known the senator was a vampire, and that the senator had been using Adam to stop me from finding and opening Pandora's Box.

"Well, you should tell her that's all on Knight and that you were picking on a girl."

As we hustled to a conference room, I was happy from the kiss and even happier to be feeling, well, clean. I was prepared to see Adam's mother—Representative Nichols. I was not prepared to see my occasional enemy, the vampire Senator Knight, or Heck Murphey, who'd been organizing the Family in Boston.

Interesting. I knew the senator and congresswoman had once been friends. They were as far apart in the room as they could be. Apparently, the brutal use of his office for personal gain, even if he believed it was for the eventual good of the Fangborn, hadn't sat well with her.

"Welcome home, Zoe." The congresswoman was tall like Adam, and her hair was cut in a bob that was blond going to gray. She looked as though she'd just stepped out of a bandbox in her bright red suit. "I'm Elizabeth Nichols. Are you hurt? I've been learning since Boston that there *are* some things that will harm the Fangborn?"

She shook my hand firmly, but I saw trepidation in her eyes. Fair enough; she'd only just learned there were such things as vampires and werewolves in the world and I'd manifested a sudden and scary power. I felt the same way, only she'd actively achieved and cultivated her power, which made her scarier to me. She had the government on her side, and I wasn't a fan of how my Family had been treated at their hands.

It didn't help that I was nearly a foot shorter than her and that I was wearing fatigues that were too big for me.

"I'm okay," I said. "Thank you. I'm getting over the effects of a particularly nasty new injection they gave me. Might want to have a vampire check my blood, find out what that is, see if we can counteract it."

"Excellent. Now, if you're up to a few questions?" She settled into a seat after indicating I should sit.

"Yes."

"Tell me everything, starting with how you left Boston."

I did, and then she surprised me by recapping them right back to me, to make sure she had it down pat. "So your powers are greater, probably, but still unreliable. You show distinct abilities usually only associated with oracles and vampires. Additionally, among other things, you moved through space and are capable of stopping time. You've been in contact with something or someone you refer to as the Makers, and you're in the confidence of creatures that are . . . dragons."

"Yes." It was actually pretty impressive when you spelled it out as she had. I was also amazed at how quickly she caught on.

"Carolina Perez-Smith funds the organization we know as the Order of Nicomedia, and that Order has basically declared war on the Fangborn, across the country, perhaps the world. How am I doing so far?"

"You got it, ma'am."

"And you managed to escape from one of her facilities, bringing with you a third . . . version . . . of their, er, Fellborn experiments?"

"Yes." I frowned. "I'd told that bitch of a guard she should let me go, before we broke out. That could be the only reason she fell for that trick. They were understaffed and ill prepared for the number of prisoners they had after Boston. And . . . I had some of my vampiric persuasion working on my side. But they were understaffed because Carolina helped organize and fund the attack on Boston. They needed more victims to advance their research on creating the Fellborn. And part of the reason Max was a failure was because Fangborn weren't drawn to him to kill or be killed by him." *And that's why no one attacked him on the chopper*, I finished to myself.

"Yes," Representative Nichols said. "She's been using the Order's synthetic copies of vampire venom to make people forget. Her news operations have been instructed to keep a lid on things, until she says otherwise. It won't last, but we need to be the ones who determine how the world finds out about the Fangborn." The representative looked down, checked her phone briefly. It was a stalling tactic, and to be fair, it was a lot for anyone to think about.

After Representative Nichols composed herself, she said, "We need to start informing the rest of the government about you. And to that end, we'd like to set up a demonstration, not only of the various Fangborn abilities, but of your own, um, peculiar talents. And I have people who might be able to help you with the artifact you mentioned—a sword? We have a lot of work to do."

"Why don't we just expose Carolina for what she is?" I asked. I probably hadn't been the first or the only one to bring that up, but I had to know why we didn't call her a kidnapper, a murderer, and a whole slew of other things. "Arrest her, shut down the Order. Bring on I-Day. With the information Max got us, we'll have all kinds of public outcry, criminal prosecutions, you name it. We take destinies into our own hands when we take her weapons away from her. It's time. Too many people know already."

Funny how strange it was to use the word "destinies" and have it be meaningful to you directly. It sounded too grand for everyday use.

"It is one option," Senator Knight said. His voice surprised me. He'd been so quiet through our discussion. Somehow, despite his tall thin build, his hawk-like nose on a distinguished face, and his air of authority, he was able to hide in plain sight, but that's vampires for you. "It's certainly the option I've been favoring for some time. We should have started immediately. I-Day will bring losses, inevitably. I'm not squeamish about the handful of dead Family and Normals the Order has."

I stared at him. He had all the viciousness of a cobra. The heartlessness of a plague. "That's not what I meant."

"We can't for the moment, for forty-seven very good reasons, as you well know, Edward," Representative Nichols said sharply. "Zoe, you may have heard how there are many Fangborn Family members not accounted for at Boston? Ms. Perez-Smith let us know she has the forty-seven missing, as well as the civilians—Normals. She's threatening to kill them and reveal the identities of all the Fangborn they know about. We go public with her, she goes public with us. Mutually assured destruction, and we want some control over how this data gets out. We're at a stalemate, even with the information you brought us."

Damn Carolina, and damn the Order, I thought. Bastards get to be evil just because . . . they're willing to be evil.

"Zoe, we're going to do both," she continued. "I-Day is catching up with us, and the cover-up is starting to get complicated. What was it they said, about Watergate? The cover-up is what kills you? So, we're going to try to rescue the prisoners at the same time we're preparing for I-Day. The government is leaving it up to this group to decide, but won't for much longer. It's getting too hot for them, too."

"The vote is a straight-up majority among the Fangborn," Herrick "Heck" Murphey said, glancing at Knight. He was an older werewolf who'd been key in organizing our trap for the Fellborn in Boston. "For now, the Family has decided to try and keep the lid on it for as long as possible. It was a slim margin, and I think everyone understands the time is short. They're preparing for it."

"Preparing how?"

"Some are hiding. Some are going through with premade plans to help with the announcement. Some are laying in supplies, in case of attack. Some are just writing their wills, also in case of attack. Some are deciding what to tell their kids." He looked at me. "What would you do if you had to tell them the world as they know it was about to undergo a tectonic shift? It's a revelation on the scale of the atomic bomb."

"My own experience has been so brief, with so much information, I haven't had time to respond at an emotional level," said Representative Nichols. "But the background emotion I feel is purely panic. Of what will happen when people learn about the Fangborn."

I shook my head. "I know how hard it was to learn about the Family, even with Claudia Steuben pumping me through with vampire venom. This is going to be tough, for everyone."

"There's been a plan in place for nearly seventy-five years," Heck said. "We've just been too reluctant to go ahead and use it. It's up to date, and we're reexamining it now to see if there's anything left to add." He sighed. "The Internet, hell, the *telephone* made our earlier plans obsolete in a hurry."

I thought about it: What do you do? Call up a reporter and say, "I know you're totally not going to believe this, but I'm a werewolf. And I'm not the only one"? Phone click, dial tone, blocked on caller ID. Even if you could contrive to get one alone and give him or her proof, which we could, it would be much harder to get that interview past the higher-ups at the station.

Then, what would they do with that information? Most people would also dismiss it immediately as an elaborate hoax, the ghosts of Grover's Mill, Piltdown man, and the Cottingley Fairies hovering in their memories. Those who didn't dismiss it will freak out, because most people don't want to know about upheaval or anything that challenges their idea of the world. If there are vampires, and werewolves, and oracles, however inaccurate or inscrutable, what else might there be in the world?

"Were there other moments when we thought I-Day was near?" I asked.

"Oh, sure," Heck said, glancing at Senator Knight, who was nodding slowly, a faraway look in his eyes. "We were on the verge a couple of times. Once, at the very end of the Second World War, but there was such a bad taste in everyone's mouth from the references to the Nazi *Werwolf* guerrilla teams we decided against it. The next time we considered bringing I-Day was during the Cold War, but still, the threat of using an atom bomb seemed less scary than Fangborn.

"Speaking of scary . . ." Heck smiled and shrugged as he handed me a schedule. "We need to take blood from you, to test that new weapon they're using. We need to organize the plan for the rescue—it's complicated, because the property we believe Perez-Smith is using is in the middle of some Family territory . . . and they're not exactly friendly to us or amenable to our plan. And Victoria Brooks came up with a few folks who might be able to make some headway with your investigation of the artifacts you're, uh, collecting. I'd like you to meet with one in a few minutes, just take her temperature, see if you can live with her. Then I'll need thirty minutes with you to work out our demonstration."

"And we need to get you in front of a camera," Representative Nichols said. "We want to bring a recording of you and your experiences to the government, as I assume you'll be too busy to be on the Hill."

I broke out into a cold sweat at all these tasks—and public speaking? "Why not just bring them a report?"

"I want them to see you, Zoe," Elizabeth Nichols said softly. "I want them to see you; I want them to hear your story in your own words. And show them your extraordinary powers."

"You've been recorded as showing an ability to blow up things and people," Senator Knight said impatiently. "You've been particularly hard on museums. We want you to do it for us. On cue."

I shot him a look of purest hate. "I'm not a weapon. I won't be a sideshow spectacle for you."

Elizabeth Nichols broke in quickly. "That's not what we have in mind," she said, ignoring the senator. "We need them to be aware of just how big this is going to be."

———

When the meeting adjourned, I pulled Heck aside. "How did you know where I was? How were you able to find that facility?"

"We'd tracked you and Fatima, and then your phone from their headquarters. Then we started listening in to the Order's calls. We got a load of chatter and found it based on that."

"Yeah, but we were in the middle of nowhere." But Fatima had told me that someone had been asking questions about us in the village. I didn't put anything beyond the Order.

As we walked down the hallway, Heck smiled, humorlessly. "I had eyes in the air."

"Must have been a pretty good pilot to see through those trees. I wasn't sure I could see the sky through them, but it felt like someone was watching me."

Heck gave me a strange look. "Well, someone was. Just . . . maybe not what you were expecting."

"In any case, I'd like to say thanks."

"Well, you get your wish." He opened the door to a room and we entered. "Jason Jordan, please meet Zoe Miller."

I couldn't make out many of the new guy's features. The heavy coat he wore had a high collar, and he was wearing sunglasses. Which I kinda thought indicated he was being a dick, but then it occurred to me that there might be a reason other than wanting to appear cool.

On the other hand, the two ravens, one on each shoulder, were a truly startling feature. They didn't make any noise, and each regarded the room as if sweeping it. I wasn't sure I liked the way they peered at me. Black, glossy, enigmatic, they gave me the shivers. The ravens looked old, reptilian, hell, *saurian* in some respects, and something in my monkey brain said "predator."

"Hi, Zoe," Jason said. "Nice to meet you." He was the Cousin with the odd headdress I'd seen in the shadows of the helicopter.

He stuck out his hand for me to shake, but his head was turned slightly askew, as if he was looking out of the corner of his eye at me.

Jason Jordan was blind, I realized.

No cane—how was he navigating? Almost as soon as I had the thought, the answer was clear. It was the ravens. The intensity of their gaze, the impenetrability of their demeanor . . .

I shivered again and then shook his hand. "Very pleased to meet you. And thank you. I could feel the breath of those guys on my neck as the helicopter came."

"We do our best." A faint smile flitted across his lips. "By we, I mean, let me introduce my friends. This is—"

"Hugin or Munin," I almost said. But I kept my mouth shut.

"Jack and this"—he nodded to his right shoulder—"is Jill."

"How do you do?" I said, disconcerted. I didn't think offering them my hand to smell would be the right thing to do. They were more likely to bite it off.

Jill stood, shook out her feathered ruff, and flapped her wings. She was . . . startlingly large, this close up, and I was glad when she settled down.

"Don't mind her," he said. "She's just letting you know who's boss."

Powers or no, I was convinced. "Can . . . you talk to them?"

"Not really. We do communicate, but it's limited. And not natural to any of us—I had to get some help from another oracle, who is better at communicating with animals. It's precarious, but it works."

"Well . . ." I said. Jill had never stopped glaring at me. "Thanks again for your help."

We all left Chicago. The flight back to Boston was uneventful; I slept and ate whenever I wasn't sleeping. At the main family compound in Boston, Heck brought me to a meeting room, where a woman with a short, blond, pixie-ish haircut and narrow features was waiting for me.

So was Claudia Steuben.

"Oh, Claudia!" I gave her a hug, and when she squeezed me back, it reminded me how tired I was and how much I wanted to just hide from the world for a while. She'd been a good friend and counselor to me.

If her brother Gerry was the very image of a regular Joe who'd been a high school athlete and then settled down to a suburban life, Claudia looked almost stern in her twinset, capris, and flats. She was tall, slender, dark haired, and light skinned considering how much she, as a vampire, loved spending time in the sun. Her hair was up in its customary knot, which wasn't quite mousy but certainly didn't make the most of her looks. I didn't think of this as the "real" Claudia, however, because once the action started, the schoolmarm disappeared and the ninja took her place.

"It's good to see you," she said. "I'm just here to do a quick introduction, then see how things go with you guys."

"More like, make sure I'm on the level," the pixie woman said. Her voice was quiet and low, but her words dripped with sarcasm.

"Zoe, this is Dr. Lisa Tarkka," Heck said. "We're hoping she might be able to assist you with some of the materials we recovered from Sebastian Porter's office in Boston and with the sword you brought with you. I'll be back to get you later, and we'll do the recording the congresswoman asked for."

"So, you're Zoe?" She looked me up and down. "I thought you'd be taller."

I automatically didn't like her. "Nope."

"I don't know why I said that. Probably because everyone's been telling me stories about you." She bit on the cap of a pen. "You don't look like a threat to global security."

"Maybe that's what freaks people out so much." I tried to keep my patience, because it was becoming more and more the sort of interaction I had these days. "But really, I'm pretty much just a person."

She seemed to wrestle with herself, before giving in. "Will you . . . Can you Change? I'd like to see it. Please."

"What will that do? Why do you want to see?"

"Because . . . I may never get a chance to see it again."

"You worked for the Order." I couldn't keep the bitterness out of my words. "I'm sure I wouldn't have been your first."

"No, like I told your friend, Vee Brooks? I worked for a company that subcontracted for a company that was an Order organization. I was just starting to do some very cool things when I started to learn what my boss was really up to. While I think it's very weird and very dangerous to have something—someone like you and your family running around killing people randomly—"

"Not randomly," I said automatically.

"Look, we can talk philosophy later. I thought I was working on how to interface technology with our central nervous systems. I've brought you this, on the off chance you can help me learn more."

She pushed a small rectangular box forward. I looked at Claudia, who nodded. So far Dr. Tarkka didn't intend me any harm, which matched my own take. I didn't get any feeling of warmth, either, and I was going to be ten times more careful when it came to the Order's hacked artifacts.

Inside was a chip. It looked like it had a half scarab gem embedded in it, and had dozens of hair-fine gold wires running in circuits. It was the marriage of antiquity and cutting-edge science, quite literally, because presumably, there would be some kind of

Order tech compensating for the missing parts. I was at once curious and repelled. "What does this do?"

"I don't know. My boss was into a lot of weird stuff, outer edges of physical and the biological, in human enhancement technologies, or HET. How far can you go, he used to ask, until your patient is no longer human?"

I shuddered.

"My specialty is neurobiology with a focus on orthotic prosthetics. Mostly the mechanical and technical, though I know the wetware side of things pretty well. I'm not fully conversant with this artifact, but I'm the last one around who knows anything about it. He was given it by Dr. Sebastian Porter, who . . . recently passed away, I hear?"

I nodded. No need to say anything more on that subject. "And . . . do we plug this into a computer, or some kind of reader?"

"Yep. You."

My heart sank. I was hoping she wouldn't say that. It must have read on my face, because Dr. Tarkka said, "Look, you can bite me if you want, make sure I'm telling the truth, but I'm just in this for the work."

Claudia and I exchanged a glance. We knew she was being honest.

"I'm going to need to examine it." I was going to be extra careful, knowing it had been Porter's. That gave me an idea: When his body was consumed by the mercenaries who hung out in my lab, the only part of him left was a gold ring. I'd have to consider what that did and compare it to this.

"Fine. I'll stay here while you do."

"I might be a while. I don't know what it looks like when I . . . go elsewhere."

"That will be interesting to see, too."

"Why are you here? Why are you doing this?"

Her face lit up. "Like I said, I'm in this for the work. Now I'm finding out that there is a whole new—species? subspecies?—of human, and I'm not giving up the chance to get in on that!"

Her enthusiasm would have been contagious if I hadn't realized that she wasn't thinking of me as a person but as a specimen.

"And if these things were made to work with your biology, I want to see what happens when it is put to the test. I'm the best chance you have of learning about these objects." She shrugged her narrow little shoulders. "If you find more notes, other scientists, I can help.

I didn't like her attitude, but she was right.

"Okay, I guess we should talk to Heck about getting you started." I stood, held out my hand. "Welcome aboard."

"Wait, what?"

"I'm hiring you. Your knowledge and experience is as scarce as hens' teeth, and we need them both. We'll pay you, put you up, but this is no part-time gig, and right now, we're on death-march schedule. In, or out?" I'd learned a lot listening to Vee talking about her work in the Normal world.

"Ahhh . . . can I have some time to think about it?"

"Sure," I said, glancing at the clock. "I have half a minute before my next meeting."

"I was thinking more like overnight."

"You don't need that long. Either you're signing up to be working on the most cutting-edge science in the world—so cutting edge, we don't even know all the words for it—or you're not. Let someone else get the Nobel Prize. I hear Stockholm is freezing in December, anyway."

"Okay, okay, you got me, I'll do it. Any chance you would Change for me?"

"Can't now, but I bet you'll see it soon enough. And wouldn't you rather see it when you can get it on video and hook me up to all sorts of monitors and stuff?"

My sarcasm didn't register. The look on her face was one of a hungry kid outside a bakery. Dr. Tarkka could only nod.

"Then let's set up an appointment for that. I'll establish the ground rules, but we'll have fun."

I had no idea if we'd have fun, because she seemed like a grump at best and a bit of a ghoul at worst. But this was the first time I'd ever hired someone and it sounded like a nice thing to say.

I had to run to my next appointment, but that didn't mean I couldn't stop in at my lab. I was getting tired of juggling all these new ideas and responsibilities and information, but there was nothing for it.

The mind-lab continued to be the space where I was able to make the most sense out of the artifacts I'd found after they became a part of the construct I thought of as the bracelet. After they became a part of me. The space was soothing and familiar and that let me relax enough to be willing to experiment with these ancient and mysterious objects. The more I tried different combinations of the artifacts, the more I learned about them.

In the lab, I put the scarab chip on the counter. I ran a diagnostic on it—well, I called it that. It was really just a list of things I'd learned to look for that were dangerous or had led to drastic changes in my powers before. It wasn't much to go on, but I didn't have a lot of time, and it did let me rule out the dangers I was aware of, like not trying to mix the powers from Pandora's Box with an extra blast of energy from Vee. Once was enough to teach me that I wanted to avoid a repeat.

The screen showed me nothing recognizably dangerous. That just left a whole new universe of elements I couldn't recognize.

It suddenly occurred to me that I'd been able to bring the chip, or maybe its essence, into the lab. Very useful to know. I called Sean, who had been cataloging the artifacts with the undergrads.

"Recognize anything? Good, bad, dangerous, odd, or otherwise? Any ideas what it might do?"

Sean shook his head. "Zoe, I can't keep up with all of this. Since the library . . . we're just swamped. We're gonna have to make some changes, you want to go any faster."

"Okay, okay."

"It's more a question for Dr. O anyway, isn't it?"

I'd nearly forgotten about my newest . . . tenant? Too early to say "friend."

As soon as I'd had the thought, he was there, in the archaeology lab. He had a chipped and tea-stained mug with a picture of Beethoven on the side and was happily nibbling a biscuit. The crumbs stuck to his cardigan indicated this might not be the first biscuit he'd had today, but there were ink stains on his fingers.

I guess he'd been busy at work.

"So . . . can you tell me about this?" I moved the scarab and chip to the workbench and tapped twice, splitting the "screen" on the surface into two parts. One showed the diagram of the scarab chip. Alongside it, on the other screen, I brought up a list of the artifacts I had already assumed into my form, their diagrams, and the powers that appeared or were enhanced after their addition. Nothing seemed to match this chip in any respect. Which was actually pretty exciting. Like baseball cards or other collectibles, you can find the common stuff pretty quickly and get a good range fast. But after a while, it gets harder and harder to find something you don't already have.

"Far as I can tell, there's no one-to-one correlation between my powers and the artifacts," I said. "It's like the artifacts are organized like those clear film map overlays that show the changing borders, or geographical details, or major cities depending on how many you put down. Or maybe like passes of an old-fashioned color printer. One pass lays down all of one color, next pass adds the next color, which also creates a third color, next pass adds more colors, and the definition of the picture becomes clearer, more resolved."

He had been watching me intently, and reached out, touching the screen that had appeared in the workbench. He tried rearranging some patterns of artifacts and then looked up at me.

"Another analogy might be the arrangement and activation of certain genes," he said. "It's not really my game, biology, but it might be like a characteristic not depending on just one gene that's switched on or off but requiring a certain combination of several switches, in the right order. More than one factor's needed to make it work."

I shrugged and nodded. "I'll take your word for it."

"Do you mind if I spend some time on this?" He nudged the chip gingerly, almost as if afraid. "This is certainly different from the Fangborn artifacts I studied . . . when I was alive . . . and the ones that have melded with you. It might give me some excellent insights, the way they came at the problem."

I thought about it and slapped the work-surface screens. A big red seal appeared, glittering in the corner of the screen, with the words "Read Only" on every "page." It didn't interfere with the text but like a watermark, was just visible behind it.

"It would be a huge help to me, thanks," I said. "For now, we're going to keep this so you can look at these things, see if you find anything by arranging them differently, but I'm the only one who can make them happen. Activate them or add them . . . to me."

"Fair enough." Geoffrey had already gotten the hang of how to flick through the pages of artifacts. The light from the screens reflected on his face, coloring his gray beard. "You know how I died?"

"You'd said you'd been studying . . . the physics of Fangborn abilities?"

"Yeah. Bit o' this, bit o' that. Whether how the Change transformation the vampires and werewolves can do is a quantum entanglement of some kind, and whether the famed identification or prediction of evil the fanged ones claim can be derived from one single, huge algorithm. Spooky action at a distance, you know? But what I was working on at that precise moment I died was how some of these artifacts might have been created." He stroked his beard, his eyes unfocused, thinking hard. "This might be a match made in heaven, Zoe, m'girl."

I nodded. "If you can help me in any way, it would be a serious relief. Right now, what would help most is some kind of index, or a schematic, or a guide for the DIY newly enhanced Fangborn," I said. "I don't know if such a thing exists, but maybe you can create a rough version? Anything that might lead me to a better understanding of how to use, make, or fake the artifacts I had, might mean, literally, the difference between life and death. And not just mine."

"I'll see what I can do."

"So what about this thing?" I held up the scarab and chip.

"Not Fangborn, not entirely. It looks like something the Order pieced together, trying to make a Fangborn artifact work without . . . the right . . . components? Energy?" He looked confused. "We're going to need a whole new vocabulary for this."

I nodded. And we were going to have to get Lisa up to speed in a hurry if I had any hope of making progress here.

Then again . . . we had no time. Claudia and I were both certain that Dr. Tarkka was not out to hurt me. And then there were my own skills in mundane artifact analysis. This was too pretty to be used in torturing Fangborn. The gold curlicues of the circuits, the way the scarab had been set into the chip . . . It almost looked like jewelry, meant for a lady.

It was no riskier than the other artifacts I'd assimilated, I decided suddenly. "Okay, I'm going to plug it in."

He was up for it. "Where do you reckon?"

I shook my head—it didn't matter. Pre-bracelet, I would have assumed it went behind my ear or I should eat it. Now, I knew, I could put it anywhere, so long as my intent was to internalize what powers it might have. I found a suddenly available square slot on my bracelet, exactly the right size for the chip. I slotted it in. It fit perfectly.

I'd had my healing powers on deck, just in case the thing was booby trapped, but so far, so good. No sparks, no smoke—or the metaphysical equivalent thereof. Also good.

I thought there would be pain—there had been a load of hurt other times, with just the straight-up Fangborn artifacts that I was pretty sure would end with my death. There was nothing here, a frisson, something barely noticeable, like clothing that doesn't fit exactly right. But it was manageable. All I felt was a vague brushing of minds outside me, very indirect, very primitive. Nothing like my own proximity sense. These minds were far away. They didn't feel like human minds, however, or Fangborn. They felt more like dragons, if anything.

I unslotted the chip and tossed it to Geoffrey.

"Nothing?" he asked.

"Not a lot. Maybe you can find something. I'll catch you later."

No further enlightened, I met up with Heck and Elizabeth Nichols, who said they wanted to record me giving a dry run of what was going on. Later, they'd review it and we'd add anything I'd left out for the official version.

I took a deep breath, tried not to squint too much, and looked into the camera, as silly and self-conscious as I felt doing it. I thought about how I was so very much the tail wagging the dog, all these important people acting on my say-so, and how I knew that I was responsible for so much happening right now. I tried not to sound too weary or uncertain as I started.

I took a deep breath. We were on the brink of I-Day. I was going to tell people in high places about the Fangborn, the Order, the Makers, the dragons, and just the thought of that was scary.

"Hi. I'm Zoe Miller and I'm a werewolf, one of the Fangborn. If you don't know . . ."

Chapter Eleven

I didn't get released from the taping until about ten that night. I ate ravenously, very glad the kitchens were used to Fangborn irregular hours and large servings. I heard a loud exclamation of "Oh, hey!" from the doorway and saw Danny and Vee, holding hands.

Danny, a Normal, was the one constant I'd had from childhood, and his friendship meant everything to me. When I'd last seen him at the Battle of Boston, he'd been badly injured, bleeding from a serious gut wound. I'd healed him remotely, hoping that it would work.

To see him now, you'd never know he'd ever had a scratch— even his glasses were intact. He was only a few inches taller than me, maybe five eight, and ten pounds lighter than me, too, and everything about his paleness and dark curling hair screamed "geek!" But in the past few months, Danny had come into himself even more than when he'd left school and found his niche in the tech world. Working with the Fangborn challenged his quick mind, and his talent with languages had proved invaluable with a global, polyglot Family.

They rushed over and Danny threw himself at me; Vee gave me a cautious hug.

"Sorry," she said after a moment. "I'm just worried . . . Last time we met, you ended up in Japan by mistake."

I nodded. "Not you. I mean, I think part of that was your extra energy, but mostly it was me just not knowing what I was doing. I'm going to proceed under the assumption that whatever happens, I'll be able to find my way back again." I held up my new backpack and my new resolution to have my stuff with me at all times.

She nodded. Danny grabbed my hand again.

"You . . . you . . . teleported! What did it feel like?" Danny could barely contain himself. "What did you see?"

"It hurt like I was in a full-body fryolator, and I didn't see anything. If I can avoid doing it again, I most certainly will."

Danny was crestfallen. "Well, that's not very—"

"Dan, let's get Zoe a drink," Vee said impatiently, "and if she wants to talk, she can."

"I love that idea so very hard right now," I said, busing my tray. "Is there a place where a girl could get a very large vodka?"

There was a TV lounge nearby with no TV, and Vee hit someone up for a bottle. After my first large gulp, I stared with something like reverence at the tumbler I had. "Dear sweet baby Jesus, this is bliss. Hey, either of you run into Max yet? You know, the guy who looks like a Fellborn but is actually really decent?"

"Oh, yeah, I saw him when I was entering him into our system," Danny said. "They've eased up on him. He's wearing fatigues, cadging smokes, and I believe I saw him badgering Lisa Tarkka about maybe changing him back, if possible."

"What's your take on her?" I asked Vee.

"Enh. She seems competent. I can't get a read on her, though. I was disappointed not to find you a Family member who could help. The ideal candidate would have been Geoffrey Osborne, who was totally brilliant and a bit crazy."

When she said the name Geoffrey, I felt my heart stop.

Vee sipped her beer and continued. "But he died in an Order attack a few months ago. They raided his lab and took the materials he was working on, notes, everything."

"Ah." A thought struck me. "Aren't there other physicists we could ask? In the Family, I mean?"

She snorted. "Oh, sure, teaching high school, working for the gas company, whatever. Do you know how rare it is to get a theoretical physicist doing advanced work in a *Normal* population?" Vee shook her head. "It's pretty unusual to begin with. We were lucky he was an oracle, because he didn't feel the Call and couldn't Change. He could focus on work. The Order didn't care that he wasn't a fighter, only that he was Fangborn."

I told them about his presence in my lab. Their faces grew increasingly worried. "Weird shit, huh?"

"Uh, yeah." Danny said, "Zoe, do me a favor? Don't trust him too much. He might be some kind of Order construct."

"A little elaborate for them, isn't it?" I asked. "I mean, I'll be careful, sure. But they're crude. They're still getting the Fellborn . . . right."

"Please . . . don't trust him too much," Danny insisted.

"Okay." I changed the subject. "You guys, do we have any idea how we work? The Fangborn I mean, sorry Danny. It's just that we look an awful lot like magic, but . . . there's never been any proof of anything like that revealed by any other physics or math, right?"

"Sweetie, we've been so busy fighting evil and trying to live our cover lives and, frankly, dying, that we know very, very little about the Change, how we heal, how the shifters can take three vastly different shapes," Vee said. "Not to mention anything at all of what the oracles are able to do, some of the time, at least. Physics . . . *our* physics, generously speaking, is still taking the first baby steps along the road to finding out. But no, there's no magic that we know of." She looked thoughtful.

I had brought them up to speed about my experiences with the Makers when I felt his presence before I heard the familiar cadence of footsteps. As I looked up, Will MacFarlane appeared in the doorway.

"Zoe!" Will ran in and grabbed me. "God, it's good to see you."

I gave him a hug and a kiss. He returned the kiss a little too vehemently. I felt a kind of proprietary quality in it that bothered me.

"Come, sit down. I'm beat. How are you?"

"I'm fine, I'm . . . You fixed me up good. See?" He pulled up his shirt so I could see his very well developed six-pack, a little blur of hair on his chest. He might have been showing off, just a little. I might have enjoyed the view another time but was aware that he was working too hard to seem like everything was okay.

"Dan," Vee said, shaking my cousin's knee, "we should—"

At the same time, he said, "Vee, it's getting late—"

They laughed, awkwardly. I didn't blame them, I thought. There had been too many strange and strained occurrences lately between us.

"We'll catch you tomorrow, okay? After the demonstration," Danny said.

"Okay." I hugged him, gave Vee a little wave, and then sat down after they left.

I brought Will up to date on my adventures and asked him about his. He interrupted me when I told him about my meeting with Dr. Tarkka.

"Zoe, Zoe—this isn't a mission debrief. Let's talk about us?"

"Yeah, but. It's just I have these really major priorities at the moment and I'm jet-lagged. I've been in meetings of the weirdest sorts today. I have to do a demonstration tomorrow and I don't even know where to begin thinking about that."

Will was not pleased, but he was trying hard to be patient. Or at least sound patient. "Look. If we are all going to be in . . . let's euphemistically call it 'in trouble,' then you should be with the person you're supposed to be with. I think that would be a nice thing, if—"

"If the world's going to end?"

He nodded. "I'm just saying."

"I get that, and all I can tell you right now is, I don't *know*. Maybe we could discuss it later, next week?" I had no idea of what would be happening next week, but between Carolina's hostages, the Makers, and I-Day, next week felt like next year at the moment.

"The last time you said that, you disappeared to Japan."

"Yeah, but *not* because I planned to!"

"My point exactly!" Will said; he thought I was getting him. "It might be worth the six hours or six minutes it would take. It would be nice, for all of us involved, to know where we stand." "All" was said with reluctance and distaste, and I knew he was thinking of Adam.

"Will, this is complicated and we don't have time—"

"You don't have time for *me*, you mean. But you have time to meet *his* mother?"

I was so taken aback by that it took a minute to realize what he meant. "I met *Representative* Nichols. It was a . . . a . . . rescue, followed by a war council. Not a trip home to meet prospective in-laws, I promise you. It was *miles* away from the sort of situation you're suggesting."

"Well, I'm sure she liked you." Will was so seldom peevish that it looked doubly ridiculous on him. I almost laughed, but I was mad, too.

"Apparently, I scared the shit out of her. The feeling was mutual, I can assure you. Have you seen her?"

"Tallish, plumpish, blondish, motherish? Yeah, I've seen her. On the news."

"Well, motherish as in mother wolverine, maybe. She sees everyone as her responsibility and she takes it seriously. She's tough and smart and suffers no fools, takes no crap." I didn't quite shudder, but I was intimidated by Representative Nichols in a personal way that even the Makers couldn't match. She stood up to Senator Knight like she didn't even care, and she went to the worst-case scenarios without batting an eye. She had a scary handle on all the angles of the situations, the situations that I was responsible for putting in front of her.

"I hate that I make you feel like this," I said. "I hate that I don't have the bandwidth to fix this right now. We both need a lot of time, and now is not exactly ideal. Can you wait? Just a little?"

"Not really."

I shook my head sadly. "Okay. Then we're done."

"Wait—what?" His face was the picture of distress. "That's not what I wanted!"

"Right, it's not the answer you wanted, but it gives you certainty. You can have that much; I can do that for you."

"Why are you doing this, Zoe?" The pain on his face made my heart contract.

"Doing what?"

And then I realized what he meant.

I'd changed. I'd become a different person. Will thought I was being petulant, giving him an ultimatum or something, and I'd been decisive and sincere, making a mature offer that hurt me to even think about.

"I'm not doing what you think, Will—aaahhh!" A blast of chaos in my head, confusion that didn't feel Fangborn, didn't feel human . . .

"What? We're doing this again?"

"No—ah, shit." I clutched my head. "It's the ravens. I'm seeing through their eyes. Jason . . . the oracle is in some kind of trouble."

———⌣———

As I ran into the kitchen area, Jason doubled over so hard, so fast, I thought he was going to knock himself out on his own knee. A second later, he slammed backward with equal violence. Jack and Jill were shrieking and flapping around him, darting, talons out at anyone who got too close.

Another Cousin I didn't know had tears streaming down her face. When she saw me, she screamed. "Get a lid on it, Zoe! If you can't use your powers properly, don't!" She ran from the room.

I stood shocked, and Jason finally staggered up, groaning. The birds however did not settle, hovering over him protectively and, if I didn't know better, squawking with concern. When Jason leaned back against the wall, Jack and Jill hopped on the floor near him. Then when he spoke to them, they returned to their perches, shrugging and shaking out their feathers nervously.

"Goddamn, Zoe," he said with a hoarse voice. "What the fuck are you up to?"

"Me? Nothing." I got him a glass of water and would have given it to him, but Jack swooped at me, cawing a warning. "Okay, okay. I won't get too close."

I set the glass on the floor and then got down on my knees and shoved it carefully toward Jason. His fingers brushed against it, almost knocking the glass over, and I got an even better idea of just how freaked out he and the ravens were. They shuffled a bit but stayed quiet—my posture was too submissive to suggest I was going to be any threat—and Jason drank deeply, sighing. His head tilted back against the wall and his face relaxed. This was the first time I'd seen him without his sunglasses on and his coat buttoned up. His red hair hung lankly, heavy with sweat, and his face struck me as surprisingly young. I slowly sat back on my heels, intensely aware that the two giant birds were eying me suspiciously.

"Thank you."

"You're welcome," I said. "Um, what happened?"

"I got this overwhelming urge to . . . do what you said." He turned toward me. "And you said it wasn't you?"

"No." I had no idea what he was on about. "Even if I could do that, why would I want to?"

"Everyone knows about your crazy vampire powers and how they're not quite normal. This was *beyond* a vampiric compulsion.

It was . . . an order, something I felt from the depth of my being. It felt like . . . It felt the way that you fangs-and-fur folks describe the Call to Change. It felt like there was no way I'd want to ignore it, even if I could."

"Whoa. Okay, well, I didn't do it." I thought a moment. "What did it say?"

"Say?"

"Was it a voice, *my* voice, commanding you?" I asked, desperate to know if I was somehow broadcasting unintentionally. "Was it a sudden urge to give me a pedicure? What *form* did this command take?"

Jason burst out laughing, which under the circumstances, was not as reassuring as it could have been. The ravens barked out harshly and flapped once or twice, and got more agitated as Jason worked to regain his composure.

"Knock it off, you guys," he said at last.

That was better. He sounded more like himself. The birds settled, only partially reassured.

"So now what's so funny?"

"You. I guess I don't have to worry about you, despite what just happened," he said. "If you were really interested in world domination, you wouldn't have thought 'obey me' translated to 'give me a pedicure.'"

I stood, getting pissed off. "You really, really need to tell me what's going on, and how you got from 'obey' to 'world domination,' and why you'd think I'd want it."

He opened his mouth to speak, and then a look of alarm spread across his face. "That's gonna have to wait. We need to get you out of here."

"What? Where? Why?"

"Up." Jason snapped his fingers, and Jack and Jill flew to his shoulders settling in protectively. "Someone's screaming pretty loud in a lot of heads—you saw, I wasn't the only oracle to get the message." He put the glasses back on and turned toward me. Both birds swiveled their heads along with him. It was eerie, being regarded times three.

"How many others?"

"Dunno yet, but from the shape of it, *all* of the oracles."

I was about to protest when I heard shouts down the hall.

"What are you doing, bitch!"

"Oh my God, Frances drove off the road! I felt her die!"

There were more screams. Will grabbed me.

"C'mon, Zoe. We need to get you some place safe."

A young boy, probably not even old enough to have finished Fangborn Academy, stopped in the hall when he saw me and went on one knee. "What do you require, Hellbender?"

I ran.

———

Claudia Steuben found us later; Jason, Will, and I had holed up in an empty conference room and I'd responded to her anxious text. She looked haggard, and I kept forgetting that just because I was having adventures didn't mean my friends weren't also overwhelmed with current events. We were only days out from the Boston battle, only days, maybe hours away from I-Day.

"How are you?" she asked.

"Confused."

Claudia's professional demeanor as a psychiatrist was still reassuring to me. "For good reason. It seems you've been reaching a wide audience, Zoe."

"It's not me. I swear." I started pacing. "Did everyone hear the same thing?"

"Yes. Every oracle sensed or heard 'Hellbender.' Which was interesting, because while no one really knows you by that name, they all had an image of you in their heads."

I swallowed. "Okay, I'm pretty sure it was the Makers." I explained what I thought I knew about them. "The uh, head one? I don't really know his name, but think of him as the Administrator. He said he'd give me some help, because he wants me to be their . . . uh, contact person, for . . . sorting everyone out."

"Sorting?"

"Well, he thinks things are a little chaotic here and wants me to make it less so." I told her about the meeting and how Fangborn were supposed to be the ones running the show. "It's just that we didn't turn out the way they usually expect, and the dragons are powerful but old and sleepy. And rather than us killing bad guys, we should be . . . ruling."

Claudia looked at me quizzically. I nodded, my eyes wide: It was exactly as bad and big as I was saying.

"Claudia, it was only months ago I found out I was a werewolf. Then Pandora's Box gave me the bracelet, and that led to finding other artifacts that are playing havoc with me, turning me into an armored monster. Suddenly I'm dealing with things—the Makers, dragons—that most Fangborn don't know about! I am talking to politicians! About I-Day! I mean, WTF?"

"Zoe—"

"We've, you've, been hiding from Normals for millennia and I'm a complete *noob* and now . . . I'm the one who's going to start outing our entire Family? I am *not* far enough up the food chain of command for *any* of this!"

"Okay, we need to tell Heck and the others. We're going to have to get this information out fast."

Claudia put out her hand. I nodded, took it, and got up. "I can add it to the formal statement I'm working on with the congress-woman and Senator Knight."

"I think you ought to. And, Zoe, you might want to brace yourself for what we run into out there." She nodded to the rest of the living quarters.

"They're angry, huh? I don't blame them." If I'd heard voices blaring in my head all of a sudden, I'd be pissed off, too. Actually, it reminded me of the dragons and their sudden appearances, which had been incredibly disruptive.

"Some are. Some think it was some kind of hoax, maybe set up by the Order. Some think you're showing off, pulling a stunt." She hesitated.

"Yeah? Go ahead. It gets worse, so tell me." I closed my eyes against the news like I was about to be hit.

"Yes. Some of the Family think they've just had a religious experience, with you at the focus of it."

My eyes opened as my shoulders slumped. "Ah, shit."

⎯⎯⎯⎯⌣⎯⎯⎯⎯

Claudia and I discussed some radical solutions to my sudden PR problem, but really, until we knew what had happened and how bad the fallout was, we had to just wait and see.

You can only get so much done pacing in a twenty-by-twenty room. I hadn't left my room after the broadcast to the oracles—which I had to assume was the Administrator's work.

The night was eaten up by putting together a basic fact sheet on what I knew—little as it was—about the Makers and the Administrator. I held a faint hope that someone else would be able to take that store of knowledge—observations and guesses, really—and find us a way to work with it.

So now, the Powers That Be—Senator Knight, Representative Nichols, Heck, and a few others—wanted some kind of proof about the Makers.

"Proof? More than what the oracles just heard?" I asked. "Well, if I can get Quarrel to show up, maybe he can tell you more. All I know is that the dragons seem to think the Makers made the Fangborn, and from what I can tell, they're vastly powerful."

"It would help. This is all a little . . ." Heck trailed off, shaking his head.

"Yeah."

"Could they be allies?" Edward Knight asked. "So far they're not offering war? You are still in the early stages of understanding each other, is that true?"

"Yes. But the fact that they can manipulate the most powerful creatures on earth is worrying to me," I said.

I caught Representative Nichols glance and felt fear a mile deep. *She's wondering, "Will we have to destroy the Fangborn to protect us from the Makers?"* I thought. I answered out loud. "Let me continue to talk with them. So far there's been no impact on I-Day. The Administrator is only doing what he said. I can ask him to tone it down."

Even I didn't sound convincing to myself, I thought, as we adjourned.

The last thing I did before I went to sleep was hit the lab.

"Geoffrey?" I took my chair by the computer, the familiar smell of cardboard, dirt, and linoleum filling my nose.

"Yeah, Zoe?" He didn't look up from the screen on the center workbench. He was still engaged in looking at the artifacts and analyzing them.

"I need to blow something up."

That got his attention. Dr. Osborne's head snapped up, his eyes locking on mine. He reached for his tea and found it, unerringly. "Oh yes?"

"I need to do it on command."

"It seems you are already capable of that."

"No, it's always been . . . in self-defense," I said. "Or in a state of high emotion. And it was never . . . against an inanimate object, a target. I need the ability to be available to me, all the time. Any ideas how I can do that?" I nodded to the screen. "Any way to make it permanent?"

"Do you want a detonation or a deflagration?"

When I said nothing, he asked, "Do you know what an explosion is?"

"Um, let's say I don't know anything apart from the boom."

"Right." He clapped his hands together, getting into lecturing mode. "An explosion is a rapid increase in volume and release of energy in an extreme manner." His eyes lit up with the words *extreme manner*. "What it looks like you're doing when you blast something is moving energy from one place and transferring it rapidly to another. Where it doesn't belong."

"Okay. I need powerful and I need showy this time. Does that help?" There was a buzzing in my ears and a kind of static rolling before my eyes. I was really tired . . .

He nodded. "Sure, got it. So what you seem to be doing now . . ." He gestured to the screens, which brought up a configuration of artifacts I'd never seen before. "This is like software. You want to make it hardware. A permanent and integral part of the machine, always on deck, right?"

I didn't like the word "machine," but let him go with the analogy. He was excited, on a roll, and started pacing.

"I think a lot of these materials you picked up in Japan? Much like the sort of thing I was investigating. My current hypothesis is that many of these artifacts have the switches, if you will, to allow you to create your own artifacts. Particularly ones related to defense and offense."

"I can do that now." The buzzing and static and sparks were worse now, and they were starting to scare me because they looked like letters and numbers. I swatted in front of my eyes, in case they were actually in the air of the lab.

"But now you can do that permanently, with these new artifacts." He went to the bench, typed rapidly, and in the air between us, a schematic appeared with the parts list. I saw the Owo lidded bowl, which had been in the Museum of Salem. There were a few more additions, including the katana and other weapons from Kanazawa, and one of the figurines from Pandora's Box.

The gnat-like letters and numbers resolved themselves into focused legibility, and I understood they were the storage numbers of the artifacts I'd need to do this. Nifty. I apparently no longer required blood to create something.

I said, "Registration numbers and schematic on-screen only." Much better; the air cleared as the registration numbers fled to the screen alongside Geoffrey's schematic.

"What I need you to do now is imagine something that will do what you want it to do. An embodiment of your idea of what makes an explosion."

I was trying to think of something along the lines of Wile E. Coyote's dynamite and detonator plunger, but what appeared ended up looking like a blaster, the sort of thing you'd see in a 1940s space opera. Big, bulbous, and mean looking, it nonetheless had the pleasing color and curved lines of a Jeff Koons sculpture.

The artifact numbers settled brightly on the schematic between Geoffrey and me. They began to slot into equations that meant nothing to me but had set Geoffrey cackling.

No longer was I in the artifact-harboring game. It now seemed that I was in the artifact-creating game. I was reminded of something Quarrel had said, that the dragons, while largely inactive, were able to accumulate the tools, as they called them, by pondering the jewels they already had and through conversation with the Makers. Apparently, that's what I was doing.

Sure enough, a band of stones in red and dark yellow, hexagonal in shape, had settled into my bracelet. I held it up to admire it. Not bad for my first try.

"Thanks, Doc," I said. I'd done all I could. I'd be able to rest now, maybe—no, certainly. I felt a terrible fatigue come over me.

"Whoa, what is that?" I sat down in a hurry.

"Hmmm. Lot of energy goes into making something like that, Zoe," Geoffrey said finally. "Probably a lot expended when you use it, too. So be careful."

"I will."

"Just two things, Zoe." Geoffrey was rotating the image of the blaster, tweaking the design ever so slightly.

"Yes?"

"There are three artifacts here that don't conform to the others. One is Porter's gold ring and one is the scarab-chip hybrid. They are similar."

"Yes, right, they came from the Order laboratories."

"Yeah, but the sword you took from Kanazawa? That's different from all the artifacts *and* it's not from the Order. It's something else altogether. Almost as if it has a different wave function from the Fangborn artifacts."

I thought about it; both my father and I had felt an affinity for the object. "Is it a Normal artifact?"

Geoffrey shook his head. "No. I get the impression that its particle spin is the opposite to those."

I had no idea what kind of equipment might be able to tell him that, or what it meant, but I got it: these three were different. "Another puzzle. Okay, good to know. The second thing?"

"If I can, I'd really love to see the explosion." There was a wistful look in his eyes.

"You sound like a kid, Geoffrey." I laughed, for what felt like the first time in forever.

"Why else do you think I went into physics?"

In my room, I tossed and turned for too long. It was so frustrating: Just as I was making headway in finding out how to manage my new abilities, just when I thought I might be getting an advantage, the broadcast from the Administrator had disrupted the chaos that was the Fangborn headquarters. That intrusion had outraged me, and I was mad at Will for making demands that I couldn't meet at the moment.

Finally, I fell asleep, wondering what Adam was doing.

Chapter Twelve

After about five hours of sleep, I turned on the news. The lead story was still about the disaster downtown—how a movie shoot had triggered a massive electrical failure and how that shoot had been catastrophically scheduled to coincide during a civil-defense drill. The questions about the possibility of an earth tremor, the problems with the destroyed sewers. The area was still closed off until the situation was deemed safe. There were pieces on the families who had been evacuated from their homes, and everyone, from the guy on the corner to the president of the United States, wanted answers.

I had hoped to have a quiet meal, but the dining room was filled with people who were working while they were eating. About a dozen were working on a plan to find the missing Bostonians, and the rest were working on I-Day preparations. Within a week, the Normal world would know about us. With any luck, it would be on our terms, because I hated to think how Carolina and her organization would be spinning this.

Many of the Family, including most of the oracles, were ignoring me. At least three oracles around the world had been killed when the Administrator's message came through. Some Family went out of their way to say hello. Adam came and sat with me, drinking a cup of coffee and saying little. Will sat on my other side, making falsely cheery conversation.

It was kind of them to be sticking up for me, but I was, literally, caught between the two of them. I went back to my room.

Having no outlet for all my nervous energy for another hour or so before the demonstration, I did something I hadn't done in a long time. I left my door ajar so anyone who needed me could find me. I pulled out my phone, plugged in my earbuds, and flicked through my playlists.

It had been an even longer time since I'd added music, so what I ended up with was a playlist that Will had made for me in an attempt to get me to go running with him. That hadn't worked, but I still loved the music, stuff he'd picked for my taste, not his.

I hit "Play." And began to dance.

It wasn't graceful—I knew better than to look at the mirror and ruin my good time. My imagination was better anyway, enhancing the experience beyond the physical expression of inward enjoyment and making me into an EDM goddess.

I heard a dissonant noise somewhere in the distance. It took exactly the amount of time for me to register that it was a knock on the open door to my room—about three beats too long—and for me to open my eyes.

Toshi Yamazaki-Campbell stood there, eyes slightly widened in surprise. I hadn't seen him since he killed Sebastian Porter. Ours had been a relationship filled with conflict and opposing ideas, but I counted him a friend. If there had been a trace of humor anywhere on his face, I would have immediately barked at him or found some other way to cover my graceless vulnerability. Instead, he came over, gave me a brief hug, and gestured, "Okay for me to?"

When I nodded, he took one of the buds from my ear and placed it in his own. An expression of satisfaction eased the lines around his eyes, and he tilted his head, showing off his amazing cheekbones and trendy, razor-cut hair, and he began to sway. Then, he took my hand, and we danced together. He was much better than I was but didn't frown or smirk or anything, just tried to work with me. His medium height didn't pose too much of a challenge for my short stature. It was fun, and unexpected. Toshi and I had fought each other, fought alongside each other, and our short acquaintance had been made complicated with politics and battles. This was a nice, new twist.

It had been a year, several years, since I'd danced with anyone. A surprise to find how much I missed it.

We were laughing, in the middle of executing a particularly pelvic swirl, when the door opened again. It was Gerry.

This time, I did stop. I didn't have any more earbuds to share, and I didn't think of him as being into electronica.

He was clearly confused, and as he tried to frame a question— probably about the approaching deadline and our seeming frivolity—Toshi spoke up.

"War dance, bro." He returned my earbud, we air-kissed twice, and he pretend-flipped long, flowing hair as he marched past Gerry.

"Ten minutes, Zoe," was all Gerry said, still not quite sure what he'd seen. "I'll see you at the truck downstairs."

Whatever break I might have taken from worrying about what I was about to do, it was worth it. A good lesson, one I hoped I'd be alive to use again, I thought. It was a short drive, and then a flight to a military base somewhere off the East Coast and to the south.

I didn't get nervous until I began to walk from the Jeep to the runway on the island. That's when the shakes and chills started, despite the warm, humid air. I was able to keep two things in mind, and those kept my head up and my nerves mostly hidden. One was that I knew I could do what I had to do next. And one was the sheer enthusiasm with which I wanted to answer these attacks on my Family, Fangborn and human. I remembered, how long ago it seemed, what the idea of Senator Knight's involvement in Sean's death did to me, the anger it brought, and how Dmitri Parshin's abuse of Danny was still so close to the surface. What had spurred me on in those cases was now a thousand, ten thousand times greater, because my concerns had spread that much further, thanks to the Makers, thanks to Carolina, and thanks to I-Day. Oddly, however, since meeting Dr. Osborne, I felt like I had a problem suitable to my skills and a mastery of those skills sufficient to deal with this specific problem.

As reassuring as that all was, it didn't completely banish the nerves I had thinking about what I was about to do. It was cataclysmically dangerous and literally could blow up in our faces.

Still, it was better than nothing, and I hadn't felt like the odds were this good in some time.

I passed a Cousin in an airman's uniform; she spoke into a mouthpiece. "Two minutes to Lightning Rod."

So that's what they'd decided on, I thought. It bordered hideously on the "too apt," and I looked around for something to focus on so I wouldn't remember that it was me drawing all that firepower. Ahead of me, several hundred yards out on the water, was the target, a truncated pyramid bobbing on the waves. No comfort there . . .

There. Amid about two hundred VIPs in the hastily assembled stadium seating. I recognized a number of faces from the news. There were uniforms from all the armed services, sporting more fruit salad than a hotel brunch buffet. I thought I recognized the vice president but wasn't sure. There were too many guys in dark suits, wearing dark glasses and speaking to no one.

There was Senator Knight. Odd that we were on the same side now. I needed his authority and influence. He needed my power.

He caught my eye and I gestured.

"Zoe," he said when I met him at the fence.

"Call me 'stray,'" I said. "It sounds more familiar on your lips. More honest, too. Plus, it makes me angry."

"Would that help?"

"I'm thinking it will."

The aquiline nose had never seemed so daunting; the hardness of his eyes was ancient. "Well, then, little stray, you'd better put on a show good enough not only to impress everyone here, from the lowliest of the enlisted to the Joint Chiefs, but me, as well. I am your toughest critic. I won't be undercut because some uncultured, unschooled orphan can't keep her promises or spins grandiose tales for some spectacularly sad reason. There are oracles who died with your name the last thing in their ears, and I'm sure we'll find more. Go ahead, I dare you to let them, the Family, and me down."

If he'd shown me the faintest amount of compassion, it wouldn't have worked. But as I met his gaze, I saw disappointment and disgust, the regret that it wasn't his power, that I'd beaten him to opening Pandora's Box, that I, a stray, had outwitted him. Had more power than he.

Perfect. I wanted to slap him stupid.

"Get going," he snapped.

"*Jawohl*, Senator, sir." I turned on my heel and muttered "asshole," knowing full well his sharp vampire ears would hear me.

I walked to the end of the runway, looked out over the water, and took a deep breath. The target was the size of a four-story building, afloat on an old barge, and made of cement blocks and mortar.

I raised my hand and noticed that while the shiny metallic blaster wasn't to be seen, there were those new stones in the bracelet on my left wrist: fiery yellow topaz and dark ruby. I had a thought and lowered my hand again.

The ensign ran over to me.

"What's wrong?"

"Uh . . . it's gonna make a mess."

"What do you mean?" she asked.

"I mean, if I pulverize it, it's going to scatter a lot of cement, and probably a lot of barge, in the ocean. Is there some way to clean it up?" I glanced at her name patch. "Ensign Hart?"

She spoke into a radio and then nodded. "Booms. They have booms underneath to collect whatever rubble you leave."

"Oh, that's good," I said. Then, "Ha! Booms."

"Yes?"

I shook my head. "Sorry, that's just me being . . . It's about to get very loud. I'd put the ear protection on if I were you, and let everyone else know to do that, too."

She nodded and then cocked her head and pulled another pair of headphones from the back of her belt. Ensign Hart handed them to me.

Good point. I might be able to bring the house down, but I didn't particularly want to go deaf doing it. "Thanks."

She nodded again and backed away, chattering into the radio.

I'd spent my short career learning how to put things back together, or cleaning them very carefully. This was the very opposite, again, of what I'd been trained to do. I couldn't think about that now. I had a target to blow up and folks to impress with how dangerous a situation we were all in.

I picked the place that Ensign Hart told me to aim for, the point at which the rest of the structure would collapse. And then I made a pistol shape with my hand, pointed it at the center of the structure, and said a little prayer.

I bent my thumb and whispered, "Bang."

I was afraid there would be nothing, because I didn't hear anything at first. Then a flash of light, brilliant, blinding. Then a push from the shockwave, hot and hard. Then came the noise, like nothing I'd ever encountered outside the movies. Death Star meets John McClane, and yippee-ki-yay.

The target wasn't there anymore. A cloud of dust and seawater hung on the balmy air.

There was silence from the seabirds, silence from the audience. The waves continued on, a little more rapidly against the shore.

That was over, at least. I sighed with relief, trying to be discreet about it; the fatigue from my effort had been far greater than I expected, and I hoped I wouldn't stumble when I tried to walk. Now all I had to do was—

"Zoe, we are here! Hellbender, the Makers will speak with you!"

If I hadn't had the opportunity to see up close how folks responded to the appearance of Quarrel during the Battle of Boston, I had now a front seat as Quarrel, Naserian, and Yuan stunned the Fangborn and Normal VIPs. Screams, gasps, and a chorus of "holy shit" came from the audience, as the black, red, and green dragons materialized in front of them. I heard thuds as two people fainted and fell over. I heard sidearms being unholstered and cocked. One gentleman jumped from the top of the seating in his haste to escape the dragons. I heard his screams after he landed, breaking his leg. There was a tangle of dignitaries as they tried to get off the bleachers. There was a much smaller knot of brave souls who quietly ran to see the dragons close up. The Fangborn in the audience were no less stunned.

These guys had actually asked to see the dragons and really weren't expecting me to produce. In truth, I don't know if Quarrel would have come if I called for him, but as it was, he'd saved my bacon. The dragons seemed to enjoy the attention and warm sun.

In other ways, it wasn't funny at all, a preview of the reactions we could expect on I-Day.

"Excuse me, I must go," I said to the ensign Cousin, who was agape. "Naserian, would you please stay here and answer any questions these folks might have?"

"Certainly, Hellbender."

"Particularly that gentleman, in the very nice blazer." I pointed at Senator Knight, who flinched under the dragon's gaze. He saw me watching him, saw me raise my pretend pistol to my lips and blow across the pretend barrel before I followed the dragons to the meta-space of the Makers.

I slowed as I approached the door to the Castle, the silent cityscape of Boston University around me. I was grubby from the explosion and frankly hadn't spent a lot of quality time with the tweezers and razor lately.

I didn't have time to think of a whole new metaphor, and I'd felt surprisingly weak after the explosion. I didn't want to waste my energy by creating a whole new meta-me; besides, if I went all badassed and swaggery and Queen Empress of Doom, rolling up in a blacked-out Escalade followed by a retinue of scary-looking troll praetorian guards, it would have been rude. The Makers had, in their way, been nice enough to show up and interact with me, heavy-handed as it had been. I couldn't afford to be rude, but I had to be . . . more of an equal. I had demands to make and negotiating to do.

I could change what I was wearing. Clean it up a little.

I was in the lab.

"Sean!"

He looked up from the catalog he was working on, smoothed his mustache. "Yeah?"

"I need something to wear."

"Like what? I'm not exactly Tim Gunn."

And it was moments like those that I realized it was only an idea of Sean derived from my memories, not his. Alive, he wouldn't know Tim Gunn from Tiny Tim. "Uh . . . something that resonates power—not like a Transformer," I hastened to add. "Like . . . worldly power."

"Like the pope?"

I took a minute to figure out how "pope" and "worldly power" went together, in Sean's mind, and then shook my head. "Um . . . less masculine?"

"Wonder Woman."

"No, jeez, not like a comic book—" Then I realized, I wasn't sure what to do. Time was drawing short, and if it was an illusion for the Administrator, it wasn't for me. Putting it off wouldn't do me any good, and my nerves were already clanging.

Fuck it.

I clapped my hands once: My jeans were new and clean and fit me as if angels had collaborated with Edith Head to design them. My old boots—tired, beat up, multipurpose hiking and digging—were replaced with cowboy boots. I hadn't ever worn them, but they were gorgeous and comfortable and were so complex—what with the brown and red detail and bronzed studs—that I felt as if I'd grown four inches and had built-in swagger.

A blouse, silk, plain, button down, tailored to a fare-thee-well. Midnight blue was a color, at least, and not a retreat into my gothic-punk attitude, so I counted that as a win. I couldn't put on my battered jacket. It was falling apart, even within my imagination, and I knew it wouldn't be long before I held a Viking funeral for it.

I knew what I wanted even before I knew it: calf-length, dark brown suede, super-simple, elegant, and it secretly made me think "Browncoat." I stuck a Swiss Army knife into the pocket, and tucked a trowel into my belt, under the coat. Metaphorical, of course, but good-luck charms nonetheless, and I felt better with them.

I walked through the outer office without a word to anyone. They were all terribly busy. Something serious must be going down. I knocked on the door, and when I heard the muffled "Come in," I entered, closing the door behind me.

The Administrator looked up from the papers he was working on. "Miss Miller, have a seat, won't you?"

"Thank you."

"We've determined to try and fix you. You have thirty rotations to effect this. You will bring the population to order and we shall consider ourselves satisfied. We will give you the power necessary, but only for one major attempt at imposing order, subject to our review. If we are convinced you are making significant progress, we will give you more."

"Order . . . can mean a great deal of things," I said carefully, trying to ignore the sound of my heart trying to beat its way out of my chest. "What does this goal look like for you?"

The Administrator frowned. "Order such that we may get what we need when we decide it's time to visit your plane of being."

Visit . . . plane of . . . holy shit. I cleared my throat. "Why not one more senior to me?"

"Because we are in contact with you," he said impatiently. "And it is easier for you, being there, being conversant with the local cultures. It saves us a great deal of energy to have you as our proxy."

I felt my blood turn to ice.

"That makes you the one we deal with directly in regards to this species," he said.

I'd thought that I'd act only as a go-between, the one who opened up a channel of communication, like Lieutenant Uhura. I thought it would be someone like Senator Knight who'd do the real talking; he was a dickhead, but he knew how to do this kind of thing.

I spoke carefully, trying to ignore my overflowing panic and hoping the Administrator would be able to hear me over the chattering of my teeth. "I appreciate the trust you're putting in me, but perhaps it would be more . . . convenient, to speak to one senior to me."

"If there were someone senior to you, they would have been the ones speaking to us," he said tartly.

Don't let Senator Knight hear I'm senior to him, *I thought. He'll call an air strike on my ass. Inspiration struck me. "It is not the way of my people to circumvent protocol. It would offend my elders for me to do as you wish." Oh, jeez, I sounded like a bad alien movie. But I was trying to walk a very fine line between insisting politely and saying "Hells to the no" outright.*

The Administrator gave me a sour look that told me that he was equally unimpressed by this effort. "I'm sure you can work it out. It's power that makes precedence."

Oof. Definitely not going to tell Senator Knight that. Looks like Lieutenant Uhura just got a promotion, I thought grimly, but it was a ship I was unwilling and incapable of handling. I wracked my brains but was at a loss. "I shall do my best."

"Good. Your full cooperation in this is expected, and we will con-fer on you what you need to accomplish this. We expect a noticeable improvement at the end of the thirty rotations."

Like I was being put on academic probation. But it was probation for . . . all of us.

I had the feeling the meeting was about to wrap up. "If I may, some of the oracles—all of them, actually—were overwhelmed by a . . . com-mand that seemed to come from me. Was that you?"

He frowned. "I said we would help you, make things clear to your kind. You are in charge. You are our proxy."

"Many of them were injured," I insisted, "and some killed by this announcement. Please, do not do it again."

His frown deepened, and he pressed the tip of his finger against his lip. "I will consider it. I presume it was effective on the entire . . . oracle . . . population?"

I worked hard, not entirely successfully, to keep the anger from my voice. "I haven't had time to take a poll."

"You've no idea the expense and time we've spent already on this system," he said, sighing. "Mostly because of your actions, and those around you."

"Which you've agreed were misunderstood by you. I misunder-stood your intentions as well."

"Yes, we agree on that. But tell me, Zoe." The Administrator tented his fingers. "How much time would you spend on a weed?"

I got a sick feeling. I knew what he was going after, and knew I had to answer. "It depends."

The Administrator sighed. "Your kind says that entirely too often."

"Because it is relevant entirely too often," I answered briskly. "At this level—my level—there's a lot to consider that might not occur to you. Depends on whether the weed is ornamental or helps keep other pests away from the garden. Depends on whether the weed threatens to take over the entire yard, is an invasive species that has outstayed its purpose. Depends on whether the weed is good *to eat. Depends on whether it is rare. Depends on whether the local bees like it. Depends on—"*

"Yes, I see your point. The analogy is more complicated for you, I understand. This is one of the problems between us. While we can communicate directly, we still lack . . ."

"A common context." I nodded. "But I am patient, and I think it is worthwhile for you to be patient, too. Here's the thing. We're usually able to figure out pretty quick if a weed needs to go or not, and the fact that you're hesitating makes me think you should consider we are a pretty weed, possibly beneficial in the long run."

"Bring your people to order. It's in their best interests that we sort this out quickly. You've clearly shown an interest, demonstrated your abilities, and you're eager for power, based on your rapid, some would say startling, accumulation of what you call 'artifacts.' You should use it to this end."

"What does . . . 'to order' mean?" I asked again, desperate to get more information from him. "What does that look like, to you?"

"It depends." He smiled a little at his use of my mitigation. "Our worlds are models of organization and structure, not the chaos you seem to have here. We'll give you the power to make them orderly. How you do it is up to you, using your understanding of their ways." He stood up abruptly. "Zoe, thank you for your time. Please stop by the desk on your way out. They'll have what you need there. We'll meet again soon and I'll work out something so that you don't need the dragons to bring us together. It is awkward."

"Wait, I—"

I found myself in the antechamber, signing forms. Just like I was checking out a library book. "One use," the assistant said. "No more, without prior approval."

"Right. How do I—"

She pulled out a key and unlocked a safe behind the desk. From that, she removed a petty-cash box, and from that, a smaller velvet tray.

I had an idea and popped into the lab.

"Whatcha doing, Zoe?" Sean hadn't moved from the computer since I'd seen him last. Geoffrey was nowhere to be seen.

"I'm thinking of robbing the Makers, Sean." I was astonished by my idea but sick of feeling powerless in the face of the Administrator. The trick would be to act with such brass ovaries that it seemed I was doing exactly what I was meant to be doing. Or to be so quick and slick, no one would notice until it was too late. It made me nervous to contemplate.

"Why not just copy them?" Sean said, glancing over. "Same as you do with the artifacts? Much less likely to be detected, and I bet Dr. O can extrapolate or reverse engineer a lot just by having that information."

I thought about it. It made sense and would be a lot of data for far less risk. "Okay, how? Take pictures somehow?"

Sean seemed to think a long moment. "No, touch them, I think—that's how Porter's ring and the sword and the chip got here, right? That will leave an impression, kinda like Silly Putty. Or making an impression of a key, so that you leave the key there but know exactly what to cut in a new one."

I nodded. "Sounds about right. But if they start getting antsy, showing the least little frown, the least concern?"

"I'll get you out of there."

"Thanks."

I was back at the desk, finishing my sentence. "—implement this . . . loan?"

"I'll plug it in for you." She put the velvet tray down; on it was a variety of jewels, like the ones on my body but far finer. Instead of flat-jeweled tiles joined with metallic solder, these were fully crafted individual pieces, like something out of the window of Tiffany or Van Cleef and Arpels. I'd never seen anything like them in person, unless you counted the jewels at the Smithsonian's Museum of Natural History.

She reached for a ring, a monstrous slab of a sapphire flanked by clusters of pavé diamonds. I darted under her hand and touched a brooch in the shape of a dragonfly set with garnet and emerald. "What does this one do?" I asked, hoping just a touch would be enough for me to record an imprint.

"That's not for you." She grabbed my wrist and pressed the ring into it. It vanished into my bracelet, leaving a smooth flat stone on my forearm. "There. It also enhances the Makers' abilities to summon you. They like to keep a close eye on things."

Like they didn't already! I thought angrily. "So if I use this power—any of my powers?"

"Anything not related to your natural, given form will cue us that you're working on our behalf. High emotional responses will, too. We must be thrifty and economical with how we expend our energy." She smiled, pleased with the sensibility of this feature. It scared the devil out of me.

I swallowed hard, trying not to think of the Makers having this direct link to me and what I was doing. "Okay, thanks."

I touched the doorknob. Alarms began to go off in my head.

Back in the lab, I asked, "Sean, what's wrong? What did I trip?"

"It's not you, Zoe!" Sean said. "It's coming from outside all of us, but I think you're going to want to get to minimum safe distance, above the high-water mark, whatever, because it's gonna hit in five, four—"

At "three," I was already out of the lab, yanking the door to the Castle open. The office assistants were swarming like ants, lights dimmed, an emergency beacon flashing.

By "two," I'd cleared the building.

It was about that point that I saw a flash of black, red, and green: Quarrel, Naserian, and Yuan blasted through the streaks of light and color that ran along meta–Commonwealth Avenue. They were descending on the Castle.

"Quarrel, what are you doing?" I screamed, still running. "You'll be killed!"

"I seek what you seek, Hellbender! If you may, I may!"

There was a madness in his eyes that I'd only seen when he'd decided he would eat me, back in Turkey. I knew then that Quarrel and the other dragons were only on my side so long as I was stronger than they were. I was just another avenue to power for another organism.

About thirty things went through my head at that moment . . .

I felt a bit sad, thinking Quarrel was my enemy.

No, it's not that he was my enemy, just . . . not a friend the way I thought of a friend.

Not so unlike Dmitri Parshin.

Not so unlike myself. We were in a survival situation, and sometimes that involved being grabby, being needy, being scared.

And I should have remembered at least a few of the stories about dragons being lustful for shiny objects and power . . .

They are not human. They don't have human values.

Could I rescue Quarrel? Did I need to?

Maybe he'd—

Boom.

The Makers tried to shut down whatever Quarrel and the other dragons were doing, which looked an awful lot to me like the smash and grab I'd considered. Being dragons, however, their attempt was on a far grander, much more psychotic scale. The assistants streamed to the Castle from all over the landscape, like ants over a dropped hot dog bun in the dirt.

The dragons were tearing up the joint. If I'd been considering stealth, they were not. They were more like coke fiends who'd just found someone else's stash, or hyperactive kids who'd been given the merest taste of sugar and then were let loose in Willy Wonka's factory. "Rapacious" wasn't the word, and I was now planning on replacing "bull in a china shop" with "dragon sees a new hoard."

Then I watched with horror as the Administrator's people began to absorb each other, growing in size and aggression. The creature that resulted was lean and horned, red skinned and scaled and many headed, with a surplus of red, gold, and orange. I had the scary feeling the colors meant it was going to be big into fire and acid attacks.

It was going to demolish Quarrel and the others. Their lust was going to get us all killed.

I couldn't let them do that. I had to try to protect them, even if what they were doing constituted an assault on the Makers and, quite probably, a challenge if not an assault on me.

I felt the call of the artifacts, especially now that the dragons were trying to extricate them and the administrators were channeling their power into their überdragon. It was a firestorm of sound, a thousand trilling notes of outrage and color.

It was like the fight with Toshi for the power of the mosaic, I realized. It was, if not a competition, then survival of the strongest, the greediest, the most strategic. I had to take them myself.

As soon as I had the thought, I knew it would be bad. But too much depended on me keeping the dragons in check and keeping my fragile, tentative relationship with the Makers intact to second-guess myself. Yelling, "Quarrel, Naserian, Yuan, stop! I command you," I braced myself.

Not that I thought me yelling or commanding anything, especially a dragon in the heat of battle and out of its mind with jewel lust, was going to help, but I had to try.

Deep breath. And . . .

As soon as I actively entered the fray, it was as though ten thousand bullets slammed into me, in the form of energy and information. Somewhere through that, I knew I couldn't possibly overwhelm the new guardian beast and three dragons who were battling each other. I didn't want to if I could help it. And I worried what kind of spillover would affect the situation at home.

I had to pick a side and neither choice seemed tenable. But despite his bad—no, dragon-like—behavior in starting this fracas, Quarrel was my friend. He'd come to my aid on several occasions, after all.

"Quarrel, I demand you cease this!" I shouted, more in the hope of giving myself some courage for what I was about to do. I opened myself up to the artifacts that had attracted the dragons, hoping that I could find some that would enhance my vampiric abilities to persuade.

Immediately, a number of things happened. Naserian, the oldest, began losing artifacts to me and turned in rage to attack.

"Naserian! You pledged yourself to me! Stop!" But she was caught up in the frenzy.

I reached into my bag of tricks and found what I was looking for: the katana from the temple outside Kanazawa. Having gotten her attention, I threw it at Naserian, and it turned, instantly, into a collar. She was now under my control. It was possibly the extra power I'd gained from battling Naserian that kept me able to act and plan, because my perspective changed dramatically.

I could now see through her eyes.

"We must stop the others!"

No time for subtlety. I saw Quarrel clobber Yuan, trying to steal the jewels the younger dragon had taken, so I replicated the collar and clapped it on Yuan's neck with a snap of my fingers and a flicker of thought while he was distracted. The more I had power over them, the more the artifacts from their hides, only newly enmeshed, slammed into me. I was knocked to the ground. No matter—I was becoming very skilled at thinking and getting the stuffing knocked out of me at the same time.

I gained another pair of eyes and another will subject to my own. I was starting to get dizzy, trying to keep the dragons under control, and I could feel blood streaming from my nose, my eyes, my ears. I diverted a small fraction of my power to maintaining me, and turned to Quarrel.

The hydra was trying to pull him from the Castle, which by this time, had grown into a cavern full of treasure to my dragon-lent eyes. I realized that the Castle was whatever the perceiver believed it to be. Quarrel was stubbornly refusing to leave the pile of treasure he was sitting on, assimilating so many jewels that he was a blur of gold and rich color over his midnight blue-black. He turned, hissed, and slashed at the überdragon. At the same time, he dug himself into the pile of jewels, wallowing, as if increasing the contact with them would speed his assimilation of them. With the combined forces of Naserian and Yuan, I felt myself growing taller and becoming heavily armored. I summoned up a weapon and found myself with a giant iron-pronged mace. I bashed at the überdragon, more to fend it off than to damage it, I hoped. A bop on the nose to get its attention, no more. We were the interlopers, and my friends were the thieves.

The hydra turned on me. Roaring, it clapped its clawed hands together. The resulting concussion knocked me over again. I skidded across the floor and rolled to my feet. I struck my mace on the floor in return. The hall reverberated and shook. A faint crack ran across the floor.

"Quarrel, in the name of all that is holy, I bid you: 'Knock it the fuck off!'" I turned and slammed my fist into Quarrel, just managing to get his attention. When he looked up, his amazement at what he saw slowed him down long enough and I collared him the same as I had the others. A faint line of spiderweb thinness and starlight brightness now ran between me and each of the dragons. Three sets of eyes and three sets of desires to tamp down. With Quarrel temporarily reined in, I now had three thin leashes in one hand, a miracle of shimmering fineness in comparison with the dull iron brutality of the mace in my other hand.

The überdragon pulled up cobblestones and chunks of pavement to hurl at me. More dings in my new armored form. More bruises down to the bone and marrow, and the strain on me was staggering. For the first time, I could really see what my armor and jewels looked like. Sebastian Porter had described a kind of golden nimbus around me; I saw the fine netting of gold and tiny diamonds as a body-covering armor of scale, platinum white and dotted with those same diamonds; it reminded me of circuits. The wrist and ankle pieces retained their many-hued jewel tones but now resembled greaves and gauntlets. I had a coif of chain around my neck and shoulders. It was so pretty, so ethereal and light, it gave me heart.

"Look, I apologize for my friends!" I shouted, swinging at the überdragon. The mace barely made a dent and I'm sure the impact hurt me a hell of a lot worse. "They got a little overexcited."

I swung again, and this time, the hydra did me the courtesy of grunting, as if surprised. Two of its heads lunged at me, snapping. Its breath was like sulfur and ammonia, and I had no intention of getting *close enough to those teeth, each at least a foot long, to identify the yellow substance dripping from them. Time to go.*

I raised a hand. All three dragons let loose with a volley of fire and venom at the hydra.

The überdragon staggered back and reared up. I knew what was coming next would be a conflagration. "Guys, let's get out of here before it fries us! Right the hell now!"

I tugged on the "leashes" ever so lightly, and with our combined efforts, we wrested ourselves away from the Castle. The dragons, now freed of their temporary mania, did the heavy lifting and, with a wrench, returned us to the here and now.

Unfortunately, I was more or less conscious through the trip, and I wished I wasn't. For one thing, salvos of hot plasma followed us through the rabbit hole and burned like sin. I had just enough mind to notice that we weren't being followed by the hosts of the Castle when I was struck by something that felt like molten lead. It was as if I were melting and, worse than that, being drained, as if the very life were being sucked out of me. Much of my newly acquired armor fell away as I moved through the void, and I grew increasingly heavy and slow, my skin and muscles flaking off in black sheets as we moved. I was being reduced to nothing. I felt as though I was collapsing in on myself in an impossible origami, and when my bones started to fold against themselves, and my muscles leached away, I had no mouth left to scream, no eyes left to close against the consuming black.

Chapter Thirteen

I came to on the debris-strewn tarmac. The sun was directly overhead, and I was staring into it.

The sky was dark blue; the sun was green.

I was cold, and when I moved, I suddenly knew why. I was covered in the stuff the dragons had used to heal me before. I sat up, and the stuff resisted, as if I was covered in glue.

When I was able to focus my eyes, I realized the only thing I could see were massive hills that eventually resolved themselves into the backs of three dragons.

Quarrel, Naserian, and Yuan had arranged themselves around me, protecting me from the curious, angry, and worried VIPs. Only moments had passed since the Makers called on me, our escape slowed by the überdragon.

One soldier had gotten too close and, stupidly thinking to threaten Naserian with a very large, very technical looking machine gun, was struggling, caged under the massive red claws of her left forelimb. Very carefully, she teased the gun away from him with the talons of her right. "Hellbender, what is your will with these men? They are starting to bore me with their insistent and comical aggression." Ever since the gift of the vision, Naserian had found it easier to communicate with me.

"It's okay!" I shouted. I coughed, and spit out the goo. It tasted like grapefruit and lavender, without any sweetness whatsoever:

bitter and dry, but not toxic, not awful. "Naserian, leave them be. The dragons are okay, guys. They're, uh, healing me. Protecting me. It's okay, really, everyone. Uh, stand down?"

The dragons immediately obeyed me. Naserian shoved the soldier away with a little flick of her bloodred talons, and Quarrel, rather ruefully leaned over and opened his mouth, releasing another soldier. The man tumbled to the ground, covered in saliva and terrified, but otherwise unhurt.

"We bow to your will, Hellbender," Quarrel said, working his mouth to get the flavor of uniform and fear-filled sweat from his tongue.

Gradually, the crowd relaxed, and Adam Nichols forced his way through. He stopped just shy of Yuan, one of the few times I'd ever seen Adam daunted. Yuan glanced my way and I nodded. Adam picked his way to me, around and over dragon tails, with a bottle of water. I took it, and as I opened it, he raised his eyebrows with unasked questions. I closed my eyes briefly and took a deep breath, and shrugged.

"Thanks," I said.

"You were gone for maybe three seconds," he said, offering me his sleeve. I wiped my face off on it and squeezed his arm. "Where did you go? After you left, the red . . . dragon blinked out. Then you all just . . . were here again."

"Later," I said. "Things got bad elsewhere, and I hope I was able to contain it. Just . . . I can't talk about it here, but I'm okay, for the moment."

Reluctantly, he nodded, and offered me his arm.

If the bath in Kanazawa was meant to be so hot as to sap the tension from your body, the fluids the dragons used to heal me were the opposite: chilly, bracing, tightening. If I'd been wounded, this stuff had cleaned me out and stitched me back together, almost seamlessly. I felt stiff, as if I'd been newly remolded and the joints hadn't been broken in yet, but considering what had chased us away from the Castle . . .

I stood. The dragons, moving unexpectedly quickly, wheeled around. Each extended their right forearm, one atop the others'. "We are grateful for your intervention, Hellbender. Were it not for you, we would be dead," Yuan said.

And so would I, I thought. I remained silent, waiting to see what their intention was.

"As Naserian has already pledged herself to you and your cause, so do we all now, for all time, obey none but you," Quarrel said. "We will grow or diminish with you, Zoe Hellbender, and our fortunes will be yours."

It sounded graceful and formulaic . . . and just a little dangerous. "Totally not necessary, Quarrel. I was . . . happy to help."

Quarrel shot me a dangerous look. I'd screwed up. "You refuse our fealty?"

I thought quickly: "Fealty" was an oath of allegiance, a very big deal. This was no polite thank-you. It was much more important than that to the dragons. "Forgive me. My mind is still filled with our battle. I would never dishonor you that way." A quick glance gave me another clue. I was fully healed; the dragons were not. They'd suffered burns from the plasma blast and had lost many of the jewels from their hides. Yuan seemed to be favoring one hind leg, and Naserian had a large gash, black with blood, down one side of her belly. One of Quarrel's eyes was closed and his claws were bleeding.

They'd expended all their healing powers on saving me. "Not after you've sacrificed so much to prove yourselves. Thank you, I accept your offer of fealty."

The dragons looked satisfied at this, and everyone breathed a little easier. "We will withdraw, then, to repair our hurts and consider our way from here."

"Okay—"

The second syllable was barely out of my mouth when the three vanished. I stumbled, and Adam put his arm around me. Then I thanked him, nodded, and carefully withdrew my hand. These important people needed to see me strong.

"So, how was that?" I asked Senator Knight, who'd pushed his way forward.

"Did you know that the target was not blocks and sandbags?" he asked. "That it had, at its core, a decommissioned tank, which had been filled with concrete?"

I looked where the target had been; nothing was there now. I suspected the booms had also been destroyed and that I was now responsible for a sizable environmental cleanup and mitigation fee. "I had no idea."

"Can you do that every time? Because if you can, you've just become a brand new sort of weapon, one that can walk in, looking just like a young woman, and cause massive destruction." He didn't seem to think that both of us could do that before all of this counted. "I think we need to discuss things in more private surroundings, don't you?"

"I do."

On the plane back to Boston, I had a quiet conversation with Senator Knight and Representative Nichols. Adam offered to stay with me, but even if he was only there as his mother's aide, it would have been too hard for me. I would have liked that, but now wasn't the time.

"Okay, so you've seen what I can do," I said. "What the Makers have promised me will boost whatever power I have by a significant factor. I'm not saying that to scare you, though it should—it scares the bejesus out of me. I'm telling you so that you'll understand how much power they have, and that it would not be a good idea to interrupt or otherwise interfere with my communication with them. Are we clear?"

Senator Knight stood there, trying not to show how shocked he'd been by the morning's events. While there was an audience, he'd held it together. Now . . . he was feeling the impact of all the ramifications of what he'd seen. "Crystal clear."

"I'm going to need some things."

"We can get you whatever you need." Suddenly that list of radical solutions I discussed with Claudia after the incident with the oracles didn't seem so radical.

"First off, I'm going to need an island. I have a short list of those that will serve." It was a dangerously short list. Every one of the entries had the things I needed, and each was state or federal property. No messing with private landowners for me; we had to move fast. There was a tiny bit of me that enjoyed watching Knight's eyebrows go up. I let myself enjoy the satisfaction for as long as his eyes weren't on me. It was almost as good as a bubble bath for my spirits.

"Very well, I'll see what I can do."

"There's more."

I handed him another list, one he'd find more familiar, I thought. It was the supplies for a moderately well-appointed Fangborn stronghold. My Family had gotten very good at creating hidey-holes that were well supplied over the years, and I was going to need some of that know-how and efficiency right away.

It had struck me that in all the fairy tales that might have revealed something of the Fangborn presence through history, in so many of the myths, the legends, there was always a stronghold. Dracula's castle loomed large in my mind as an example, or the dragon's lair, or a deep, dark dungeon. Who knew? Maybe even the troll who lived under the bridge and menaced the Billy Goats Gruff was Fangborn, colored with menace to protect him from the Normals and distract from his real purpose.

Recalling the setup that Okamura-san and Ken-san had in Kanazawa, and what Gerry had told me about the major Family strongholds around New England, I put that knowledge to work for me.

"How soon?" Knight's patience was wearing thin.

"Immediately. As soon as inhumanly possible."

Representative Nichols gave me a stern look. "You don't want much, do you?"

"Just enough. It all has to be done as secretly as possible," I said. "Also, we're going to need sovereign status. I don't care how you do it. Make it a reservation; create an embassy. Something. But my team—me, the dragons, and anyone I say—has to be inviolate. If the Makers want to come here, this is where they'll come. If I have to act on behalf of us—Fangborn, Normals, everyone on this plane of existence—I need to be subject to nothing but my own law. It's not like you can make me president, or king, or whatever. But you might be able to make me an ambassador."

"Sovereign status?"

"Or diplomatic status. I'm not sure exactly what it is, but make it so I have authority without breaking too many rules. Make something up." "And you'll want some kind of distance from me," I almost said, but didn't want to give him any ideas about what could happen if I failed in whatever happened with the Makers next. "There's got to be some fancy word for what that is."

"Without breaking rules," Knight said, "I believe your fancy word may look like 'treason,' or 'secession,' or 'act of war.' What you're proposing violates many, many federal laws and more than a few international treaties. The president, NATO, the EU, the United Nations . . . all will be very interested."

I wanted to say, "Since when do you care about the UN, Senator Knight?" as he pretty much played out his games with very little thought for the rights of other nations. But I thought that would be childish and I wasn't here for my own vengeance. I felt that much of the ill use I'd had at the hands of the senator would be easily repaid now. But I took a deep breath and settled for signifying, implication, and passive aggression instead. "I have complete confidence in your abilities as a lawmaker and Hill player and am certain you are capable of organizing this. Of course, I'll look to you and the rest of . . . my advisers. I don't plan to go into this without a lot of help. But never forget, I'm working to save us all, and whatever help you give me will be considered . . . an act of friendship."

Senator Knight looked thoughtful. "Given the special status and laws regarding the Fangborn that have been on the books, however secret, I believe I can craft some language that might do."

"And I would like a cat," I said suddenly. I surprised myself; I had no idea where that came from. "I mean, it's not top priority, but I've always wanted one, and now I'll have a place for it." The wistfulness in my voice was pathetic, even to my own ears, but I figured, I might not be alive to look forward to having a cat at some point in the future. There'd either be plenty of people left to look after it if I died, or the world would be gone, and it wouldn't matter.

"A cat." Huge disdain. "Any particular color?"

"I dunno. I've always wanted a black one, but just a youngish one, from a shelter or something. Doesn't need to be a fancy breed, you know?" I realized I was getting kinda soppy. "And whatever it needs in the way of . . . cat stuff."

"That's it?"

"Beer. Vodka. A *lot* of liquor, basically." I shrugged. Knight looked downright dangerous now. "And you can make *that* as fancy as you want."

⌣

I headed to the lab; I needed a moment to collect my rampaging thoughts. "Dr. Osborne?"

"All right, Zoe?" He was there, rubbing his hands, dancing a little dance of glee. "Now that was *wicked*! What else can we explode? Let's do it again!"

"Trust me, we will," I said. "Did you catch the stuff with the dragons, and what happened after, too?"

"Oh, *yeah* I did!"

"Well, I need a little help sorting that out. As in, what. The. Fuck."

"I think it's pretty clear. You're getting powerful enough that acting in your best interest is rewarded by the acquisition of artifacts. It's what predators get for being predators, right?"

"There's that word again. I don't like it."

"You don't have to. But I'm not wrong, am I?"

I thought about it. "Like what dragged me away from that staked-out child molester in New Jersey, so that I could find the information about the asylum where Porter Senior was raising my mother. Which led to me realizing a whole new set of abilities."

"Exactly. Perhaps there's both a Fangborn reason for you to pick up on an artifact or a bit of information that will help you become a better, more evolved Fangborn, combined with a personal desire to be near that same place? Knowing what happened to Richard Klein was hugely important to you. That drew you to Kanazawa, but mostly because the katana and the other artifacts could . . . reel you in. I think the stronger you are, the more the artifacts are attracted to you."

"There was a lot drawing me to Japan," I said, nodding. "Finding the short Celtic sword, whatever that is. Killing Jacob Buell. Not a bad haul."

"And that's why you had the instinct not only to consider nicking a few extra baubles but it's also what inspired you to rescue the dragons. You got many of their jewels, even if a lot were burned up in the attack and retreat home. This connection between you and the artifacts is getting stronger, and I wonder if this might not be adjacent to some of my research on how the Fangborn Change. I've been playing around with quantum entanglement as an explanation for that phenomenon."

Geoffrey and I had very different ideas of what "playing" meant, apparently. "Yeah, you said . . . spooky something?"

"Yes, spooky action at a distance." Then he launched into an explanation that used words like "remote steering," "qubit states," and "buckyballs." It was when he began discussing the possibility that we were dealing with a "landscape multiverse" that I held up my hand.

"You mean . . . like a parallel universe?" I hazarded.

"Yes, but . . ." He was baffled. "It was William James who came up with the term, "multiverse." He was *American*. Do you even understand that time and space are the same thing? How can you not know any of this?"

I was starting to lose my patience. "Yeah, archaeologist."

He waved his hands. "Okay, okay, never mind, it doesn't matter. Quantum entanglement is the faster-than-light communication of an entangled system with the time dilation of special relativity, allowing time to stand still in light's point of view . . . Alice asked, 'How long is forever?' And the White Rabbit answered, 'Sometimes, just one second'—"

"I'm sorry," I said. "I'm trying, but even that—"

"Let me just say that there might be important relations between you and these objects, between states of the Fangborn Change, that could enlighten us as to the nature of the universe, multiverses—"

He finally twigged that I needed more specific, concrete ideas, for now. "Let's focus on you and your experiences. There are connections among these multiverses—you call them your mind-lab or meta-realm or voids or whatever. I think that the Makers might come from another multiverse superimposed on our own, and that they've found ways to bridge between theirs and ours. Just streams of particles would be all it took. You, the dragons, the artifacts all have some way of communicating across these spaces. That's why you're able to play with time, and now, space. I'm trying to define how you're doing it."

"Um, okay. The how isn't so important as the how come, to me, though."

He waved a hand. "It's all part of the same problem. Take the name the dragons are always calling you. Why Hellbender?"

"I don't know. I looked it up. It's some kind of ugly giant lizard."

"Salamander," he corrected automatically.

"Whatever. I thought it was just what I look like to Quarrel. But . . . it's got to be more. He once said I would become the Hellbender and none but my Makers could overtake me. Or something like that."

"Well, have you ever thought that it might be hell you are bending? Not fire and brimstone, but the place where time and space get *really* weird, beyond our brains to comprehend? Maybe that's what it refers to. You're learning to do in a very short span what he came by naturally after centuries of communicating with the Makers. He understands *you* have real power, to be able to do that."

Geoffrey seemed very excited, but so far, not a damn thing he'd said trying to reassure me had worked. In fact, quite the opposite. I didn't like the idea of bending time and space, and I most certainly didn't like thinking about bending any hell, either. I made a note to ask Quarrel what he meant as soon as possible.

On the other hand, if Quarrel could explain it to me, the answer might be even worse. That's how I was finding it with dragons.

"Now tell me about these shifts of temporal perception you've experienced," he said.

I mentioned seeing the rebuilt oracular temple at Claros—or maybe I should say the original structure as it was back when it was first standing. I described the seeming lack of time passing for Adam while I was in the house in Roskilde in Denmark. After a moment's consideration, I described the fight with the two Fangborn there in nineteenth-century costume, and how they vanished, the swirling chaos, the flickering sight of a giant snake.

"But I don't know what that was, really," I said, half-apologetically. "Some kind of hallucination, or some trick of the artifacts to protect themselves? I don't know."

Geoffrey stared at me. "Well, the idea of a wormhole springs to mind. A wormhole is a shortcut through space/time and wyrm is another word for "dragon"; maybe there's a connection in the stories of the Fangborn . . . What do you call it?"

"Um, culture?"

"The way that these things move between multiverses. I mean, I've never actually seen one fly—and I'm not sure they are structurally sound for flight. The wings seem more, not vestigial, but not quite developed yet. So, if you want to look at the different myths and legends about dragons flying, I'd say it's more like teleportation." Geoffrey took a deep breath, and a disbelieving grin just about split his face. "And now you can do it. This is awesome!"

At the same time I said, "Terrifying."

"Zoe, it's all in the name. You've got to learn to bend these things, these hells, to your will." He nodded. "Now's no time to be timid; that's all I can say. When you need to use these powers, go in big, like you own the place; that's the only way."

"It would be nice if I knew exactly how to do it and end up not scattered across the universe. Multiverses," I corrected myself.

He nodded. "I'm working on it."

I'd spent so much time thinking about abstractions and hypotheses that I needed something physical, concrete but not life threatening. I went to the gym, where I found Dmitri Parshin jumping rope. He'd always been an imposing figure to me. His muscles had suggested steroids, and so did his viciousness. I'd thought of Dmitri as evil—and he had been once, until I changed that—but now I recognized the discipline that backed up his ego and his ambition. Clean shaven, dark hair carefully cut, he moved with practiced ease even though he was sweating from the intensity of his workout. I was surprised to see him there, but he and the men under his command who had survived the Battle of Boston were staying with the Fangborn. Eventually, they'd move to the island with me.

It was cheaper for the government to have all their criminals in one place.

"I'll come back later," I said. "I don't know what I'm doing here anyway."

"Here." He wiped off his face and went to a bin. He pulled out a pair of boxing gloves and threw them to me. He donned a pair of training mitts and held them up. "Work on your combinations."

"I don't have any." But that wasn't true. "I once learned some boxing, from a friend."

"Then it's time you added to that." He gestured with the mitts. "Give me jab, cross."

We'd worked our way up to speed, and I relaxed a little. Thoughts crept in, though, when I was doing a "jab, jab, cross, duck, uppercut." I didn't duck fast enough and Dmitri caught me on the side of the head with the mitt and knocked me over.

"You're not concentrating. That will get you killed." There was nothing of pity in his voice.

"Yeah, I know. This is just practice."

"Practice concentrating on not getting killed. What are you thinking about?"

I wanted a distraction, so I turned it around on him. "What's your long game, Dmitri? Because I know you have one."

"Power. I go where power is. Sometimes it's me. Right now, it's you."

I nodded and returned my gloves to the bin. "And what if I gave the power back to the Makers? What if I used that power they're giving me to take myself out of the running? And they'd have to wait another ten or fifteen or thousand years for the next Fangborn who gets all the goodies?"

He stared at me, no expression on his face. Finally, the hint of a smile. "You're not going to do that."

"Let's say I am."

"I suppose I would find my own way of communicating with the Makers," he said. "Ally myself with your friend Quarrel."

"Maybe you would." I thought secretly that the first thing I would do after I rejected the Makers' power would be to kill Dmitri. Just in case. There was no way I was letting him get near the Makers or the dragons or anyone powerful enough to communicate with them.

Communication—I suddenly remembered the impression of reaching other minds when I'd experimented with the scarab chip. I didn't want more abstract physics, so I turned my thoughts to Carolina Perez-Smith. "Carolina. Logic isn't enough to deal with her brand of crazy. Reason isn't nearly enough."

Dmitri removed his mitts and wiped his face. "What do you mean?"

"I'm thinking about Carolina, her whole machinery. It just seems there's no good way to deal with her and her brand of narcissism.

He regarded me with pity and humor. "You can't win with logic, Zoe. With her, we go in, full throttle, and tear it down, burn it, then salt the earth for good measure."

It was so easy for him. Violence was always the solution.

I nodded, slowly. Then, "No, we can't do that. We can't give her anything more to use against us. Check that—it doesn't matter if we give her anything. If we don't, she'll make shit up, spin hysteria from speculation and rumors. We can't feed the monster, either. We can't feed the beast; we can't destroy it . . ."

An idea hit me. "We starve it. We take its food away, we starve it, then feed it poison. We cut off some heads, bury the others."

"What do you mean?"

I'd forgotten about him, struck by my idea. "Nothing," I said, running down the hallway. "Thanks for the lessons."

Chapter Fourteen

I showered and then asked Danny, Vee, Lisa Tarkka, and Claudia and Gerry Steuben to join me in a meeting room.

"The Makers," I said. "I've told you about what I know of them. What do *you* think they are? And please . . . use simple words."

Danny focused on a space on the wall above my head as he thought. It was a familiar habit, as though he were concentrating on the answers that hovered outside of our perception. "Maybe the Makers are a kind of megapathogen, a complex biological organism, that spreads. Maybe they need real estate; maybe they need information. Maybe they just want to see what's out there."

"And it would take a lot of energy for them to move or create something, right?" I remember how exhausted I was after the construction of the blaster and using it. "So . . . how did they make us, if that is true?"

"Maybe it's just a"—Lisa flicked her wrist, in a gesture of throwing—"series of very little messages. Maybe they send out genes like spores, to turn worlds to something useful for them? Maybe they change your human DNA with a couple of switches on, or off. Or maybe they're a virus that takes over in some ways, to their advantage. Something that doesn't take a lot of effort. We know so little about the full range of genetic information; we can't identify something like fifty percent of the bacterial or viral information in your gut. It's biological dark matter, doesn't look like anything we know about now."

Eeeeewww, I thought. *Like puppet masters or . . .* "What is that cat disease? You know, the one that's supposed to make you want more cats, so it gets more hosts?"

Lisa's face cleared. "Ah, *Toxoplasma gondii*. Well, that's popularly misunderstood, but the analogy of a host and parasites might be accurate here."

"We could just think of them as aliens," Danny said. "With advanced technology and understanding of the fabric of the universe; it makes the most sense. I mean, he talks about planes of existence and the like."

I knew he was right, of course, but I felt my stomach flip. It was bad enough for me and the unacculturated Normal population to grasp that the Fangborn existed, stretching taut the already straining fabric of credulity. Now aliens? "I wish that wasn't the case."

"Zoe, you've already encountered vampires and dragons," Vee said. "And you're already on first-name terms with the Makers. Why is that idea so distasteful?"

"It's irrational, I know, but I don't know what they want for all of us." I understood that was exactly how the Normals will feel on I-Day. "But the massive expenditure of energy they'd need to communicate with us. . . That might explain the reason that older Fangborn, like Senator Knight, don't feel the Call to Change, don't seem as driven to pursue evil. There could be a stretching of the connection between the Makers and . . . what the Fangborn were meant to be? I mean, they've . . . become so much their own selves that they no longer feel the influence of the Makers?"

"Or it could be they're becoming more specialized tools for the Makers," Lisa said.

I tried hard not to dislike her, but Dr. Tarkka was making it difficult for me.

"Okay, okay, more immediately, more concretely. Carolina and the kidnapped Family. What plans are in place?"

"Senator Knight has a spy in her camp," Gerry said. "We've

been told that the Boston victims were moved to a place on private property in New York State. That's why the Midwest facility we rescued you from was so full. The folks there had been moved to free up a place closer to Boston to whisk the Boston Family to.

"That property is within . . . well, let's just say, some Family believe they have the rights to certain places. So tonight, you and some others are going to talk to the Adirondack Free Pack about this." He shifted, looking uncomfortable.

"Since when are there separate 'packs'?" I asked. "Do they only have werewolves or something?"

"These guys are unusual," Gerry said. "Claudia calls them the Cousins who live in caves and cast bones."

Claudia shot her brother a dirty look. "Not that there's anything wrong with that," she said hastily. "It just seems . . . archaic. To me."

"And patriarchal, right?" Gerry said, like he was repeating back a lesson. He looked pleased with himself for remembering, but Claudia's pursed lips shut him down. "Anyway. The majority of the Family, well, we try to keep things democratic," Gerry said. "Like, Heck's running things in Boston, because we've agreed he should. The Free Pack, they keep to themselves, isolated from humans, and they feel very strongly about other Fangborn coming onto 'their' territory. They tend to keep Fangborn varieties segregated. In this case, the werewolves are dominant. You'll go with Senator Knight—they know him and respect him. You'll take Jason with you. The idea is that one of the ravens can be observing Carolina's property while you're in talking to the Free Pack."

"Okay, but why me?"

"They're curious about you, the senator said." Gerry looked through a very messy notebook. "After that meeting, we're all going to storm Carolina Perez-Smith's compound tomorrow. Remember, the goal is to rescue the kidnapped Fangborn and round up whatever Order members are there—no killing, no casualties, if possible. We just want our people back, and if we can find a way to make Carolina and the Order pay for it later, so be it."

"The rescue is the priority. Vampires will be supplying a lot of alternate narratives, but we want to keep the memory changes as slight as possible. We can't have the Order all doing a complete turnabout, because it will let everyone else know what we're up to. We're just trying to contain her a bit, is all."

There was a clamor outside, and the door opened suddenly. "Zoe," a werewolf said. "There are two kids named Dickson who want to see you. Shall I send them up?"

"Yeah, sure." Why on earth was this person—was her name Ryleigh?—asking me? "Kids? Who—"

Rose and Ivy Dickson appeared. "We needed to come," Rose said.

"We felt an emptiness, and since you established that connection between us . . ." Ivy said.

"You thought being here would help?" I said.

They looked at me, acknowledging that I'd just filled in a space that was left open by Ash's death.

"That's totally . . . I didn't do that," I said hastily. "I was just trying to figure out what you meant."

My protest didn't convince either of them. "See?" they said at once.

"Besides, Rose said we needed to be here," Ivy said. "She's always dragging us around."

"We *are* racking up the frequent-flier points," Rose said.

"Okay, well, I won't lie," I said. "We can use you in the rescue operation tomorrow."

"Just don't try to give us venom or a suggestion that we forget," Ivy said fiercely. "About Ash."

"They kept trying it at home. Why would we want to forget?" Rose added. "Why would we not want to feel this? You wouldn't ask someone who'd lost a limb or an eye to just get over it. We've lost much more than that. A third of ourselves."

"And don't tell us Ash would have wanted us to feel better."

"I would never say that," I said, shaking my head. "I hate that. 'Oh, you're mother would have loved this' or 'She would have wanted it this way.' People say that at funerals because they can't bring themselves to say that *they* like something, or that the person who died might have been unhappy at the idea of death. It's a stupid thing to say, and if you ever catch me, you can punch me in the head."

"Zoe's right," Claudia said, with a disapproving look at me that suggested she didn't think I should be talking about punching people in the head or funerals.

I shrugged. "So we have no desire to try and jolly you up about your brother's death. We desperately need all the help we can get."

"No problem," Gerry agreed. "We'll get you a room; it's getting crowded here, but when we are set up on Flock Island, it'll be easier. Dan, Will and Adam will be here in a moment. Can you give us five minutes on how the provisioning of the island is going?"

"Sure," he said.

Everyone looked at me as if I was supposed to do something. "Uh, thanks for stopping by, folks." Apparently, I was running this meeting, and since we were finished, I was the one to dismiss it. It was another new experience, almost as unsettling to have people looking to me for guidance and authority as to deal with dragons.

"Hey, Danny? Got a quick minute?" I said as everyone was leaving.

He stopped and turned. "Yeah, Zo." Vee stood by as well.

I was shivering as I thought about what was coming. I took their hands and pulled them close so we wouldn't be overheard. "Do me a favor. Go. Run, now. Danny, take Vee and run as far away from me as you can."

"*Take* Vee? I don't think anyone's *taking* me anywhere," she said.

"Zoe, what the fuck?" Danny's indignation was enormous. "No."

I spoke quickly, before I lost my nerve. "Look, at this point, I'm responsible for the death of a lot of people—Ash, Fatima, and oracles I've never met being the latest. That number will go up, significantly, in the next couple of days, unless I can find a foolproof plan and execute it exactly right. The chances of those two events happening are microscopically small, minute to the point of utter improbability."

Danny looked like he was going to correct me on my logic, but shut his mouth when I held up my hand.

"It doesn't matter. What I'm trying to say is that I feel unbelievably horrible about all of this, but on top of it all, Sean died in my arms. Danny—Dan, I mean, that's what you're going by now, right? Everything's changing . . . I'm the last person who should be making these decisions. It wasn't so long ago, a lot of people didn't think I was capable of making decisions for my own life; you know that better than anyone—"

I choked up then, and shook my head, tears filling my eyes. "Forgive me if I tell you I don't think I could live if I added you guys to the body count, too."

Danny didn't seem fazed, however. By my tears or my problems. Neither did Vee, who looked at me like I was crazy. He just shrugged. "You're the only one who can make them, Zoe, so it's no use pretending you can't or you shouldn't. It's not something that's going away."

I wiped at my eyes angrily. "Yeah, thanks a pant-load."

"You know it's true. You just gotta take it one apocalypse at a time, Zoe."

Apocalypse was a good word. "I just wish . . . it wasn't me. Wasn't now. Wasn't near you guys."

"Zoe, there is *nowhere* to run away to that will get us away from this," Vee said. "You know that."

"You're right," I said, embarrassed now. "I'm sorry, I just . . . I'm sorry."

It was at that moment that Adam and Will walked in, and stopped when they saw I'd been crying. "Do I want to know what you all are talking about?" Adam asked.

"Almost certainly not," I said. "Adam, Will, I would like you both to go away from me, leave me to the *mishegas* that is my life, and live until well in your nineties, happy and safe. Will you both do that for me?"

"Um, no," Will said. "And never ask again, please."

Adam shook his head. "What is this about? I'm not going anywhere."

"Without you," Will added, as if it was some kind of competition. The tension between them was palpable. They were cooperating, because they had to, but that was it. "Why do you ask now?"

I shook my head. "It's just the short version of the conversation."

That sealed it for me. If they weren't going, I had to be the best I could possibly be, and then a whole lot better. As Geoffrey had told me, I had to act like I owned the place.

———

We spent the afternoon loading up truck after truck with materials from the Boston house to bring to the wharf, and from there, to be shipped to Flock Island. It was amazing what Fangborn habits combined with military procedure could effect. The place wouldn't have permanent buildings for some time, so there'd be tents and temporary structures. There was a kind of contest between the groups working on opposite sides of the island to see who could get more done faster. The Fangborn had centuries of practice in establishing hideouts and bolt-holes; the military had almost as much time to perfect the quick establishment of a base with housing and communications.

A box full of books fell, spilling and splaying all over the street. I looked up—more thuds and crashes. The Fangborn carrying them had all gone stock-still, frozen in their tracks, their faces blank.

Their mouths opened, but nothing came out.

Suddenly I dropped the box of blankets I'd been carrying. I had to cover my ears, but it was reflex, because I heard the cries of thousands of Fangborn souls coming from within me.

When I felt a tug, I knew that I was being summoned by the

Makers. I gave into the impulse to follow, as I had before with the dragons, and found myself back at the Castle.

———⏑———

It was like being called into the principal's office times a hundred thousand. I remembered one or two trips home in the back of a police car causing less concern than this, and because I was out of my head with fear both those times, I was now recalling them fondly.

This wasn't good, but . . . it was familiar. If I hadn't gotten into trouble as a kid, I wouldn't know what I know about getting into trouble. Meaning, yes, there might be bad things about to go down, but at least I knew from experience that the anticipation wouldn't kill me. My fear was unpleasant but manageable.

Still didn't mean I wanted to be here. The outer office was a hubbub of assistants trying to clean up and repair the damage that had been done by the dragons. Several of them were limping, and I saw black eyes and broken arms.

In the inner sanctum, the Administrator was not pleased. "The incident with the elder beings," the Administrator said. "The ones you call dragons. Most regrettable."

"Yes." I decided I wasn't going to say anything more than politeness dictated.

"A great deal of damage done, resources expended, and, well, general unpleasantness."

"Yes."

"It's shown me several things, however."

"Yes?"

"Clearly, those dragons were acting on their own. They were not part of any . . . plan of yours."

Like I was incapable of a plan, *I thought. I was planning the same thing; it was just that the dragons were far more direct. But now, anything that might have stuck to me, artifact-wise, would be blamed on them.*

He turned, distracted, and hit a few keys on a computer keyboard. "You also got them under control, if in a rather . . . self-interested manner."

"Yes. They won't be any more trouble. You have my word."

"So it is also apparent that while you were not in control of them, you are now."

"I suppose so."

"Then you'll be held responsible for them from now on."

"I understand. But I must ask you . . . The way you called me? It has a terrible effect on my kind. My kin. Some have been killed or injured when you . . . possess their minds so."

"But it got you here?" The Administrator was annoyed; the dragons' rampage had caused an upset and he craved order. "It reinforces the idea that they must look to you and obey you. It is a lesson to you as well, not to be distracted by their petty business. You answer to us."

"Yes, but perhaps you could—"

"We shall do what is necessary. That's all."

———

Back in my here and now, the sidewalk outside the Boston safe house was a mirror image of the outer office at the meta-Castle: It looked like moving day gone wrong. Boxes were scattered where they'd been dropped, causing a snarl in the traffic and a mess on the sidewalk. Family members were dazed, a few sitting down on the ground, trying to figure out what had just happened. This time it was everyone: oracles, vampires, werewolves.

The Normals going about their business in that part of the city had no idea what was going on. Adam, Danny, and Will had been the only ones in our crew left unaffected, wondering what the hell had just happened to the Fangborn around them.

As they recovered, I yanked Gerry aside and told him what had happened. He told Claudia, and she organized the vampires to tell any onlookers that they'd felt a tremor in the ground, a minor earth-quake that had caused the mess. When I asked Jason what he'd picked up from the other oracles, he said there had been casualties. More had been hurt or killed, distracted or dismayed by the Makers' call.

That did it. I headed to Flock Island with the latest shipment. My team said they'd join me later, but for now, I needed to be alone to think the unthinkable.

Whatever else happened, I had to make sure that disruption didn't happen again, especially with I-Day around the corner. We couldn't have anything that would make that worse than it was going to be already. I can't have the Makers yanking the leash of the Family.

Flock Island had been my first choice. It was off the coast of Massachusetts, just beyond sight of the Graves Light. Its use by Europeans had started in the seventeenth century; through the centuries its use had changed. It had been a fishing station, a fort, a whale-processing station, a prison. In the twentieth century, it housed a lighthouse, a fort in both World Wars, and a boy's work camp. Then it was abandoned and avoided because it was also rumored to have been a hazardous chemical-waste storage depot. This was a rumor spread by the government, because it was always handy to have a strategically located island off the coast near your major cities. The name may have come from when there were lots of seagulls attracted to the fishing processing or it may have referred to a former owner. Once upon a time that would have been the first thing I looked up. Now there just wasn't time.

In other words, it was remote, yet close to Boston, New York, and Washington by boat and helicopter and small plane. There would be no problem keeping day sailors and adventurers off the island, because not only would I have navy protection, but marines and coast guard as well. A correctional facility, a slaughtering place, a fort.

Sounded about right for me.

There was a patch of garden land, oddly enough, a relic of its days as a work farm. I can't imagine how much manure or seaweed had been hauled out there, because there were boundaries still visible and a riot of bird-picked squashes and matted corn stalks. Clearing that out would give me something to do, because basically, I was now a prisoner of my own making, as securely defended from the outside world as they were from me.

I didn't like it, but I could live with it. I would camp out on the island with my army of honorable werewolves and vampires and dishonorable humans who'd sworn to obey me because their real boss Dmitri was paying them a lot and he was much scarier to them than I was. A handful of them knew better, but for the moment, I was glad to have the air cover of Dmitri's bad reputation.

True to his word, the senator had found me a cat. I took the carrier to my room at the building at the bottom of the lighthouse and, making sure the space was closed in, let him out. A streak of gray-blue, a flash of coppery, panicked eyes, and the cat found its way under my camp bed.

I didn't blame him—her? It was an attractive idea to me, too. I needed peace, I needed quiet, and I needed a big dose of inspiration. The assault on Carolina's to rescue the Family was tomorrow, and I-Day would follow shortly after. There was pressure on all sides, and too many variables. I unpacked a box of books and papers and began to pace.

I had on a table in front of me a pile of, well, scraps. Copies of every written and recorded Fangborn prophecy and prediction going back to the beginning of Fangborn recorded history, and the list of my own information, gathered directly and indirectly from the Makers.

I had one chance to please the Makers, and I had to pick from a long list of potential global catastrophes to do that. Could I use that borrowed artifact to create a vampiric suggestion that would make the entire world forget they'd ever heard anything about the Fangborn? Probably too many factors involved in doing that, never mind the scope of reaching out to six billion minds. I was bound to screw that up. It had to be a smaller population. What about the Order? Could something be done there?

It was remotely possible I could remove all Fangborn powers everywhere. That would be one way of resolving the issue with the Normals. Everyone the same, all over again. But I couldn't just save the Fangborn from Carolina and then leave them powerless to face the Makers. Or maybe I could download all of my abilities to the Fangborn. That would be another way to resolve things, but I didn't think that adding a load of superpowers to the mix would help.

No. Too radical, too visible a change. It had to be something no one, or virtually no one, knew about. I knew it had to be something I did to the Fangborn. Something to help, something small. I'd been making the most of small things all my life. Crumbs— of information, of kindness—can take you a very long way if you know what to do with them.

This was worse than the hypothetical question, "If you had five seconds to change the world, what would you do?"

I suddenly hated hypotheticals—the people who asked and answered them were just fooling around, toying with what was now my real responsibility.

I walked over to the window and looked out. Quarrel was there, soaking up the sun and sleeping. I could see wisps of steam—I hoped it was steam, and not acid vapor—rising from his mouth, which I supposed meant he was snoring. Naserian was helping out, rooting out a bunch of stones and moving them. We would have to bring over heavy equipment to do more of the construction, but for now, Naserian was happy to assist, or so she said. Until I could find them a place of their own—I was officially responsible for them now—I'd have to let them do pretty much what they wanted to keep from getting bored. A bored dragon was a dangerous dragon.

Seeing the copy of the Orleans tapestry prophecy, the one I'd learned about in Venice that said whoever claimed the golden disc hidden there would "unchain" the Fangborn, got me thinking about the nature of prophecies. Everyone always described oracles as tricky: They gave predictions that were either unintelligible or so vague as to be generalities. No one in any book I'd ever read ever had any luck with prophecies, either. Just thinking about examples of unhappy prophecies didn't give me much more confidence or more of a clue. Predictions are usually described as obscure, almost legalistic, so that they were riddles. A play of words, a loophole, and the fabric of prophecy was undone.

I figured that something, some bit of memory or information, had been passed down through the ages, and been transformed into a prophecy. I had to consider whether it was a garbled message from the Makers. Someone was trying to tell me something, and I had to figure out what it was.

I had choices. I could "fix" the Fangborn, make them over into what the Makers intended. I could make them into something else. I could subjugate the human race, which is what I assumed the Administrator meant by "my people." I couldn't do nothing.

What about the Makers? Could I banish them from our collective psychic and/or physical presence? Right. That would be like trying to push a grizzly bear out of your way—not realistic and truly unwise. Should I attack them, maybe bite them so hard they would think twice about coming back to haunt us? I had no idea about the scope of their power; what they'd shown me should be warning enough.

It was a horrible idea—the repercussions would be ghastly— but I could not scratch it off my too-short list.

I prepared for my meeting with the Adirondack Free Pack.

Chapter Fifteen

Our goal was to request the Free Pack's permission to enter their territory when we attacked Carolina's compound and to ask for their help in the assault. I wasn't convinced we'd get either, from what I'd learned from Gerry. They were so conservative that they were actually in favor of taking over custodianship of humanity.

They requested three of us in the envoy: vampire, werewolf, and oracle. Senator Knight was the vampire—the Pack knew and respected him. They would have been very pleased if he'd been the one to open Pandora's Box. They had asked for me personally, Knight said, because they were curious about me. The oracle, it was decided, would be Jason, the plan being for the raven Jill to observe Carolina's property while we were so close by. It was fitting: In many cultural traditions, ravens and crows lead wolves to prey. We had maps, and we had intelligence—the senator's informant on the inside—but no one would ever suspect Jill was working for us.

We took a small plane to the nearest airport, then coptered from there. I was getting used to traveling in helicopters and it was a wonderful way to get a close bird's-eye view of the world. But the noise . . . It would always remind me of Fatima's murder by the Order. We set Jill loose, Jason giving her specific directions, he claimed, and promised to meet her back at the landing site shortly.

We hiked in through the woods, coming to a clearing. A number of roughly organized structures, in no way uniform, were clustered around a central open area. We were greeted by a number of Family, who were eager to meet Senator Knight but eyed me and Jason Jordan with suspicion.

A tall werewolf stepped forward. "I'm Eli Passey, and I speak for the Adirondack Pack." Blond hair and blue eyes and his flannel shirt and jeans were normal enough, but Passey was a scary-looking bastard, whip thin with the kind of muscles that come from hard use and aren't just for show. He must have been hurt badly as a child, as a human, before he could Change, because he had a long white scar that ran from his left temple to his jaw line and down to his neck. A scar that size meant that the wound should have taken off the side of his head; only being a werewolf had saved his life. Maybe that counted for his behavior now, the Fangborn-first chauvinism and the clannishness that went beyond Family ties.

"I know why you're here," he said. "Present your case."

Senator Knight handed him a file folder. He flipped through it, his face contorting with anger. He handed it to his second, who looked at it and swore, throwing it to the ground. I picked it up when no one else went for it. One photo showed a large barn on what I assumed was Carolina's property, covered with some kind of mushrooms.

Then I realized the things on the wall were ears.

There had been an orderly pattern, lined up neatly in rows. The oldest ones were now just blurs of weather-beaten flesh and rusty nails that punctuated the ancient wood of the barn.

I'd never really understood the notion of tacking animal hides or ears or tails to a fence to "scare off" would-be interlopers, but I got it, a little, when situated in the context of fear, superstition, and a struggle for survival. But these days, I was less sympathetic to the gesture, if not outright hostile to it, and I felt my blood boil over as I realized what these trophies were.

They were human ears, and the reason they'd been hung up next to the wolf ears and snakeskins was because they had been taken from Fangborn.

As much as I'd like to think we might some day as a species find our way out of the pits of hatred and ignorance, it wasn't happening anywhere near here, anytime soon. It made me think twice about I-Day.

I was experiencing something I felt certain was very close to the hatred the Order felt for Fangborn. The killing impulse didn't fade with that understanding, which distressed me for about a microsecond, and I knew I was heading into murky philosophical waters. The urge to do violence didn't go away, but I could channel it to suit me: I wasn't necessarily going to slaughter whoever'd done this, but I was going to give myself a lot of leeway in how I addressed the situation.

The senator and Passey shook hands on the deal. As the senator turned to go, Passey said, "Will you stay a moment longer, Zoe Miller?"

Not liking the feeling of danger that suddenly coursed through me, I looked to the senator, who nodded. "We'll see you at the landing point," he said as he and Jason left.

I expected to be asked about my unexpected trip to Japan, or introduced around as a courtesy, a stray to a new group. Instead, I was confronted with a picture of Fatima Breitbarth's body in the snow.

"You left your friend, your Family, to die, while you escaped?" he demanded.

I gasped, shocked by his accusation. "No! The Makers—"

There were uneasy sounds in the rest of the group, as if I had invoked some holy name.

Eli held up a hand to quiet them. "I've heard about your powers, everyone has, and still you didn't save her. What, were you trying to get some of her abilities for yourself? That's what you do, isn't it? Suck the power from other Fangborn. You're some kind of vampire now? Or are you in league with the Order?"

Stunned by his accusations and total lack of understanding, I said, "What? No, I never—"

"What about Toshiharu Yamazaki-Campbell? Everyone knows that you assaulted him."

Passey suddenly reminded me of a Fangborn version of Buell, and I was shocked at just how much that frightened me. Logic didn't enter into addressing something as deep as a cultural bias. It was more dangerous than religion, because in this case, there was no higher power, no rules to temper his response. It was Passey's ideas alone driving him, and it made him dangerous. Disagree with him, and he'd claim you were anti-Fangborn, which, with this crowd, was something you didn't do.

"What? No! He and I were . . . competing for the power from an artifact. I won. He's still Toshi; he's still got all his vampire powers. That's just a false rumor. He's in Boston now! You can ask him!"

"We're not in contact with him."

"That doesn't make *me* a liar."

"Uh-huh. Well, I'm not convinced. In fact"—Passey glanced around at the crowd of angry Fangborn around me—"none of us are convinced. I'm calling for Examination."

Whatever, if it would just get us moving. "Great. AP English or history? Trivial Pursuit?"

Passey looked aghast. "You take this very lightly. Too lightly. Call your Family together; let them stand with you."

"I'm a stray, you know that. What am I supposed to be taking so seriously?"

"Examination is our justice. If you're found guilty, you undergo a shedding."

I shook my head at this sudden madness. "I don't know what that is."

He looked shocked. "How can you not? Stripped of your *powers*. A group of vampires drains the life from you, almost—and injects certain chemicals. It has the effect of permanently removing your powers, your ability to Change." Passey smirked. "No more Miss Showboating Stray."

"But I didn't do anything!" I insisted. "And you'll be able to tell I'm telling the truth. You bring those vampires in here right now!"

"We know you're not lying. But if you've broken our laws, you pay the price."

"I was trying to help!" I looked around desperately. "Ask them! Ask Toshi!"

"Not necessary. We ourselves have proof of your lawbreaking. Your image, your name is what was broadcast to all of our people, on two occasions now. That resulted in the death of several Family members, thus breaking the law." He spat. "We abide by the law, even if you don't. Resign yourself."

I didn't have time to waste with this. I knew I'd done nothing wrong, and I didn't have the time to work it out by trial. But I couldn't risk any ill will that might jeopardize our mission tomorrow.

I had to get out of here.

I could feel the antagonism toward me building, and knew that it wasn't going to be talk that got me out of here.

I couldn't kill or hurt them. We needed them in the fight against Carolina and the Order. I needed another way out.

The bracelet flared; I recalled the brightness of it underwater in the bath at Kanazawa. It was camouflage. I needed camouflage now . . .

The idea seemed to feed into the bracelet, making it alive, glowing brighter, and brighter, until the colors washed out and went to—

Blinding white light, as everything went online, burned *on*. I felt a thousand suns light up inside me, as if floodgates had been opened, a connection made, a damper removed.

If I thought I was the only one who could see it, that this was a private showing, I was wrong. The rest of the Pack could see it, too, and threw their hands up over their faces, threw themselves on the ground to keep from being blinded.

"Don't lose her!" I heard Passey shout.

Five more seconds, and I could feel the light softening, going dim again. I cursed myself for not having the brains to run when I could have. I hurried as far over to the gateway as I could, trying not to step on too many people as I ran. I didn't oppose squashed toes or crunched fingers, not at the moment. I was just trying to keep as inconspicuous as possible while I fled.

The light vanished, and I was face to face with three very angry werewolves and a vampire. I stopped short, wishing I'd thought to run along a wall, and at least be able to fight with my back to that.

"Who has her?" The vampire in front of me Changed, gone to gray scales with yellow streaks. He was so huge, I couldn't imagine what kind of snake he resembled. Maybe he was the Loch Ness monster.

Then I realized he was staring right at me and still couldn't see me. Couldn't smell me. Maybe he was still blind, suffering the aftereffects of—

He turned and made eye contact with his equally confused partner. They could see each other . . .

No time for questions. Time to jam.

I started to tiptoe around the trio, when one of them, searching for me, whirled around, his arm out. I braced for the impact and the brawl that would follow.

It never came. His arm went straight through me. In fact, now he was standing exactly where I was.

I couldn't feel him. He couldn't feel me. So I needed to get the hell out of here while I could.

I ran while they were still hollering and groping for me. I ran until I was pretty sure I was safe, then ran some more to confuse my trail, and then ran a bit farther because I was scared to death.

I kept running, also, because at least it felt like I was alive. My heart pounded, my chest heaved, the sweat rolled off me. I was afraid if I stopped running, I wouldn't be able to feel the ground, that I would be stuck otherwhere, out of sight forever. I was afraid I would learn I'd turned into a ghost.

It was tripping and measuring out my length on the pine needle duff that finally convinced me. Ghosts can't stub their toes.

The bracelet went from living color to dull, so that it looked like an ordinary mortal accessory. I could see myself solid, again.

I raced for the landing site.

"What did they want?" the senator asked. His question was all innocence but with no surprise that I'd been running.

I eyed him, half wondering if he hadn't offered me up to them on purpose, especially after the demonstration, when I'd seen him lose his cool. I caught my breath. "They wanted to subject me to Examination and shedding. I escaped."

"Did you kill anyone?"

He didn't ask why, I noticed. "No. I knew better. That would void their contract. Will my escape affect your deal?"

The senator leaned back and shook his head. "As long as no one is dead, they are allowed to fight with us, and if I-Day comes within the year, they are content."

"Fine."

We sat in silence, waiting for Jill the raven to return with her intelligence, and then left for the island.

I had been fast asleep that night when suddenly the alarms sounded in the lab. I materialized there immediately.

"What the hell is that?"

Sean stared at a screen flashing red, lighting up his face. "Intruder alert. They're coming in from all over."

"What? We don't *have* an intruder alert. We can't have intruders, because we're . . . me?"

"Dude, I can only tell you what the screen says. Anything else, you have to figure out yourself. The software is only as good as the user."

"Yeah, whatever, shut up a second." I thought furiously. "Okay, Sean, stay with me."

We were in the coffee room, the space where the men I'd killed—some from the Order, some mercenaries from Dmitri's employ—hung out. Basically, if their blood was on my hands, they were here and I had access to their memories and knowledge. "Whatever you guys used to do back in the day, you're doing it for me now. We have intruders, and we can't afford that. If I go, you go. We've got to get them out of here, ASAP."

"Zo, are you sure that is a good idea?" Sean asked. "What if they belong here, came in with the other artifacts? New abilities, new minds, like Dr. Osborne?"

"I wondered about that, but it was the fact that *you* called them intruders, Sean. New rule: anyone who wants to be in here has to introduce themselves to me, shake my hand. Got it? No skulking in around through the lab without a pass, which . . ." Suddenly badges appeared on everyone around me, including me. "Which you all have. We'll sort out levels of access later. Sean, where we got them?"

"Five different points. Here." He raised a hand, and suddenly a plan schematic of the lab, now a full-on office park, appeared. It was far bigger than I thought, even with the new lab attached.

"Okay, five teams, divvy up according to abilities."

Instantly, the mercenaries who worked for Dmitri Parshin in life now formed teams in their afterlife to fight for me. They appeared to be armed again, but that was my intent. No weapons allowed in my mind-lab but those I authorized.

A group of ten interns stood there. "You guys—just keep out of the way."

"Zoe, hang on," Sean said. "The lab rats, the undergrads—they're not dead, remember? They're constructs, kind of subprograms you created to sort some of the information so you could study it."

"Yeah? Right, they're not mercenaries, not trained soldiers."

Sean looked pleased with himself. "But they can be."

Holy shit. They could be anything I wanted. I was still figuring out how all this worked, but the bigger I could imagine, the better they'd be. "Right. You guys . . ." I pointed to the undergrads and interns and waved my hand. "You now have the skills those guys have. And you're all on my side, no divided loyalties here."

Instantly, they wore gray fatigues and snapped to attention.

"Okay, good enough." I'd been hoping for white-armored storm troopers or giant battle bots, but this was all I was capable of mustering up at the moment, apparently. "Break off with the other teams, same drill. All of you, ask questions first, but return fire if the intruders get aggressive in any way. Got it?"

"Yes, sir."

"Go."

I was going to have to train them to say, "Yes, ma'am." "Sean, let's go find the biggest ones."

Sean kept an ear open and told me when the other teams found humanoid invaders in areas around the lab; my guys were doing a competent job of containing them. What the invaders seemed to be doing looked to me like sabotage, a rogue demolition team. They ignored my guys until their pry bars and toolboxes were taken away from them, and they attacked. This is exactly what Dmitri's ex-mercenaries wanted, and the first three groups of invaders were crushed to dust. Too easily. They failed so quickly that I had to assume that was intended: There was nothing left for me to examine or interrogate.

The invaders Sean and I found, on the other hand, looked like a couple of industrial-sized yeti and I suspected were much tougher than the ones Sean had reported elsewhere. They'd made straight for the boiler room, their intent clearly to shut us down.

I hauled off and punched one in the head. He didn't even look up. He wore green overalls with no markings; his "skin" was traffic-cone orange and his head was hairless as well as featureless; there was nothing but a kind of fuzzy flatness where his face should have been. I felt a little sick, like the time when I saw the little bumps all over my arm and realized I had caught chicken pox.

"Zoe, our guys are back in the lab," Sean reported, pointing out that the faceless goons we were confronting had materialized there as well. I noticed he now had a very flashy military-looking earpiece with which he was communicating with the other teams. "They couldn't even make a dent in these guys. They sort of . . . bounced . . . right off them."

"Okay, Sean. You go help that team, pronto. Then I want you to divert all the power you're not using to repel any other invaders to tracking and nailing that last team. Anything left over, you ship it straight to me!"

Sean vanished.

On my own, I took a deep breath and tackled the one nearest me. He was easily twice my size and removing the plates from what looked like old-fashioned fuse boxes and control panels. I bunched up both fists and slammed him in the back of the head. He backhanded me without even looking, and I sailed across the room. I picked myself up and put a hand out to steady myself. I felt teeth moving under my tongue.

I Changed to my werewolf form and decided to use his own power against him. While he worked, I snuck up behind him and pulled a file from his kit. Using all my might, I rammed it through his neck at the base of the skull. I felt the blow reverberate through my whole body, and then I felt like I'd been hooked up to the electrical mains myself as a jolt of power about fried me to death. The file sizzled, and I let go. He collapsed in a pile of pixels and sparks and flaming circuitry, which flared up and then zapped out. Nothing but a pile of dust left.

The last one was twice the size of his friend, and he was busily disconnecting ductwork. I knew enough not to go in barehanded, so I picked up the hammer that he wasn't using—he had a fine, daunting collection of scary tools—hauled back, and swung.

Not so much as a grunt, no break in his concentration. He was doing very bad things to the beating heart of the lab facility and I had to stop him . . .

But the hammer I'd taken from him was suddenly much bigger, like Mjölnir's cousin. It stood to reason if these guys were here to bust down the structures of the bracelet construct, then the tools they had were related, somehow. I had those powers, so I could use those tools against them, too.

I swung, and it felt . . . like it was part of me.

I squashed him like a bug. He dissolved into dust.

No time to think about this new development. "Sean! Where is the last group? Have you got them contained?"

No answer.

"Sean?" Panic welled up in me. Had I scrambled my own systems, using the bracelet inside the lab, using the invaders' own power against them?

Static in my head. "—facts—" was all I could make out.

At least it was Sean's voice. The last of the intruders were in the artifact storage area, which struck me as the true brain of the lab. I found myself there and got just a glimpse of the two invaders, easily as large as the ones I had fought just now, as they vanished.

Sean and the rest of my makeshift security team were picking themselves up off the floor. They were covered in bruises, some bleeding, and had clearly been no match for the invaders.

"Sean, where did they go?"

He just shook his head, trying to catch his breath. Sean's arm was shredded pretty badly, and I realized that he couldn't talk because some vital part of my systems, my 'verse, had been compromised.

Okay, think, think . . . "Hey, Doc?"

Professor Osborne showed up. I figured as the newest addition, there was a possibility that the intruders weren't aware of him. "What's up?"

"We've had visitors, and they're not nice. I've apparently taken some damage . . ." It was at that point that I realized that my own nose was bleeding steadily. "Ah, shit, they managed to screw up my healing abilities. Okay, these guys are fast, and as soon as a real threat pops up, they vanish. What can I do?"

"I'll work on plugging up any holes," Geoffrey said. There was something in his demeanor that said he liked the action, that he might have excelled in scenarios and simulations classes at the Fangborn Academy. And then there was that reaction to the explosion at the demonstration . . . Maybe all of his life hadn't been spent in an ivory tower or another multiverse.

"Could it be the Makers?"

"I'm not one hundred percent sure, but yeah, could most certainly be," he said as he examined the schematic of the lab. "But I wouldn't worry about it. You've got that thing, there, and whatever it is, it's doing a lot to keep them out."

"Wait, what thing? What do you mean?"

He pulled up the image of several artifacts. "I noticed that gold signet ring. Very posh. And the scarab microchip. Those are Order creations; they're not something the invaders understand, and those pieces were confusing them."

Porter's ring, the last thing I took from him as his body disappeared under a flurry of violence from my lab assistants. He didn't belong in the lab, I remembered, because he'd been jacked up on Order chemicals and enhancements. The scarab was the same, and it was keeping the Makers out.

"What about the sword, from Kanazawa?" I asked. That was on the screen, too.

"They were positively terrified of that."

Interesting. I recalled that Quarrel had referred to "that alien thing" in Kanazawa, and now I wondered if he was referring to the sword or the ring Porter made.

"I've been studying that sword. Zoe, that's crazy stuff. I have no idea what that is or does—but it's *major*. Like I said, it's not Order, it's not Fangborn. Okay to keep working on that?"

"Sure," I said absently. Then the timing hit me, and my stomach clenched. "Geoffrey, you're the translator the librarian told me about, right? You came with the papyrus. Were you sent by the Makers? Were you sent to fix me? To control me?"

Dr. Osborne looked surprised I hadn't asked this before. "Yeah, Zoe. Yeah, 'course I was."

Chapter Sixteen

I was about to dissolve into a panic when Geoffrey said, "But I can't function the way the Makers want, because of those objects. So basically, I get to play, hang out, think really big thoughts. You've given me so much new material—this is much more fun."

"But they have access . . . to *me*." I wasn't ready to give up on that panic just yet: I'd given the Makers even more direct access to me than they already had.

"I'm telling you they don't," he insisted. "If they had . . . those things would not have failed. There's something about you—and you said your blood had been tampered with by those TRG scientists, too, correct?—and these artifacts that keep the Makers at bay. You've got a natural resistance *and* an acquired one. Otherwise, you'd be doing what they want."

"So . . . can you tell me what they're thinking?" I asked, still worried, only a bit reassured. "Are you in contact with them?"

He cocked his head, as if listening. "Not really; I was supposed to have a mission, and because it didn't work out, they removed that capacity. I do get flashes, like they don't understand if they're trying to fix you with their repair teams, why you don't let them. They see it as further proof of your . . . brokenness."

Just because I wouldn't let them interfere with my lab, my construct, without my say so? I bit my lip; I had to trust what he was saying, for the moment. "I just hate being enmeshed in their plans, whatever they are. I hate being entangled with the Order—"

As soon as I said "entangled," an idea came to me so vast in scope and scale, it took my breath away. I sat down and put my head on the work surface, trying to keep my thoughts straight.

"Zoe, you okay?" Sean asked.

"Yeah . . . give me a minute, okay?"

The Orleans prophecy had featured the word "unchaining," but I'd never known if it meant that I would let someone off the chain, as in set them loose on someone? Get off my land, or I'll set the dogs on you? Then I thought what Geoffrey and Lisa had said about flipping the switches on certain genes, and that made me think about the strands in DNA. Maybe I could do something with that?

Meanwhile, Geoffrey wasn't quite tapping his foot, but he was waiting for me to connect my dots. Sean hovered over me uncertainly.

And once I figured out that yes, I was all about the metaphors, the idea came to me. Everyone stays the same, everything stays the same, except for one small thing.

Easy peasy, in theory; terrifying, in reality. Any reality.

I left the lab and found myself sitting up in my bed on the island. The cat, who had snuck up to the foot of the cot while I'd been asleep, stared at me suspiciously. I offered my hand for him to sniff and he stretched forward just out of reach. It was a start.

"I need to find out what your name is," I said softly. "You need a name. I could call you Demo, because I got you after I demolished something."

The cat turned his back on me and curled into a tight ball.

Not Demo, then.

I took a breath. The potential of the Makers to mess with my lab, to mess with me at this level, was scary and only made me more anxious to do what I understood had to happen next. I fell back to sleep still worrying.

The next morning, light streamed into my rooms at the base of the lighthouse through every window. I ate breakfast and thought hard, paced a lot. When I finally figured things out from all the angles I could, I found the others who were staying on the island and invited them to my rooms. The island complex was starting to come together, but the odd assortments of temporary structures, military tents, and camping tents, as well as the reuse of existing structures still gave the place the feel of a refugee camp. No one looked particularly rested, but there were temporary plumbing and generators for electricity, and we were all able to sleep inside at night.

I made a special effort and got one of the early-morning launches to bring doughnuts. I was learning what was important in a meeting.

Max looked good, much more chipper than the last time I'd seen him, and his fatigues had done a lot to minimize his "permanent werewolf" look. The island was a good place for him, away from Normal eyes and some place he could be near people and be "useful," as he put it. Gerry still looked raggedy and I worried that he wasn't eating enough; Claudia and Toshi, on the other hand, were positively radiant. The bright sun on the island was a dream come true for the vampires among us.

Danny and Vee had Wi-Fi and electricity, so they were able to keep up with their work, and I suspect, keep an eye on me. Will was working with those responsible for the planned rescue tonight and had kissed me rather determinedly when he arrived.

Senator Knight, who was the government's chosen liaison with me, was not staying on the island. He'd come over with the early launch, as had Adam, who was working with his mother's temporary office in Boston, helping with the I-Day preparations. Theirs would have been a very interesting conversation to hear, former employer and former employee.

I took the doughnuts from Adam, who brushed my hand superstitiously, a secret smile on his face. "What?" I asked.

"Nothing, just that some misguided soul, not knowing who he was, asked the senator if he'd please bring the doughnuts to you." Adam looked very pleased at Knight's discomfiture.

We pulled up mismatched chairs in the large room outside my "bedroom." The cat wandered in and jumped into Gerry's lap.

"What's his name?" he asked.

"I don't know what to call him, or her, yet," I said.

Gerry hauled up the hind end of the cat. "Yeah, it's a him, if that helps."

The cat jumped down, flicked its tail in annoyance at this usage, and stalked off.

I did my best to explain what I was planning.

My friends looked at me like I suggested broiling up a few kittens, but they heard me out. I spelled out the reasons as best I could, and almost wished I'd made a PowerPoint presentation just to keep everything in order, but I didn't want to risk having notes of any kind around. Telling folks, even my nearest and dearest, what I might do was dangerous enough.

When I finished, there was nothing but silence. "So . . ." I said, to fill up the vacuum. "The Makers are intensifying their attempts to keep me on their plan. *My* goals are to make sure the Makers can't use you directly against me or against Normal humans again, to make that possible with as little aggression as possible, and to keep everyone else on the planet out of this."

No one said anything. "There is no good way to predict what will happen in the long term, based on any decision I make," I said. "What might work for a while might turn bad in a decade or a century or a millennium. But I can only make choices that are the best for the moment, taking the immediate future into consideration. I really don't want to."

"But, Zoe," Max said. He took a big slurp out of his Dunkin' Donuts coffee mug. His knee jiggled nervously. I didn't allow smoking in my rooms. "You *have* to change things."

"I'm going to, but I'm worried about unexpected consequences, and there are two things that come to mind. One is knowing that I don't want to spend all my waking hours trying to undo what I might have screwed up in wishing for the world to change. And the other is the tale of the monkey's paw. I just get a bad feeling about trying anything so drastic, because of what could bite us in the ass. I want to keep it simple." I couldn't come up with anything else but my plan that seemed to cover these bases. "What do you think?"

"If the choices are for you to change us so the Makers can't, or change us so *we're* more powerful, I think you're right," Claudia said.

"This is all very . . . iffy," Gerry said.

Will nodded. "You shouldn't rush into this. This is dangerous for you."

"It's *all* gonna be dangerous," I said, impatiently.

"Right, but if you can act, you have to," Adam added. Will glared at him.

"Hold on," said Toshi. He was wearing jeans that I guessed must have cost a fortune and an even more expensive leather jacket against the chilly fall air. "Why shouldn't we ally ourselves with the Makers? How do we know it could be any worse than what's going on now? It could be the answer to everything. Everything, Zoe. You seem to be skipping right over the fact that you could single-handedly make this world a better place."

"It's the words 'single-handedly' that bothers me, Toshi," I said. "And I don't like sweeping, all-inclusive solutions. They all seem too dangerous to me."

"And we don't know how the Makers will respond to your plan." Senator Knight was pacing slowly, shaking his head. "That disobedience in itself might constitute rebellion, treason to the Makers—and bring worse upon us all."

Suddenly I was angry. "You know, I'm not here to make all your political dreams come true, Toshi. And, Senator, I know you don't like me or anything I stand for. I'm the opposite of you, who are the . . . living old guard. You're so old guard that you actually gave birth to those rules, codified them from your dreams of order. They're not working anymore, so you can't criticize me because I'm hanging on to the trapeze with no training and no safety net. You can't criticize me for *not falling*. I'm here, I'm making it work, on my own, and you don't get to piss on that and second-guess me because it's not you."

I took a deep breath. "So here's what's going to happen. I'm not here to fix everything you think is broken, especially when I'm not sure that's the case. And while I value your opinions, I do not care for this strong-arming, emotional blackmail shit." I darted a look at Will.

"I'm caught in the middle here, and it's up to me to decide. You may forget that it's only me between us and the Makers. That puts me in a tough spot, and I welcome your support and advice. But I don't ever get to forget that it comes down to my decision, my skin in the game, and I have to live with the outcome, no matter what happens. So a little empathy for my situation rather than looking out for your own selves wouldn't be amiss. There are enough folks ready to screw all of us."

I looked around. Nobody said anything. Toshi dropped his gaze; Knight didn't. Will looked majorly pissed off. "Fine," I said. "I'll take some time to think all this over and get back to you if I need anything to get ready for tomorrow. Thanks."

Before anyone could do anything else, I made a beeline for the door, and was down the stairs so fast, I had to wonder how many steps I'd actually touched.

I didn't stop until I reached the picket guard, who looked confused. I waved him aside, let him know I was okay, and pointed to the rocks that marked the edge of that part of the cliff.

I sat down. It was warm and there was a small flat space that made a pretty good seat. I watched the seagulls fighting for a while, until they took the squabble to the shingle and fought over whatever stolen treat they had. I watched another hover on the updrafts, hardly moving a feather, and envied him. A narrow range of responsibilities, being a seagull. A limited set of requirements and tasks.

A shout jarred me out of the daydream. The guard was waving at me, and I saw Dmitri Parshin waiting as patiently as he could to get my attention, which wasn't very patient at all. But another time, another life, he might have just shot the guard and then held me over the cliff by my hair. So respect of this sort was an improvement.

I waved him over. He glared at the guard—not one of his men, apparently—and stood by the rock, his arms crossed, while I watched the seagull hovering on the wind.

Out of the corner of my eye, I could see him scan the ground and glance back up at the seagull. Before he could indulge his instinct to find a rock and throw it at the bird, I sighed and turned.

"I just came from the lighthouse," he said.

"And no doubt someone tattled to you," I said. "I behaved poorly, but don't tell me they're just trying to do their best. That they just want to help and got overexcited. It's starting to get personal, and they're starting to get scared."

"I would *never* tell you they're doing their best." Dmitri laughed, and it was a harsh, barking sound. "I'm a cynic. I believe everyone is acting in their own self-interest. And more than that, I'm generally deeply suspicious."

"What are *you* going to do?" I was curious what part of the truth he would tell me; I would know if he was lying.

"I'm going to stand by you," he said simply, "as I promised. More than that, tomorrow, the day after . . ." He shrugged. "There's no point in lying to you, but you're making me nervous, Zoe. Not many things do, and it is not something I care for."

I had to smile. I couldn't deny that making Dmitri Parshin nervous gave me terrific satisfaction. I shrugged back, making it as European looking as I could. Because a European shrug said "sophisticated mystery" and an American shrug said, "Huh?"

"I do not like the idea of you deciding to subjugate the human race," he continued. "I do not like you giving even more power to the Fangborn. I do not like you thinking about giving that power back, leaving an . . . an alien force unchecked and us powerless against it."

"Me, neither."

I braced myself. If he tried to push me over, I'd blast him. Even if that didn't work, I'd take him with me, and I had a much better chance of surviving than he did, despite the rocks, the waves, and the height. He could try to do it and think he was saving the world . . .

"I do not trust people," he said, "but I think you are not a bad choice to be the one deciding. It's as close to a fair chance for the rest of us as I can think." He put his hand on my shoulder. I tried not to tense. "Do you want to go back now? The others are worried."

"No, thanks. I'm going for a walk. You can reassure them if you're truly concerned." I smiled; he was very convincing when he wanted to be. "You solicitousness is deeply gratifying, Dmitri Alexandrovich. It is a comfort to me in this time of grave concerns and fear."

He laughed again. Danny had told me no one used that kind of archaic address anymore, that it was just in old Russian novels, but I didn't care. I had learned it from a Russian novel.

"I only ask that, once you have ascended to be queen of the world, Zoe Richardovna, you will remember that it was poor Dmitri Parshin who was there for you."

"Remember the little people, that it?" Dmitri towered above me by about a foot and a half and outweighed me by a hundred pounds.

He bowed, a sweeping gesture. "If you would be so kind."

***

We set out for Carolina's retreat in upstate New York, following much the same route as I had the day before. When we rendezvoused with the Free Pack, Passey growled at me. I ignored him, as if he was beneath my notice. I was learning from the best, Senator Knight and Carolina Perez-Smith. I did notice some of his fellows making gestures, but whether they were blessing themselves or trying to avoid the evil eye, I did not know. They did not like the look of Max, who was so eager for retribution he hadn't smoked since we left, or of Claudia Steuben, who was dressed in black and ready for battle. Her serenity scared me.

Gerry was more like a football player before a game, pumped up and pacing, until Toshi irritably asked him to stop "jumping about." We all had our ways of warming up, I guess.

A group of oracles, including Rose and Ivy, were near our landing spot, ready to lend their talents. One was known for luck, so his presence was very welcome. Some were able to communicate with others and helped keep us all on the same page. Danny and Vee were with them, to help with the more mundane aspects of communication and monitoring the emergency channels. Only a small group of us knew she was there in case I needed her gift to help boost my powers.

Will dogged my steps, as did Adam, who had insisted to Representative Nichols that he be the one from her office to "observe."

I was glad to have allies.

The main goal was to rescue the prisoners and raid the lab. After that, it was about locating and containing Carolina herself and any Order personnel.

We approached cautiously, and slowed when we saw too many cars, too many lights.

"There's some kind of event tonight," Senator Knight said. He was at the most casual I'd ever seen him, in a sports shirt, pressed khakis, and lace ups. "My informant did not tell me. This will complicate things."

I did not think his informant was any longer in Edward Knight's good graces, and suddenly I knew who it was. Zimmer—"Clean-head" as I'd once called him—had done dirty work for Knight; sometimes this involved beating me up. Old as the senator was, Zimmer's evilness didn't bother him.

It stank to me.

"We need a distraction," I said. My gaze traveled to the large barn and the door covered with hateful trophies.

Passey shot me a look of pure joy. "We will set fire to it."

I reached out to the barn and sensed many beating hearts in there. "Wait. I think the prisoners may be in there, so check for hidden rooms if you don't see them at first. Remember, this is a rescue—and we're rescuing the Normals, too."

Passey frowned with distaste.

"Even if they're not there, keep in touch," I continued. "I need all the information we can get."

He looked at Senator Knight, who nodded slightly. Passey nodded, gestured, and they took off with a troop of his werewolves.

To hell with them both. "Will, please go with him? I don't trust either of them."

"I'm not leaving you!" he said.

"I'll go," Adam volunteered.

"Thanks, be careful with Knight," I warned. "Remember, he thinks you betrayed him."

"That's because I did. But we're all on the same team now," Adam said, with a pointed look at Will. Then he ran off, almost silently, through the woods.

Will and I joined the second team, who were beginning to close around the house, and waited. Any minute now our assault would begin.

"Zoe . . ." My earpiece crackled and the senator's voice was strange. "There's . . . a hide on the wall."

"Yes, I saw the pictures."

"No. This is new."

I'd never heard him so strained. "Yes?"

"It's a dragon hide."

I took a moment to digest the enormity of that insult, the utter disrespect for the beast, the colossal affront to the dragons and the Makers.

It suddenly made sense, and when I realized what was going on, I felt myself swept away on a flood of anger. But that emotion was working for me, because it joined several thoughts together, making them whole in an instant: The scarab chip had been to reach out to unearthly minds. Dmitri's words about going where the power was. Carolina's ultimate goals.

That was her plan.

Shaking, I reached out psychically for the dragons. "I believe Carolina has killed a dragon and is intending to use its power to communicate with the Makers herself. Do you sense anything that might indicate where she is?"

Naserian answered. "Hellbender, I can taste his stolen jewels."

"Can you guide me?"

"Yes, but it is a difficult trail, made by one who does not know fully what she's doing."

A rifle shot, followed by an alarm and shouts. We'd been discovered. The Order guards were firing back. I could smell the foulness of the Fellborn unleashed to find us; soon my Family would be drawn to their evil scent.

"Go, everyone, now!" I shouted. "Hit them now!" I shifted my focus to the dragon. "Naserian, take me now!"

"Hellbender, I obey!"

More shots. A light—I saw him.

Bald, scarred . . . Zimmer, the man whose footsteps had dogged mine through Europe, the senator's spy in Carolina's retreat, had now betrayed us all.

I raised my hand and got two blasts off, but Zimmer had moved as soon as he saw me in his scope.

He raised his rifle, pointed at me. Then swung it around.

He shot Will three times, center mass.

Naserian began to follow Carolina's trail to the Makers, taking me along with her as I stared, horrified.

"No!"

I was drawn helplessly away from the fight, from Will dying, from the here and now, and on my way to find Carolina.

⌣

As soon as we had found ourselves in the metaverse Carolina was using, I shouted to Naserian. "Go, back, please! Get Will out of there! Heal him if you can! It's his only chance!"

Naserian nodded, a strange thing to see a dragon do. "But how will you get back if I leave, Hellbender?"

"I have a lot to do before I can even think of leaving. Go, please!"

With Naserian gone, I found myself in a train tunnel that felt generically like New York, London, or Paris. That confused me, because I'd believed I'd find myself at the Boston University Castle, which was Carolina's goal. Then I realized that she was far from adept in her acquisitions, that she had stolen the life and knowledge of a dragon, but her use of it was imperfect. Her transition wouldn't be automatic because of how she cobbled together the means to get here.

I glanced in the train that was just pulling out. Carolina wasn't on it. It was a subway train, not an Amtrak train, so it wouldn't be a long journey to the Makers. I wouldn't have much time to stop her.

Carolina appeared on the platform a moment after that train departed, and cursed, looking around in bewilderment. I had a moment to observe her and remarked the rank of chips that had been mated with fragments of Fangborn artifacts, like the scarab hybrid Lisa Tarkka had given me, along her arm. The scar from the surgery was still stitched, red, and angry. When she saw me, she turned purple with fury and threw a bolt of energy at me.

It was ragged, unfocused, and fell short, scorching a wide swath of the platform. Even as the thought crossed my mind, I was across the platform and had Changed. Before she could move, I jumped, spun, and kicked her in the gut.

"You can't do this, Carolina," I shouted.

"I am doing it! I'm taking the future in my hands!"

I grabbed at the chips, hoping I could snag one from her, but she was very quick, almost Fangborn quick, and I knew she'd taken the Order's best speed and strength synthetics. She snarled at me and lashed out, but I jumped away.

"The Makers!" I shouted. "They're talking only with me! They don't like . . . disorder."

"But I don't talk to lackeys," she said.

I aimed a blast at her, but she dodged that, mostly. There was a whoosh of exhaled air as she leaned forward clutching herself, sparks flying and blood flowing. I'd already used up a lot of that energy on Zimmer, but no mind. I followed up with a two-fisted hammer blow to the back of her neck and then ran to the wall. I pulled out the fire hose and spun the crank, blasting her full strength with it, trying to wash her off the platform.

A train was coming.

Somehow she managed to withstand the stream and force her way toward me. The hose suddenly turned on me, like a living thing, and the force hit me full, though I kept my balance. I don't know how, but the fire hose twined around my ankles. Carolina appeared behind me and shoved me toward the train tracks.

I flailed, grabbed her hand, and pulled her into the ditch with me.

I could feel the train bearing down, the rumbling devastating; I couldn't hear, couldn't think. I had to find a way to stop her long enough to get away.

I could see the lights of the train behind Carolina. I could see my fear reflected in her cracked glasses. She was going to keep me busy, long enough to shove me into it, and scram out of there before she was hit.

Her strength was scary and unexpected. It was clear that she had as many of the enhancements as Porter and Buell did. It was too much like fighting Porter—ahhh.

She had enjoyed the fruits of his research but lacked one thing he had. Bingo.

Porter's gold signet ring.

I had the ring, and now I knew what it was for. Porter had created something to keep only for himself, an object that could remove the synthetic powers he'd given to his colleagues if he decided to.

The ring was Porter's version of Fangborn shedding.

I pulled it out of thin air and slipped it on my finger. It was laughably too big, but it made a dandy knuckle-duster. I ate a couple of punches, which hurt like hell, but I needed my hands free. I grabbed Carolina by her expensive haircut with my left hand and slammed my fist, and the ring, into her forehead.

"We're done here," I said.

Time froze, literally, for the both of us. I didn't feel anything but the sweat on her forehead stinging my cracked knuckles. When I tried to pull my hand away, to try and get away or drag her up to the platform, I couldn't. And then shit got glowy.

I realized that the rising fog before my eyes wasn't because I was about to pass out, but that there was a reddish mist accumulating around the pair of us. I closed my eyes, just a second, to make sure; then, when I opened them again, I could see that the mist was coalescing into tendrils.

Tentacles, really. They were moving, waving individually now, about a dozen of them, moving from my hand and the ring—which presumably was creating them—and hovering around Carolina's head. They hovered a second longer, before all twelve—or was it twenty?—drove themselves into her forehead. More extended, and began to curl around the chips in her arm, plucking them out delicately.

Carolina screamed. In this weird communion, I screamed, too, a chorus of pain to hers. It felt as though something in me was digging through her bone, brain, and psyche; it reminded me of trying to grab something valuable before it got lost in a trash can filled with glass fragments and metal industrial waste.

The world around me blurred, which I assumed meant that she was getting weaker, or at least her hold on the reality she'd created was getting weaker. I didn't like betting, so with a great deal of concentration,

I jumped? Teleported? Moved us to the platform again. At least we'd be out of the way of the train.

I felt good, felt like I was getting the upper hand, at long last, but I couldn't seem to keep my balance. Carolina weighed virtually nothing, but she dragged on me like a laundry bag full of anvils. But that still wasn't it. She wasn't fighting me; she'd gone limp and I couldn't let go.

The ground, the platform beneath us, was shaking. Disintegrating.

Shit. I was going to have to take her with me. I couldn't go back to the lab—there was no way I was going to let her in there, no matter how dead or unconscious she might appear to be. I didn't know what would happen if these two worlds—multiverses—collided. I had no idea of how to get to some neutral territory . . . some place that wasn't me, and wasn't Carolina's fractured simulacrum of her internal world.

I cast about, desperately. Like an earthquake, the whole tunnel was collapsing around us now, and God only knew what was on the surface that might come crashing down on us. Worse, maybe there'd be nothing and we'd cease to exist.

But then I saw what looked like a ray of light, a ray of hope, and not the oncoming train. "I don't know what or where or who you are," I shouted. "But this is an emergency and I'm coming in!"

I looked down. The tentacles had transformed once more and were now terribly fine circuits that were running through the skin on Carolina's face and neck. It was terrible, an alien intrusion into her body and mind, and I didn't dare break it now. "Hang on, bitch."

Grabbing her tight, I made with another one of those jump/morph transitions I still didn't quite understand and felt myself hurtling toward the light. Maybe it was sunshine, maybe it was a firestorm, but I didn't have a lot of choice.

The trip seemed to take an awfully long time, but eventually, the light grew larger and stronger, and I heard a voice so welcome, I thought my head would explode.

"This way, Hellbender! It is safer for you here!" I heard Quarrel's commanding voice.

"Quarrel, you are the very best power-hungry demonic manifestation of a friend a girl could have," I muttered to myself. I redoubled my efforts and found the going easier, and finally, I found myself settled on a grassy hill, overlooking a meadow.

My hand—the ring—was no longer stuck to Carolina's head, but a connection remained. Those red electrical circuits remained, line segment geometry, laser-pure glow eating up the last of the Order's implants. Carolina didn't move, but she was still breathing, and I was glad of that. I hurt all over.

I Changed back to my skinself. I noticed that the tendrils had evaporated and whatever connection Porter's ring had made was now broken. I needed to think about finding a way to get her home—or at least back in her own little world—but that didn't stop me from wishing, just for a minute, that I had a marker so I could draw a penis or write "douchewaffle" on her forehead.

"Any thoughts on how I can get her home, Quarrel? We can't keep her here."

Quarrel snorted. "Why not? She will cause less trouble here than in your world."

I had to marvel at a dragon's pragmatism. "She'd cause more by being missing; we'd be the first ones suspected."

"You only have to push her," he said. "Her inclination is to go back where she belongs."

"Okay, how do I—"

"You really are not very skilled, are you?"

"I've come up in the ranks suddenly," I said, at once realizing the way I needed to behave with Quarrel and the others. I continued with a coldness to indicate he shouldn't be fucking with me. "It's to be expected that I will need advice from older, if lesser, beings."

At first I was afraid I'd gone too far, but Quarrel simply nodded. "You are correct, of course. I meant no disrespect."

"I understand."

"I'm not sure how to explain it, but if you think of how you used to track an evildoer, in your wolf form—"

"Yes, I know. And I still do." I said it as much for my sake as Quarrel's.

"That's very unusual, for a dragon of your considerable abilities . . ."

The floor fell out of the reality elevator as I grasped what he meant. "Quarrel, what do I look like to you?"

"As I do to you, no doubt. A fine beast with an aura that indicates your strength."

"Tell me what you see? For I do not think my perception is the same."

"A fine young beast—quite small, but the quality and number of the jewels in your armor more than impresses. As for returning that one, if you imagine you are scenting her track, you can . . . urge her to return that same way. It should not take much energy."

I nodded, doubtful. I let my eyes unfocus, and after actually sniffing with no result, tried feeling around for her trail. I found a slender iridescent blue thread, almost like a strand of spider silk, leading out of the space I could currently perceive. It reminded me of the threads that bound the Dickson Trips' souls. There was a light of blue at the end, which I realized was Carolina. I shoved gently and watched the light fade as it followed the trajectory back, I hoped, to wherever it was Carolina was supposed to be. Before she vanished, however, I reached out, as I had with Dmitri Parshin, and nudged Carolina Perez-Smith's being.

I was going to change her mind.

When she disappeared, I suddenly got nervous.

"Quarrel, she's okay, right?" I asked, suddenly worried. What if I'd sucked too much . . . whatever out of her?

"Oh yes. You've merely removed the . . . alien artifacts from her. And given her a new way to think about things." He snorted contemptuously. "She is no worse—or no better—than she was before she assumed the powers of that dragon."

And now I'd found what I was looking for. If I was in the field, doing archaeology, I'd say I'd defined the edge of a feature. I'd identified that I'd found something, still not knowing what it might be—a rubbish tip, a post hole, a privy, a fire pit. I'd identified what I needed to do about the Makers.

"Thank you, Quarrel, you've been of tremendous help to me today. If you would help me return to the fight I just left?"

And I was back in the woods.

———⌣———

Because of the ill-conceived space that Carolina had taken us to, it took much longer to return than I expected. Nearly ten minutes had passed since I'd left, and I arrived back spent and battered from my own fight and the long journey between meta-realms.

A lot can happen in ten minutes. Too much.

As soon as I got there, I smelled smoke from the barn, and heard screams and shots. I thought I'd slow things down to suit my own pace, but stopping time really had lost its appeal for me after Kanazawa, and I couldn't risk taking myself away from here again. And I suspected I was too weak to do that anyway.

I could still Change, however, and felt better immediately. Claudia Steuben was suddenly by my side, her hair streaming out of the braid she'd had, her black ninja wear torn and matted with blood. She was smiling broadly, and it had nothing to do with humor.

"Zoe! I was afraid you'd popped off again!"

"Not as far as Japan this time. What's the situation?"

"We're winning," she said. "We've found the Boston Fangborn and Normals. The vampires have started coordinating memories so that we can turn this into a dinner party gone wrong."

"What?"

"For some reason, Carolina Perez-Smith is trying to calm everyone down. Says her house caught on fire, and she's concerned about her guests. Nothing so far about the Fangborn." Claudia gave me a look. "Was that you?"

I nodded.

"Well, now there are reporters, firefighters, and police officers here. We're going to keep all trace of the Order out of the news, but we Fangborn, we're going to star in the late news. We've decided that we might as well be caught on camera, saving folks from the burning buildings." She looked at me. "I-Day."

I nodded again. "Still lots of details to work out with Carolina—just don't let her get away."

"Oh, no. All the folks who were Order, they're all offstage, so to speak, and Max is guarding them." Another smile let me know how much she was enjoying that thought. "Gerry is rounding up the ones who got away. Everyone so far is safe; some bad wounds, but nothing we can't handle." She hesitated.

"Will?"

"He's fine; that giant red dragon came back and kept him from dying." Claudia frowned. "I'm very glad he's not dead, but we needed that dragon to help us fight."

"I know." A thought struck me. "Where's the senator?"

"I don't know."

"Then that's where I'm going. Thanks, Claud."

Without waiting for a response, I tore off through the woods, heading toward the barn where I'd seen the senator heading with Eli Passey. Their scent trail veered away from the crowds and lights at the main complex. I followed.

When I found them, they were in a dark clearing. With my keen eyes, I didn't need lights to see what was going on. The senator had Changed; I'd never seen his fangself before: His ordinarily carefully groomed hair was now wild, stripes of green amid the gray. His scales were also gray, with those same green streaks. His prominent nose had vanished to a nubbin, and his fangs were shockingly long. The senator's clothing was torn. He'd been fighting and he was in a rage.

I could see the reason. His former henchman, Zimmer, was lying on the ground, bleeding and unconscious. Eli Passey was also Changed to his wolfself, his shirt missing entirely. He was standing over Zimmer and snarling at Edward Knight.

"What's going on?" I demanded.

"This old fool of a vampire doesn't want me to kill this traitor," Passey said. A smell of scorched fur told me he'd been in the fire, but another smell told me that the senator had spat venom at him.

"I want this man brought to justice," Knight said. "Get away! And you, stray, this is not your business!"

"It's entirely my business. Back down."

To our surprise, Knight actually relaxed, whether it was because of my limited ability to use a vampire's voice of command or some new authority, I didn't know.

Passey took that moment to snap Zimmer's neck. He glanced at me, looking for approval or a fight.

I nodded, wondering whether Knight had actually been trying to rescue Zimmer. "We have work to do. Passey, take the body with you, but keep it hidden, away from the civilians we rescued."

Without another word, I turned and left.

Chapter Seventeen

All my life I'd wanted to be some place stable, for good. Own a house, something. And now I was finding out what a responsibility running a household—hell, an island castle, complete with retainers—was. A small price to pay for what I needed to do, but a very steep learning curve.

The morning after the fight at Carolina's, Will knocked on my door.

"I came to check on you. You barely said a word last night. Are you okay? Why are you hiding, Zoe?"

I looked up from the documents I was studying. "Is that what you think I'm doing?"

I stretched, feeling a thousand years old. "Will, it's over. We are over. From the very first, I was right, that I was a danger to you. I was right to leave you the first time. And when I ran into you in Berlin, and then in Greece, I was thrilled."

"So was I!" Will's face lit up. He didn't have a scratch on him, not after Naserian's ministrations. "Zoe, this is good!"

"You don't understand, Will. I wanted you. I wished for you to want me back. I didn't know I had vampiric powers, and so might have compelled you to love me. So, yeah, I dragged you into this even more than you dragged yourself. I was right to leave you that first time, because if I wasn't a serial killer, something—call it intuition, call it prophecy—was telling me I wasn't going to stay plain old Zoe the werewolf, either. There were just too many things . . . off about me."

He shook his head, quite sure of himself. "Vampires can't . . . make someone fall in love. Give them an idea, yes, make them inclined toward someone, want sex, even, but not . . . fall in *love* love, like we had."

"Nope, they can't, Will. But you forget. I'm not a vampire. The rules don't seem to count for me." I picked up where I'd left off with the inventory. "So it is over. I love you, but I am not the same girl who loved you a year ago, or three years ago."

Okay, so I wasn't expecting that hesitation, that tightness in my throat. This all sounded so reasonable—how could it hurt so much, when I knew in my heart I was right? I promised myself a good cry at the end of the day. I love a good shower cry; no one can hear you, and it's easier on your eyes.

Will was still denying my words. "Jesus, Zoe. You're so wrong. We can make this work! You were right before; you just need time. So you take your time, all the time you want. Lick your wounds; give yourself a chance to get your head around all that's happened. You've done enough, more than enough—let the rest of us handle I-Day." He smiled confidently, now certain he was right.

It struck me. Will thought I was trying to be alone because I was tired and confused. And I was, but not the way he thought. Not about him, not anymore.

I was so stunned at his naïveté, his complete lack of comprehension, that it took me a moment to collect myself. I was so used to being the one who was playing catch-up with everyone else around me; this was a novelty that took me by surprise. But that only underscored the knowledge that I was right.

I'd changed, profoundly. Little *c* change, but every bit as cataclysmic as the Fangborn transformation.

Especially to those around me.

"Will, I'm out here because it's the best thing for everyone." I held up my hand before he could interrupt. "No, no, not that way. A much bigger scale. Remember the demonstration, when I blew the shit out of that target without even trying? Now I could take out all the humans on the planet. They'd be orderly then, wouldn't they?

"For another thing, you and the whole Fangborn Family need distance from me, deniability, if I can't do what I need to do next. You all need a lightning rod, to keep the shit-storm that would follow that failure away from you all. If I screw up, I can be the scapegoat, you can say I was a rogue, you can throw me under the bus, and there'll still be a chance for the rest of the Fangborn to be safe. There are too many variables, between Carolina, the Makers, and I-Day. Too much can go wrong. This is insurance.

"The other thing is that physical distance from the mainland and population is a good thing, in case someone—Normal, Fangborn, or Maker—comes after me. Someone wants to declare war on me, they can, and it's not gonna take out Boston or New York or London as well.

"Also, we need the perception that I am in fact the representative of the Fangborn. Again, separate is good. And if for some reason the Makers decide to show up, somehow, in person, we're gonna need a place for them to land. A place for them to have their embassy or something—I'm not really sure about the politics. That way, they're separate from the US, from the rest of the world, and we can say that we're being impartial."

I rubbed my head. "I don't know if that will work, or whether I actually want the US to be in charge of that discussion, but for now, this is how we're going to go. We can worry about 'most favored nation' status or whatever after."

Will's mouth hadn't closed the whole time, and he sagged back against the stack of crates. He closed it, and then started to speak, but nothing came out.

Finally: "Oh."

"Yeah, I got a big promotion, Will. And it's also high risk. So I'm learning a lot and trying to keep up with what *could* happen in addition to what is happening this instant." *I'll cry later, I'll cry later, I'll cry later,* I promised myself. *Just keep going. Just do this.* "Last night showed me something, when you insisted on sticking with me, wouldn't take my orders, still wanting to protect me. You don't see me as I am. And I've changed."

"You sent Naserian—"

"Of course I did. I wouldn't let you die. You're too dear to me. After what we've been through?" I shook my head. "But I don't have the option of staying out of things, and that's all you want for me. I can't do that. I'm sorry."

After he didn't say anything, I did. "Please, Will."

"No, I got it. I'm good." He glanced at me, still not quite sure of anything but the notion that he'd completely misjudged the situation, a situation that had depths he couldn't begin to plumb. "Okay, well, I won't say I'm thrilled about this, but . . . okay." He raised a hand in farewell, slapped his leg with it. "See you, Zo."

It was seeing Will so nonplussed, again, that did it for me. I could fix this, and I couldn't fix other things, and I should make the most of that possibility while I could. Better to be right than happy, sometimes.

"Will . . ." My voice cracked. "I'm sorry."

"For what?"

"Everything. Just . . . everything. Turning your world upside down—"

"Not your fault."

"Sure it is." I tried a small smile.

Will smiled back, but he didn't mean it. He was trying to be decent about it. "Yeah, okay, it's on you." He looked away, cleared his throat. "Well, I'm going to go back to the Boston house, help Heck out. I-Day's here."

I nodded unhappily. "Happy I-Day, Will."

He nodded, turned, and left for the launch.

———

That was the last quiet moment of the morning. Everyone was nervous and busy. Phones and computers were overworked, preparing for the official moment when the Fangborn Identified themselves to the world.

I excused myself from breakfast, saying I'd be back shortly, that I was going to my room at the lighthouse. If I succeeded in what I was about to do, they'd barely notice I'd left. If I failed, they wouldn't know about it until it was too late.

That thought haunted me as I sat down. I was in the mind-lab.

"I have to do something, and I'm not sure it's right," I said to Sean. "I'm not sure I can. But I have to do something."

"Most people would pray," Sean said.

I shrugged. "You know that's not me."

"Well, it's a lot of folks, and Zoe, do you *ever* need to get out of your head."

I gave him another look that suggested he should be the last one to suggest it. "What, and leave all this?" I gestured around me. The lab was looking more chaotic than ever, and it occurred to me that with all the new things I'd been learning, acquiring, I'd no time to sort things out. There was a direct correlation between the state of the lab and the state of my psyche, because, well, they seemed to be the same thing. Or at least they were carved out of the same multiverse.

But he had a point. I only had a short time until I had to do whatever it was I was going to do. I could go for a run, but me running would look like "Zoe's fleeing danger" and I wanted to avoid freaking everyone out. I made a note to get a treadmill in there.

But for now . . . I needed to empty my head of everything but the job ahead of me. I remembered my moment dancing with Toshi and knew immediately, that was it.

Some percussive music has the ability to stimulate the mind to want to move or dance; your participation in that movement causes you to fill in the musical gaps, to make connections. People in many cultures use music with repeated rhythms, along with drugs, a lack of sleep, movement, and special environments to create both a trancelike state and a sublimation of the self in favor of shared spiritual experience.

I liked techno as a way to get into a different head space, and heaven knew I was running on a sleep deficit. All I needed was to dance, and maybe I'd find my way to do what I needed to do.

The landscape shifted so quickly that I almost fell over with vertigo. No more lab—and that brought a heart-pounding nanosecond of terror—because it had been replaced by an anonymous industrial space. I was only reassured when a heads-up display showed me my new lab-campus complex with Dr. O's research lab, mine, and a new dance club.

Inside, screens flashed images of flowers—on high speed, opening and closing, but never dying away—psychedelic patterns in orange and green, and superimposed over consumer ads from the early sixties. A DJ, a young man in bare feet with his hair tied in a knot at the back of his head and dressed in flowing trousers and tight tank top, played trance that had the crowd moving, swaying, their arms tracing out intricate patterns only they could see.

Close, but not enough. Too mellow, more like something for the early morning, watching the sun rise after a long night.

I needed more.

As soon as I had the thought there was another shift, more subtle than the last one. The DJ was a shorn and shaved young blond in a hoodie and jeans, with Nike Air Force Max Area 72 kicks that would go right back into a carrier when his set was over. The screens were more on the order of spray paint dripping and being sucked back into the can and film stock of a family vacation burning and turning different colors.

The depth and loudness of the bass were better, and I could feel the urge to dance take me.

But it just wasn't fast enough, loud enough, anything enough . . . I couldn't focus.

The crowd got bigger, more lively, and now the DJ was a young Asian woman who looked as though she was dressed for speed skating. The new song was pressing the outer limits of the speakers, in a way that was both pleasing and in no way approved by the Underwriters Laboratory. I could feel the beat driving my feet, felt the base changing the rhythm of my heart, filling my head.

Still, I wasn't getting there.

Suddenly Geoffrey appeared. He handed me a couple of green star-shaped pills and a bottle of water, putting another into my backpack. "This is what you need. Don't take anything from anyone but me."

"What is it?" I asked a little suspiciously. Was this an attempt by him to derail my planned attack on the Makers?

"It's a metaphor, silly girl, a little energy in reserve, a little push over the edge. A little confidence. You can do it," he said. "And there's this."

He opened a long, thin, flat, brown polished wooden box with an ornate latch and hinges. Inside was a replica of a Time Lord's sonic screwdriver.

I laughed, shrugged, and clipped it behind my trowel. Might as well take it; I needed good wishes and encouragement. "Thanks. But why do you say not to take anything from anyone but you? The crowd is cool; this is inside my space. No one but me, nothing to be afraid of."

"Not anymore. And those guys . . ." he nodded to a couple of the large cone-orange intruder types standing on the sidelines, craning, looking. "Those guys are big trouble."

"Oh, shit."

"This is no longer your own private preserve. It could be the same as the others—someone sent by the Makers; they may be getting worried about you. In any case, they've found a way in. Did you eat anything at the Castle, ever? Take anything from there?"

"Not beside the—oh." I remembered long ago, I'd taken the lighter and two joints and drunk a beer with the Administrator.

"Ah, there's the problem," Geoffrey said. "The clock is not only ticking, Zoe; it's sped up. You got about fifteen minutes now. Get busy, child."

I blinked and realized if Fatima could know about the Hulk, Geoffrey could know the Chemical Brothers lyrics. I nodded. "You got anything that can slow those thugs down?"

The two guys were starting to press through the crowd and not in a "May I?" fashion. Just the feel of them let me know he was right. They weren't me; they didn't belong here. "Slow them down a lot?"

Geoffrey smiled, a secret, nasty smile. Maybe there was a little more werewolf from his father's side affecting him than he thought. Maybe I was affecting his afterlife more than either of us wanted to admit. "I'm yours to command."

I suppressed a shiver. I didn't need any more distractions now. "Just keep the collateral damage down, 'kay?"

"You just take the pills and get to work."

The BPM kicked into the 160–180 range. I swallowed the pills. The music went past 200 BPM, to 500 . . .

I began to dance. Things started to blur, lights began to trail, and I began to see the individual bands of light prism and sparkle. I began to taste the music and feel numbers as parts of me began to melt away.

I have to see if Geoffrey has any more of this, I thought giddily. *I've never taken anything this good, have never been able to afford it, and now I have my own private chemist who is turning out some* seriously *good shit . . .*

I started to feel nauseous, a little throw-up in the back of my throat. *Only to be expected,* I thought, *a small price to pay for this—*

I turned inside out. My brain split in half.

I was outside the club—or was it above?—watching things unfold there. There was a blank area beyond that indicated where I needed to get to. Geoffrey was using moves straight out of a Hong Kong action film, keeping the bad guys at bay. It was like being outside of two different theaters, watching two different plays, while I was simultaneously acting and directing them. I'd be lying if I said it didn't hurt, if I said it was easy. It felt as if my skull were being cracked open, but the fact that I could do it at all gave me the motivation to keep going, see how far I could take it.

I couldn't stay here; I needed to get to that ominous blank space. I reached out for the dragons. "Quarrel, Yuan, Naserian? If you could get me where I need to go, and I'll take it from there."

"We will escort you, Hellbender," Yuan said.

"No, I need to be stealthier than that. They see you guys, my chances are blown. But thank you."

In an instant, I was there.

I didn't recognize where there was and was afraid that I'd miscalculated. What I saw was a rippling wave of black, so black, I could barely detect that it was moving. But very rarely, every here and there was a break, a line of bright red or silver or pale blue that showed me the black was billowing in waves, like a silk sheet being shaken out. I tried to look beneath it, but no matter how far I followed it down, I couldn't find the underside of it, and there were curves that made me wonder if I weren't moving in circles, or some trick of the near light that altered or distorted my perspective. So I followed one of the red lines back, finding no end.

I pulled the sonic screwdriver out of my pocket—I would have used a rock if I'd had it—and threw it at the blackness. It caused a furious rippling, and now I could see, very distantly and less faintly, how the lines were interwoven, warp and weft.

A crack appeared in the fabric; there was a noise like ice creaking and glaciers calving. A flare of color like the aurora borealis and a portion of the dense black nothingness shattered, falling away to nothingness. I could see many of the fine threads now, bundled into very large groups, like individual strands twisted into a heavy rope. The larger bundles were like wires or circuits interconnecting, overlapping against the wider darkness. All the lives I knew or could imagine in the multiverse, intertwined and overlapping. Geoffrey had suggested there might be streams of particles bridging the overlapping multiverses, and maybe this was it.

I recalled the fight with the Administrator's überdragon. My dragons had been on silver threads, ever so much finer than these cables, when I'd taken over command of them. The Trips had a red thread binding them together, and Carolina had a pale blue one associated with her.

I saw a heavy silver rope quivering and glinting starlight in the darkness of whatever meta-space the Makers and I shared. Strands emerged from that main rope to form new connections with other, crossing cables.

I followed the heavy silver cable until I found three cut edges; three cobweb-fine loose ends fluttered from the main rope, but already a kind of self-healing was occurring, reweaving new threads grown from the cut end into other circuits.

This is where I'd freed the dragons from the Makers. This is where I'd seized their power.

I traced their threads back to where they connected into the main rope. The silver threads of the dragons and many other silver threads were bound up with a blue one, barely perceptible, that was wound around them.

This blue thread was the Fangborn connection to the Makers and the way they could control us. While it was probably not the only one, it was the most obvious and easiest one for them to use.

I was going to cut the thread. This is how I would unchain the Fangborn.

I had no idea what side effects doing that might have. Most of the Fangborn systems I'd encountered were redundant, many times over, so this might not be the only way for the Makers to reach us directly. It probably contained elements of other powers in ways we didn't understand.

But for now, it wasn't a matter of prophecies or being the chosen one. There was no chosen one; Fangborn prophecies were fragments of communications intercepted by the oracles, imperfectly received or understood by them. They were not so much prophecies as someone getting a sneak preview of the workings inside the machine, the grand scheme of things. Maybe the prophecy that seemed to fit my situation was a part of a warning label for that thread: "Danger! Do not cut!" or "Caution! Live Wire!" or "Broken, removed for repairs." But why were the Makers so intent on repairing it?

I didn't know if I was acting as Atropos, severing a fateful, fatal thread, or if I was acting as Perseus, freeing Andromeda from the rock.

I summoned the katana and drew it back, ready to cleave that binding blue thread. I pressed the sapphire jewel I'd been given to do the Makers' bidding.

The power surged through me and I suddenly had a good idea of what it was like to be in a jet going supersonic. I had no idea of the proper way to use the katana in real life; here, with that loaned power, I was a master of what it represented. The sword was no longer perfect steel, folded over and over ten thousand times; for my purpose, it had turned into black diamond, flecked with moonlight. I Changed, not able to wield this power without summoning some of the strength my other nature represented, and stood on top of the blue thread, which was now as massive as a drainage pipe with my new perspective. I swung with everything in my being.

I brought the katana down.

It bounced off the thread, as if it was made of rubber. Just like the intruders in the mind-lab.

I tried again, feeling the borrowed power course through me.

Nothing.

Squinting, I could barely make out where I'd hit the blue thread. I reached out and tried to pull it apart with my hands. It burned with cold to my bones.

The katana wouldn't do it. Like the tools that belonged to the orange demo crew, it was a product of the Maker influence on its Fangborn artisan.

I summoned the hybrid Celtic/Anglo-Saxon sword I'd found in Kanazawa; I knew it had tremendous power, but not from the Makers.

I swung.

A cut appeared in the blue thread, like a notch axed from a tree. My arm went numb at the blow. I summoned all my reserves, feeling the strain pulling at the core of myself, threatening to tear me apart, and swung again. Sparks flew, blinding me. A cacophony filled my ears, the sound of worlds exploding. I prayed it was not indicative of what was happening in the here and now.

There was a bellowing in the void around me; the überdragon, even larger than last time, was on its way. I'd woken up the Makers. This was not what they thought of as orderly. It was not what they wanted. Three hydra heads of the überdragon appeared, followed by its massive body, the noise like a bomb blast.

I was a sitting duck. I swung again at the cable.

Halfway through, this time. One more would have to do it; it was all I had strength for.

A blast of energy appeared so powerful, it lit up the void. Heading my way, it fell short and dissipated, but the überdragon was following, preparing another blast.

Flashes before my eyes—I couldn't tell if they were from the silver thread or my brain collapsing in on itself. I lifted my arms, feeling them wobble under the weight—what weight?—of the sword. I felt about as tough as a plate of soggy pasta. My heart pounded so hard, so fast, I thought it would break out the cage of my ribs.

Last chance, Zoe.

The überdragon was nearly on me now, and I knew I would perish with its next burst. I paused, pulled out the blaster, and fired at the hydra. I felt myself go weak as it drained my energy. I could barely move but had bought myself some time.

I swung, and this time, the sword cut cleanly through but only to the last core of the strand.

It was not going to give under the sword. Any sword.

I had one trick left. I pulled up the bone-and-soul-chilling thread and bit it. My werewolf fangs sheared through the last fragment.

The thread was broken.

I howled, even as my life was leaving me. I felt a tremendous rushing, like rapids heading for a waterfall, and my feet were knocked out from under me. I grabbed at what was left of the thread; it turned white and disintegrated. With a planet-shattering rumble, the black waves rearranged themselves and swallowed up the hole left by the vanished thread. I was unmoored and unsupported. A tiny pop of emptiness deep inside told me I'd been successful. When the wave hit me, I was knocked far away.

I saw Dr. Osborne hovering near me. "I think it's time to jump ship, Zoe. Unless you want to get sucked up into the vortex."

"Good idea," I croaked. "Dragons?"

"We're on it."

A volcanic roar in the void as my three friends appeared, straining, screaming with indignation at the überdragon, who was struggling to get one last blast at me. They grabbed me and I followed them back home.

I found myself in a pile of blood and sweat on the floor of my room on Flock Island. My clothes were limp and soggy, as though I'd had a fever. The cat hissed at me.

Oh, gross. *Cleanup in aisle five*, I thought before I passed out.

Chapter Eighteen

I woke up, stiff as hell, with a terrible hollow feeling inside and out. A soft moist snuffling under my nose; I snorted, and sneezed. The cat, who had been inspecting me, took off.

It was as if there was nothing inside me, and nothing in the outside world capable of sustaining my skin, a leaky balloon. I just wanted to ooze into the floor, but it kept falling away from underneath me. It was the definition of misery.

I was on the floor, having fallen off my chair. By very carefully flexing one muscle at a time, I was able to determine that none of my bones were broken, but I was bleeding from the nose and chin, where I'd landed. While it had not been a physical battle, a serious toll had been taken nonetheless.

I lay there hating the feel of the gritty floor under my cheek but unable—at least unwilling—to get up. Faced with the prospect of spending the day there, I have to say, I gave it considerable thought. Not only did I feel like a sock full of hammered shit, I had another bunch of high-risk, no-reward tasks to do before I dared to rest. I shoved myself up and fumble-grabbed a bottle of water and drank it all without stopping.

I coughed, and called out. Claudia poked her head in the door, saw the blood on my face.

The cut was already starting to heal. That was a good sign.

"Holy God, Zoe!" She ran to me. "What the hell did you do to yourself?"

"Later," I said. "What's going on?"

"Lots. Same as a minute ago. We're on for I-Day." She shook her head, frowning. "Are you okay?"

"No, I mean, maybe. I mean, did anything happen? Out here, with you, with any of the Fangborn?"

She shook her head. "What do you mean?"

I swallowed my frustration. I had to know. "Like, did you sense any disruption here, in this world? No flying squids in the sky? It's still just after breakfast on I-Day? Can you Change?"

"No, yes, hang on." Claudia Changed, as effortlessly as ever, her face shifting from human to violet and serpentine. I felt the familiar frisson of energy and felt the urge to follow her suit. I did so, and then Changed back.

"Okay?"

"Yes, thanks," I said. So far, so good.

She Changed back.

"I think I did it." I said the words, dazed, not believing them. "Claudia, I think I did it."

"Did what?"

"Unchained the Fangborn."

She looked astonished and scared and excited. "Okay, the prophecy—how—I don't know what . . . but you did?"

I nodded.

"So, I-Day?"

"It's on, as planned." I took a deep breath. "It's been a long time coming. The Normals could use a little excitement."

Claudia frowned, but nodded and took off.

I dragged myself up to the table, sat down painfully, and found my phone. I made two calls: one to Senator Knight to tell him I'd succeeded and one to Danny.

I noticed there were little indentations all over my bagel where the cat had licked off the cream cheese. Someone was settling in to his new routine.

Finally, I texted three words to Vee: *The game's afoot.*

I waited until the phone binged, letting me know Vee had texted me back: *Done. The game is ON.*

I grinned weakly, amazed at how much that simple act hurt. Without many Family ties of her own, for I-Day Vee was going to involve her Normal friends, whom she'd once described as her "techies and geekdoms." They were going to solicit a little help from the willing uninitiated, crowd-sourcing the problems of I-Day and integration via several online communities. The social media blasts had been carefully planned, hashtags ready. Additionally, certain groups of scientists and researchers were going to get very interesting emails with carefully selected information about history and biology. It was going to be done quietly, resembling more an IV drip into a bloodstream than a series of press releases, so certain folks would get a head start on what was coming and hopefully take our side. I'd also put Vee in touch with Ariana, my Italian vampire friend, who was going to release her new game, "Wolf, Raven, Snake." The card game looked remarkably like Fangborn adventures to me—with us as the good guys, of course.

All of this was quite possibly a futile gesture, but it was the only way the two of us personally had to soften the ground. We hoped to gain allies by introducing the idea of the Fangborn with the lure of science and entertainment.

At seven o'clock tonight, President Rozan was going to read the statement she, her staff, Representative Nichols, and the Fangborn in the government had been working on. After that, Senator Knight was going to hold a press conference on Capitol Hill to discuss the presence of the Fangborn and the secret treaty status we'd all been living under since the Fangborn had been in America. He'd explain that the Battle of Boston was just the latest example of the Fangborn fighting for us all against unknown foes called Order and Fellborn.

Until then, the news outlets were going crazy with the footage of the fire at billionaire Carolina Perez-Smith's country retreat. She too had been attacked by the Fellborn, and had been rescued by Fangborn-American citizens. It was the first time there was good footage, shot by reliable sources, of the Fangborn performing heroic actions. It was pretty nifty to see a vampire carrying out Carolina on his shoulder and a werewolf braving the flames to rescue a kid. No need to mention that the kid was also a Fangborn and was only there because Carolina had kidnapped him in the first place.

Carolina was on our side. For now. She and Senator Knight were working together to craft our story, one that would leave out the Order's experiments. Someone else would get pinned with the kidnappings; her business acumen, paired with the change of heart I'd inflicted on her, would ensure that. She'd play the concerned citizen, grateful for what the Fangborn had done for her and working to see how our presence could benefit the country.

I didn't like it and thought she and the Senator were a match made in hell. But it was I-Day, today, and things were going to be tough. I'd live with that pair if we had her influence on our side.

I wondered if I could restore the Fellborn—and Max—using the ring as I had on Carolina. I would be very happy to be able to make that visible contribution.

It had been a very busy day, I decided, and it wasn't even nine o'clock yet. It wasn't every day a girl got to sever connections with a controlling nonhuman entity and throw the world into upheaval by helping to out her entire Family.

I flicked on the news, still too tired to move much. Soon the world would be seeing vintage tape prepared by the TRG to showcase the Fangborn. There was the World War II newsreel about the new allies in the war against Hitler, showing werewolves doing boot-camp stuff, medic-trained vampires, oracles translating and looking into crystal balls. There was the 1960s advertisement talking about everyone working for a better world, getting in touch with that beyond you, and expanding the mind. Then there was the 1980s Cold War propaganda bragging about the arsenal of missiles and Fangborn allies we had on our side to stop communism, working shoulder pad to shoulder pad.

I worried about what other historical images might also repeat themselves: the Salem witchcraft trials, the Japanese internment camps in the '40s. Protests for civil rights turned to riots all through the '60s, '70s—hell, even today. After all, how do you identify a threat, an enemy, when he looks just like you? Humanity did not have a great track record when dealing with those who were different, or even suspected of being different.

There would be public violence in some cities and vigils in others. There would be some suicides and there were some folks who thought we were on the verge of some kind of golden age. There would be arguments about traitors and vigilantism and about the nature of humanity.

I understood all of these responses. I had to worry about becoming a dragon myself now that I was no longer under the control of the bracelet, no longer driven to find other artifacts that might be out there. I wanted them, but I could find them in my own time. There was a lot to do, and on top of it all, I also had to worry about Family like the Adirondack Free Pack thinking I was some kind of prophet. Or a demon.

All that could wait. I needed a shower. I owed myself a good cry.

I got up from the table, stiffly, looked out the window. Adam was moving toward the house. He paused, and when I nodded, he came in. I hobbled to him, leaned against him. Let him kiss the top of my head.

"Zoe," he said.

But something was tickling my brain; I had the urge, as I had at the Battle of Boston, to reach out, to see what was going on now, locally, with that astonishing footage of the Fangborn being shown everywhere. "Just give me a second, okay?"

He nodded. And I projected my consciousness out and over Boston.

The colleges and coffee houses were abuzz. Arguments, just as I suspected, and there was excitement, too. Eagerness, on some parts, and I began to wonder if the generations raised on the space program, comic books, and CGI special effects might not be ready for us.

A blink, and I was over a neighborhood to the west. A fire had been started outside the town hall; protesters were warning the end was here. Another group was praying just as loudly for peace and patience. A rock was thrown, and the sirens began as the crowds clashed.

So I knew: It would not be smooth transition, this I-Day. An old world gone, any number of new ones loomed possible. It would not be one thing. It would be complex. It was the end. I'd severed many connections today. But there were maybe new ones to make, too.

I returned my focus to where I was, and to Adam. I nestled my head into his chest, enjoying the quiet, for the moment.

The dragons, who had been lounging on the cliff, began to pop in and out of sight. Then I heard Quarrel cry out in my mind.

"Zoe Hellbender! The Administrator wishes to speak with you!"

"He can take a flying fuck at a rolling doughnut—no, Quarrel, don't say that. Let him know I'll visit him later." Might as well get chewed out or blasted from existence with a clean shirt on.

"No, he comes swearing truce! He will not break it, but he is very anxious to speak with you. I think you must not ignore him."

"Okay, let me see what I can do." I turned to Adam. "I'm going back in, for a second or two. I need to visit with the Administrator, and I'd rather be sitting."

"Is there anything I can do?" Adam said.

"Just be here when I get back. Just a minute, I promise."

I stood up on tiptoe and kissed him, and smiled as he kissed me back. I hobbled into the house.

"Hellbender . . . you move so slowly!" Quarrel's concern filled my brain. "What is the matter?"

"I'm actually doing fine, Quarrel, healing up nicely. But . . . fighting Carolina, severing the connection with the Makers, and now I-Day? It's enough to take the starch out of anyone. I'll be fine."

"What is 'statch,' Hellbender?" Quarrel asked.

"'Statch?' I don't know—oh!" I laughed. "Sta*rrr*ch. Sorry, my accent is getting in the way here. It's an expression meaning my efforts have left me tired but not seriously wounded."

"Your accent is one marking the elite of your kind? A superior or high rank?"

I laughed, as much from fatigue-silliness as at the absurdity of the notion. "I would say, it is more a source of pride of my people, a regional indicator."

"You are not wealthy? Powerful?"

"Not wealthy. Powerful, maybe. But I can talk real pretty if I have to."

"Now you are the Hellbender, and that confers as much honor as you would want."

"Honor is all well and good, but influence . . . That's something else. And it's taking some getting used to."

"Do not be too patient while you are learning. Better to eat a few enemies, assume their power, and make an example than be too timid. The Administrator is still waiting."

"Thanks, Quarrel." I sighed. "Hang on."

I was in the lab, in clean clothes, my face clean. "Sean, can you fix us up a meeting space?"

"Sure, Zo. Auditorium or amphitheater or what?"

"More intimate. Think . . . study in a Craftsman-style home."

"Oooh, nice." He vanished.

"Doc?"

"Yeah, Zoe?" Geoffrey looked a little beat up but eager. He had reams of new data to play with and the promise of occasional fights and explosions in my company.

"Can you make it secure, so that the Administrator can't attack me from inside?"

"Sure. After you unchained us, the attackers vanished. The lighter vanished, too. Anything else comes up, and I can use the sword to fix that."

"Then do it, and thanks."

Sean said all was ready, and I found myself in a small, cozy study. Warm wood and heavy textiles characterized the furniture and floors; the walls were lined with filled bookcases. The ceilings were low enough that I felt safe, not overwhelmed.

I opened the door. "Administrator. Please come in."

"Thank you." He looked nervous, very like a parody of an Edwardian gentleman about to propose. He took the chair I indicated and I sat.

"How can I help you?" I asked, hesitantly.

"There's a problem we'd like your help with."

"I'm sorry, the Fangborn are to be left strictly alone. No more suddenly interfering with them—"

"No, you made that clear, and you made it impossible. Not them. You." He fiddled nervously, out of his element, clearly distressed. "It is terribly important to my . . . our . . . continued survival. Perhaps even that of your people. Of course, I can make it worth your while."

I sat back and sighed; my eyes closed for what seemed a long time. I recalled the email that Ken-san had sent me last night, with the translation of Okamura-san's reading for me.

It was, roughly translated, "Going far beyond our house."

Then I sat up and reached for the teapot that was, along with its service, on the low table in front of me. I poured two cups and offered him one.

After he sipped, I asked, "How can this werewolf . . . this Hellbender be of service?"

Acknowledgments

My husband James Goodwin and I have been talking about books, life, the universe, and everything even before we started dating. I'm so thankful for his love, support, and the decades of conversations. Mr. G, you inspire me every day.

My beta readers are awesome. James Goodwin and Josh Getzler always offer good advice and it's scary how often they both tell me the same thing! My friends Charlaine Harris and Toni L. P. Kelner (a.k.a. Leigh Perry) read carefully and thoughtfully. It's a wonderful privilege to have amazing writers like them on my side.

I'm very lucky in my literary agent and coconspirator in all things Fangborn, Josh Getzler. I love that we can talk about the business, the many versions of Sherlock Holmes, and werewolves all in one call. I'm grateful to the excellent professionals at HSG Agency: Carrie Hannigan, Jesseca Salky, and Danielle Burby.

I wish everyone could have the great experience I do working with the brilliant folks at 47North. A very big thank-you to Jason Kirk (editorial lead), Justin Golenbock (PR specialist), Ben Smith (senior marketing manager), and Britt Rogers (author-relations manager). Clarence A. Haynes is my developmental editor; he is a wonderful reader and, quite simply, the bee's knees.

Camille Minichino, MarySue Carl, Debi Murray, and James Goodwin offered terrific advice on the (increasingly!) complex science of the Fangborn. Hank Phillipi Ryan and I spent a wonderful, exciting hour discussing how the Fangborn might announce themselves to the world. Playing what-if with talented people is one of the very best parts of writing.

I'm so grateful for my reading and writing friends in mystery, SF/F, and Sherlockian communities. It's such a pleasure to get to see members of the Teabuds, MysteryBabes, BuffyBuds, the Crimespree Family, Mystery Writers of America, and Sisters in Crime at conventions and gatherings. Going to conventions like Malice Domestic, Bouchercon, Boskone, World Fantasy, Murder and Mayhem in Milwaukee, and the BSI and Friends Weekend also lets me say thank you to the booksellers, bloggers, and librarians who spread the word and turn me on to new reading addictions! Special thanks are always due to my promotion group, the Femmes Fatales. They are: Donna Andrews, Charlaine Harris, Dean James, Toni Kelner, Kris Neri, Catriona McPherson, Hank Phillippi Ryan, Mary Saums, Marcia Talley, and Elaine Viets.

A great thank-you to the convention attendees and participants in online events who bid on the chances to name characters in the Fangborn novels and short stories. I'm delighted when readers' generosity in supporting good causes overlaps with their having more fun with the Fangborn.

And thanks, so very much, to my readers. Y'all rock. Awooo!

About the Author

Award-winning author Dana Cameron lives in eastern Massachusetts with her husband and two cats. Cameron was short-listed for the Edgar Award in 2010 for "Femme Sole," and has earned multiple Agatha, Anthony, and Macavity Awards for her work, including several Fangborn short stories. Her Fangborn novels, *Seven Kinds of Hell* and *Pack of Strays,* and short stories, "The Serpent's Tale" and "The Curious Case of Miss Amelia Vernet," were published by 47North. Trained as an archaeologist, Cameron holds a bachelor of arts from Boston University and a doctorate from the University of Pennsylvania. When she's not writing fiction, Cameron enjoys exploring the past and the present through reading, travel, museums, popular culture, and food. More news about Dana Cameron and her writing can be found on her author website and blog, at www.danacameron.com.